# CATCHING FEELINGS

Visit us at www.boldstrokesbooks.com

**By the Author**

Changing Majors

Catching Feelings

# CATCHING FEELINGS

*by*

Ana Hartnett Reichardt

2022

**CATCHING FEELINGS**
© 2022 By Ana Hartnett Reichardt. All Rights Reserved.

ISBN 13: 978-1-63679-227-9

This Trade Paperback Original Is Published By
Bold Strokes Books, Inc.
P.O. Box 249
Valley Falls, NY 12185

First Edition: September 2022

**CREDITS**
Editor: Barbara Ann Wright
Production Design: Susan Ramundo
Cover Design By Jeanine Henning

# Acknowledgments

Sports have always been near and dear to my heart. Growing up, being a part of a team felt special and helped to solidify my confidence—no easy task for a teenager. A huge shout out to all the coaches who had an immeasurable impact on who I am today.

And to all the teammates I ever crushed on, thanks for the fodder. I had such a fun time writing this book and creating the amusing, boisterous family of a team that is the Alder Lions.

Endless gratitude to Bold Strokes Books. I never imagined I'd be writing novels. And now, I can't imagine stopping. Thank you, Rad and Sandy, for allowing me the opportunity to pursue this passion. I feel so lucky that I ended up with BSB. Thank you to my editor, Barbara Ann Wright, for being brilliant and having patience with me while I continue to master the comma. And thank you to Morgan, who has been the most helpful, generous mentor I could have hoped for. And a great friend, too.

To the whole BSB production team, thank you.

To the folks whom I trust with my messiest of manuscripts. My wife, Sarah, for always keeping me on track and being my biggest support. My mom, Carmen, for being my number one fan and never mentioning the steamy scenes I write. Amy, for making me believe I could do this thing and being my first beta reader. Zach, thank you for being my writing date over one too many negronis. Steve and Rose Ann, thanks for…everything.

A very special thanks to Tom. You showed up for me at my very first reading and helped to calm my nerves. I hope to see you soon at the Squealing Pig. Next round's on me.

Most importantly, thank you to my readers. I'm excited to continue to build this—already awesome—relationship. Cheers to you.

# Dedication

H,

The higher they go, the faster they do.
A million dedications couldn't capture
How much I love you.

## CHAPTER ONE

The crinkling of cellophane tickles my ears as my team settles in the Lazy. We call it the *Lazy* because it's our meeting, eating, and between-drills room. Basically, it's the only place in our clubhouse where we slow down. Someone might think it impolite to whip out a Nature Valley bar when the coach is about to announce the starters for the season, but as college athletes, we eat whatever we can whenever we can. I wipe the sugar crumbs from my sweatshirt and stuff the sticky plastic wrapper in my softball bag.

I'm a sophomore now, but I'm not really expecting to get the starting catcher position. My role on the team thus far has mostly entailed being a support wherever I'm needed: making sure the field is clean of stray balls after practice, talking up—or down—my teammates, keeping stats for the coaches. I'm basically the Duct Tape of the team. Slap me on most anything, and I can make it better. My job may be ill-defined, but I'm handy as hell. My dad was diagnosed with multiple sclerosis when I was eight, so I learned a long time ago to be useful. To be a presence that gives energy instead of takes it. It only took my mom calling me a selfish brat one time when I was nine to solidify that trait in me.

Coach Clayton clears his throat. "All right, ladies, since our meeting had to happen later tonight, study hall is canceled." The sound of happy sighs fills the Lazy. "We've had a good August. Everyone worked hard over the summer and showed up to campus in shape," he starts, using his "team meeting" voice, low and grumbly. He insists on tucking his Alder U T-shirt into his gym shorts, ballooning his small beer belly into a maroon blob overflowing his waistband. "And we had a strong month of strength and conditioning and solo drills. We want to go ahead and list positions and starters so we can begin specializing solo practices and preparing for October, when we'll begin team practices and scrimmaging."

He grabs a blue Expo marker and bites off the cap.

I pop my knuckles in my lap and steal a glance at my teammates. Everyone pretty much knows who's starting at each position. Kim and I happen to be the only real wild cards fighting for catcher. She sits next to Maya, our fiery ace pitcher, who lounges with one elbow hanging over the back of her chair like she owns the place. Maya's hips spill over the edges of her seat, her body formed of the kind of curves that no pair of baggy sweats can hide. And who would want to?

I love catching for her. And I truly hate catching for her. She's a self-centered, entitled hothead with an incredible arm.

And she's devastatingly attractive. *Ugh. I'm staring.*

I crushed pretty hard on her last year. We were both freshmen from Atlanta when we joined the team, so we gravitated toward each other, and I felt like she tolerated me more than she did most people. I remember the little grins she used to give me around the clubhouse, crooked, as if she kept half the smile gripped between her teeth. It was cute as heck. I wanted her to let go and give me the whole smile, teeth and all. Instead, she swallowed that grin completely.

I swear, Maya Gonzalez liked me. Until one day she just *didn't* anymore. Since then, our interactions freeze in the air between us and shatter into icy shrapnel, and I don't know why.

Kim snickers in her ear about something ridiculous, I'm sure. Those two feed off each other's intensity, and there's not much space for anything else when they're together. Even though Kim is just a freshman, she was heavily recruited by our coaches and is favored to start over me. At least, that's what I assume. From the way Maya and Kim have been inseparable lately, it's clear they don't think I'm starting, either.

With such a talented senior ahead of me last year, I was happy to take the back seat and learn from her, but I'm not sure there is much I could learn from Kim. In fact, I believe I'm the better catcher, but if the coaches think she's the best pick for the job, I'd be okay with that. I have to trust them.

Coach Clayton scribbles the starters of the outfield and the infield.

"Maya will be our go-to pitcher. Start as many games as she's able. We'll find that sweet spot, May. Daniella, you'll be our number two." He writes their names and turns to face the rest of the Lazy, scans us as if assessing possible damage, then pulls off his cap and runs a hand over his tired hair before shutting it back under.

"Andrea will be our starting catcher. Congratulations, everyone."

My heart explodes and drops at the same time. I get to start, but I also have a target on my back. Kim's front chair legs slam against the linoleum with a crack, and Maya pops an impossibly loud bubble with her Trident. I still in my seat, uncomfortable at being the impetus of their resentment.

"Girls." Coach Williams, the pitching coach, bites at the divas, her eyes cutting into them. "Kimberly, let's go chat. My office."

Coach Clayton watches them leave and tries to move past the moment. "One last announcement. I am very excited to name this year's team captain, Andrea Foster." My mouth dries, and my cheeks burn as if someone traded the spotlight I'm under for a heat lamp. My team applauds half-heartedly. Everyone is confused.

I'm confused.

I look around in disbelief. My teammates glance at me from the corners of their eyes, as if they think I rigged this somehow. Naming a sophomore as team captain is unheard of, and naming a sophomore who didn't start as a freshman is as rare as a freak accident. I'm not even sure if it has *ever* happened...maybe it is a freak accident. Maybe Coach Clay huffed that marker one too many times before this meeting. The truth is, I don't want to be captain. Being in the spotlight, taking up that space, commanding a team, these are not my strengths. I'm more of the quiet soldier type.

My heartbeat thrums in my ears.

I have tricks for moments like these, for moments that threaten to gallop out of my control. When I was younger, I suffered from "white coat syndrome." Every time I had to go to the doctor, my body would turn on its burners and boil me over into an intense panic attack. When the nurse took my blood pressure and told me that if I wasn't fourteen, she'd rush me to the emergency room, my parents decided to send me to therapy. And it was great. I learned the skills I need to avoid artery-bursting anxiety.

In this particular moment, I press my open palm against the wood of the table and try to feel every atom of myself that is in contact with the cool surface. I breathe. And I breathe.

And I swerve. I swerve away from what's bringing me stress and recalibrate.

Maya throws her bag over a shoulder and stalks to Coach Clayton. I can't hear what she says as I zip my bag, but by the way her thick ponytail lashes from side to side, I gather it's about me, her new subpar partner. Her new subpar captain.

Only I'm not subpar. I'm wiry and fast, have a .350 batting average, and a knack for stealing bases. Not only that, but I am a solid catcher. Sure, my arm could be stronger, could be a bit more accurate, but I know that, and I work on that every single day.

But being named captain? That has me stumped…and terrified. I can't blame her for having a reaction to Coach's announcement. Maya huffs and storms out of the Lazy. I'm surprised Coach's gray stubble isn't smoldering from her dragon breath. I give him a quick nod as I hustle by.

"Andy. Hold up. I want to have a word." He catches me before I can escape back into anonymity.

"Sure, Coach. No problem."

We wait for the last couple of girls to clear out before he sits and directs me to do the same. "How's your dad doing?"

I stare at the little mole planted on the side of his nose. I don't want to talk about this. He doesn't want to talk about this, but ever since he found out that my dad has MS, Coach Clay feels obligated to start every conversation with a check-in. Not that anything ever changes for the better with MS. It's a slow, degenerative grind. My dad is not well. He hasn't been well for the last ten years, having a more aggressive case of the disease. Some folks get away with a mostly normal life with MS, but not my dad. He's in almost constant pain and recently transitioned to a mobility device. And I'm not there to help him or my mom, which shatters me. *Shatters* me. But they wouldn't let me stay. Forced me into early retirement.

The ticking of the plastic clock on the wall wiggles into my brain, and I use the little metronome to center me back in focus with Coach Clay.

"He's good."

"Good, good." Coach clears his throat of the sludgy cigarette muck that clings to his trachea. He pretends he doesn't smoke—thinks some minty gum and Old Spice can hide his vice—but his gunky cough and tobacco breath, however minty, give him away. "You looked surprised when I announced you. As a starter and as captain."

I scoot back in my chair and dig my fingers into my jeans. I love wearing jeans. In a world consumed by sport, wearing jeans signals to my brain that it's break time. Time to chill. While other girls throw on their team sweats when we're done for the day, I always pull on my jeans. I get a little crap for it, but it's worth it. "I guess I am surprised. Thought maybe Kim would—"

"Did we ever lead you to believe that Kim would start over you?"

I try to recall any conversations with the coaching staff that would have led me to that conclusion. I guess it was just Maya's attitude and my own underestimation of myself. I shake my head. "No. I don't think so."

"Look. First of all, you are an excellent catcher and a deadly base runner. Plus, you have a great batting average. Just based on that, you earned the job."

"Thanks."

"There's something else that we really value about you." He steals a glance at the door and adjusts his cap again. "Maybe you've noticed that Maya has had a hard go of it here."

I clear my throat, a little uncomfortable to be involved in whatever this conversation will end up being. But I can't lie; I know exactly what he's talking about. Whenever Maya starts, there is a constant hum of anxiety on the field. In the dugout. Shoot, probably in the stands. When she gets down, she spirals and robs the rest of the team of our energy. It could be over something as small as an iffy pitch.

"I noticed."

He nods. "You're cool and steady. She needs a catcher who can reach her and help her through her anxiety or whatever it is that's getting to her. I'm hoping that's you." He points to me and blows out a deep breath that crinkles my nose. "And that's why you're the captain. You're good at holding people up. I can't put the leadership of my team under a negative attitude. This will force her to work together with you, and I'm hoping it will elevate her in the end."

If coach thinks I have any sway when it comes to Maya, he is absolutely crazy. Out of his mind. I don't want that responsibility, and I *definitely* don't want my success on this team to be tied to her attitude. "Coach, I can't control her. She—"

"I'm not asking you to *control* her. I know you're surprised, Andy, but you have to trust the coaching staff on this. Isn't your major Sports Psychology?"

"No. I mean, not technically. I'm double majoring in Psychology and Exercise Science. Then I'll get my PhD in Sports Psychology."

"Jesus. We allow athletes to double major?"

I shrug.

He shakes his head. "Well, we need you to calm her and help her harness all that power and passion. Just because she didn't get an offer from UGA out of high school doesn't mean she can't get where she wants to go in life."

I knew Maya wanted to go to UGA. She was heavily recruited by them, but they dropped her at the last second to go with a girl from Montgomery, and she clearly has not recovered from the rejection. "Where does she want to go in life?"

He tilts his head a little, and I tilt my head a little because I don't know why the heck I asked that. It may have something to do with the crush I had on her. *Have* on her? I don't know. She's like a car crash. I don't want to be anywhere near her, but dang, I can't keep my eyes off the girl. So I want to know every detail about her life.

Doesn't mean I like her.

"Hell if I know. It doesn't matter. Just try." He stands to emphasize the end of our conversation and slaps a meaty hand on my shoulder. "Okay, Andy?"

"Yes, sir."

"Don't make me regret putting my team in the hands of a sophomore."

"I won't." *I hope.*

"Right. Now get out of here."

I grab my softball bag and walk past the indoor batting cages and into our locker room. I wish they'd change the floor in here. For some reason, the locker room sports the same green Astro Turf as the batting cages. The little blades of dummy grass scratch at bare feet, but I can't complain. It's gorgeous in here. Our lockers are built of the type of handsome oak that inspires no-hitters and RBIs and that makes us feel like we could be champions. We are assigned them by year and alphabetically when we join the team. That means, to my undying regret, that my locker is next to Maya's.

I tuck my bag in my locker and finger the crisp practice uniform that hangs in all its Alder University maroon and navy glory. I shoulder my backpack and consider Maya's locker. Consider mine. I want to call hers messy, but I know that's just me being rigid. It's not that bad. Her roll of pre-wrap spits its tongue out of her bag, and her pitching mask lies abandoned on the ground, but she was pissed-off earlier. It probably fell when she stormed out of here.

I tuck the face mask next to her glove. A Gonzalez family photo hangs from a piece of athletic tape on the side of her locker. A true family of athletes. Her oldest brother, Miguel, is on the Patriots' practice squad with promise of suiting up for the real deal soon, and her middle brother, Robbie, is the senior starting first baseman at UGA.

And Maya is here, at Alder University, not UGA.

I pull my head out of her locker, make sure mine is clean and orderly for tomorrow, and tap my name plate. *3 Foster.* Tap the faded *Lion's heart, Lion's courage* placard to the right of the locker room door frame and leave.

My white Adidas practically glow in the dark as my eyes adjust to the night. A small but constant breeze makes known all the oaks and pines and maples that surround and overflow onto our old campus. This campus must be in every student's top three reasons for attending Alder. These woods, these mountains, they hold us. And the old gray stone of the buildings inspires us. Every day, I feel nostalgia for this place, and I haven't even left. I wish I could memorize every detail of the campus and hold them with me forever. The way the old cobblestone pathways try to trip you up, how the warm puff of steamy Tide from the laundry room smells flamboyant and out of place compared to the usual dank stone and pine sap, and the feeling that I am *exactly* where I am supposed to be.

I walk past my dorm. I know I should get back and finish my kinesiology homework, but it's not every day that our team study hall is canceled, and it's only eight. As important as it is to maximize every hour in my day, sometimes it's equally important to drink hot cocoa.

I bound up the big steps before I can change my mind and order a cup from the café in the library. After I pay, I sit on the far end of the front steps and pull my homework from my backpack. I don't actually do it. I just set it on my lap while I sip my hot chocolate and look at the stars. They're bright here. Not quite ocean bright but small town bright. A group of students laughs and jumps on each other's backs on the sidewalk across the street.

Do I wonder what it would be like to be one of them? Sure. Do I sometimes question whether I made the right decision committing my whole college experience to playing a sport that won't lead me to any money-making career?

You betcha.

I wouldn't trade my experience on the softball team for anything, though. I'm just adjusting to my new responsibilities, to the new massive weight on my shoulders. I used to just be a happy passenger on my team, with no way for me to screw up too badly. Now I'm driving the entire bus, and if I crash...if I crash, I don't know what would happen. If I fail at helping Maya lead us to regionals, what good am I to the coaching staff? I'd probably lose my position.

Not being named a starter is one thing, but losing your starting position is a completely different beast. It's a failure.

I shake my head.

If only she liked me. The way I know she used to.

I shove my homework back into my bag and enjoy the moment. Focus on how the sugary chocolate coats my tongue and fuzzies my teeth. Sports psychology is full of all these little tricks. Mechanisms for finding calm and confidence just like the ones I learned from my therapist. I think the general population calls it *mindfulness*. When my body starts to react to my anxiety before my brain knows what's happening, I can use my mindfulness tricks to slow down my heart, my breathing, and the numb tingling that spreads to my arms. I keep them in my pocket like stale hard candies.

People think I'm quiet. But when something like MS has a grip on your family, how do you complain about the trivial things going on in your life? There's always something more pressing to focus on. I learned to keep it tight. Don't be a burden. Don't be *loud*. The three of us are a team. The Fosters versus MS. And I am a good teammate.

My phone pings from inside my backpack. It's Emma. *Coach obliterated us. Obliterated. I'm dead.*

*I'm drinking hot chocolate. Study hall was canceled.*

She texts back immediately. *Wow. Rub it in a little more. How'd it go? Are you starting?*

*You are talking to the starting catcher and team captain of the Alder Lions fastpitch team.* I force myself to smile as I type. Maybe I can train myself to only see the positive of being named captain.

*Holy hell. Congrats, Andy! When I get a minute off, I'm coming over to hug you.*

*Thanks, Em. Hang in there.*

I toss my empty cup in the garbage and walk back to Wilder Hall, one of the athletic dorms at Alder, with Emma on my mind.

We went to the same high school. She played softball and basketball but chose to pursue basketball at Alder. She's damn good, too. I used to go to her games and try not to drool over her. If I was lucky, she'd offer me a ride home, and I'd get to sit in her dark car while her fingers stroked my knee, and we listened to some cool band I'd never heard of. I wanted so badly to be hers, but she just didn't feel the same way. Just wants someone to flirt with. Otherwise, we would have explored more than holding hands. Alas, here we are in college, just two good friends.

My dorm is empty like I knew it would be. My roommate, Rachel, is the center on the women's basketball team, and their season starts in November, so she and Emma are in the heat of training. The three of us make a nice friend trio. Plus, it's a comfort to live with a fellow athlete. Someone who understands my life and doesn't make it harder with invitations to parties or a bunch of friends in our dorm room or alcohol or whatever. Rachel trains, goes to class, lifts, goes to practice, and attends mandatory study hall.

Just like me.

They're all I really need.

## CHAPTER TWO

R unner on first. One out. Count is 1-2.
Time to get her with a rise ball. Coach Williams calls pitches in games, but sometimes, I get to call them in practice. I show three fingers between my legs as Ashlyn takes her sign from Coach Clayton. She takes one more swing through the air before she steps into the batter's box and digs her cleats into the dirt. I doubt that Kim will steal second. She's not that fast, and with this count, Maya isn't going to throw Ashlyn anything she can hit. She'll think she can hit it, but at the last second, the ball will soar above the strike zone, and she'll miss completely.

This is our first team scrimmage and the first opportunity I have to show the coaches they made the right decision starting me. If I'm really lucky, I'll be able to show them they made the right decision naming me captain, too. Though, I'm still trying to convince myself of that one.

Maya spins the ball in her glove, finding the right grip for the pitch, and I lower into my squat, fingering the dirt just in case I have to throw Kim out at second. Maya bows, rocks forward, and launches off the pitching rubber. The ball catapults from her hand, and I realize from the spin that it's not a rise ball at all, it's a *drop* ball. I sink a knee into the dirt too late as the ball dives into the ground in front of me and escapes to the backstop. I tear off my mask and leap to retrieve it. No one shouts a base for me to throw to, so I grab the ball, cock it, and check. Kim is safe at second, and

Ashlyn is now at 2-2 because not only was that a drop ball instead of a rise, it was a terrible pitch.

"Time, Coach," I call to Coach Williams, our unofficial ump for the scrimmage. She nods.

I grab my mask from the dirt and walk to the pitching circle. Maya watches me approach with a bored look on her face, a piece of thick black hair stuck to her neck, and her hip cocked to the side.

She pulls off her own mask, rolling her eyes when I step into the pitching circle, which is starting to feel more like a boxing ring. "You have to stop those balls, Andy."

I look around the field. Some of our teammates are chatting, some are watching us, and I can feel Coach Clayton's eyes on me. *Thanks for throwing me to the wolves, Coach.*

"I called a rise," I say.

Her brows clash like swords over her eyes as she stares, sweat glistening on her perfect dark skin like moonlight on a midnight ocean. *Stop staring, Andy.* "Well, I threw a drop. Ashlyn can't hit the drop."

*Yeah. I know you threw a drop. You threw a freaking gutter ball into the dirt.* Time to put on my boxing gloves. My blood heats, but I got this. Controlling anger is just like controlling panic.

*Breathe. One. Two. Three. Swerve.*

I nod and blow a piece of hair out of my face. "I get it. But I need to know what pitch you're going to throw, so I can adjust. Next time, just call me off until I signal the pitch you want. I'm totally cool with that." I mean, come on, we're college athletes. I should not have to explain this.

She shifts her weight to pop the other hip, and I expect a crack of thunder to accompany the move. "Call better pitches, *Captain.*" She spits into the dirt.

Only she doesn't exactly spit into the dirt.

She spits on me. On my cleat.

Brown dust coats the little blob of salvia as it shakes like jelly in the wind. My face heats, and I throw on my mask to hide under its thick wire cage. It takes a lot to make me angry, but right now, I'm livid. I hold my breath. I *have* to stay in control. Maya pulls on her face mask, too, and it takes all of my willpower not to tackle her in the dirt. It's just a stupid power play.

The pines sway in the breeze around our field like thousands of cheering fans.

*Breathe. Swerve.*

I take a step toward her and hold her gaze—dark brown eyes glued to mine—as I drop to a knee and wipe her spit off my shoe with the back of my mitt. When I stand, our masks are only inches away from each other. No one can hear us.

"That spot was dirty. Needed a little spit shine. Thanks, May." I wink and knock her glove with mine before I retreat back to my post.

"All right. Play ball," Coach Williams hollers.

I squat, a little shaky from the adrenaline rush, and flash Maya two fingers. A good clean changeup. She doesn't nod. Do exactly what I ask? She would never submit like that. I prepare for whatever pitch Maya throws, and when her hand leaves her glove, I see it's going to be a curveball. Classic.

Ashlyn cracks it into the gap between second and first, and Kim easily advances to third.

"Time, time, time," Coach Williams calls once the play is over. She walks toward me from the visitors' dugout and waves for Maya to join us at home. I pull off my mask and wipe my hair out of my eyes. Not my best work with the French braid this morning.

"A curveball, Andy? That's Ashlyn's bread and butter. And with two strikes, she was going to swing at anything that wasn't in the dirt." She sighs. "I know you won't be calling pitches in a real game, but what the hell was that?"

Maya's face is locked, eyes glued to Coach Williams, not a single twitch in her lip. I want to call her out so badly, to throw her under the bus where she belongs, but I can't. Getting Maya to chill out is one of my main priorities as captain, and making her look bad in front of a coach is not the way to do that. Instead, I try to think of why Maya wanted to throw the curve so I have an answer for Coach.

I wipe my hand down my thigh and meet Coach Williams's questioning stare. "I guess I thought she wouldn't expect the curve. Um, because it's her favorite to hit."

Coach Williams plants her hands on her hips and shakes her head. "With a batter like that and a 2-2 count, off-speed or out of the zone. Understand?"

I nod. "Yes, Coach."

"Shake her off next time, May. A curve? You know better."

Maya nods once, then trudges back to the pitching circle.

The rest of practice drags. Maya throws the pitches I call, but anger hangs thick like smoke between us. Why is she angry at me? I'm guessing it's the big "C" printed on the breast of my practice uniform. After that performance from me and Maya, I'm not so sure that "C" belongs on my jersey at all. Hopefully, this is rock bottom.

❖

I shower in a rush, wanting to escape the team, to escape Maya, as quickly as possible. Not that I can actually escape; we have mandatory team study hall Monday through Thursday, and since today is Thursday, I have one more joyous evening of studying in the same room as her. I towel dry my hair and pull on my jeans and a sweatshirt. The freshmen are still waiting to shower, and the rest of the team is dressing and chatting, a low hum of Drake spilling from the Bluetooth speaker that lives in our locker room. At least I can get to study hall early and pick a spot in the corner, away from her and Kim.

My teammates trickle in to study hall, laughing and playing around. Someone plays music from their phone, and a mini dance party forms. I watch, a little annoyed at their disregard for the rules, and wait for a coach to tell them to get to work.

Katie, our junior second baseman, takes the seat next to me and pulls out her notebook. "I don't know how you do it," she says. I like Katie. She has an ease and confidence about her which I'm drawn to. I would consider her my best friend on the team, and right now, her presence brings me some much-needed relief. I don't have to try so hard around her—don't have to don my captain facade.

"Yeah, well, I'm not really doing anything at this point. Today was a disaster." I tuck my hands into the sleeves of my sweatshirt.

While this old stone campus is gorgeous, it could be a little warmer inside these buildings. More teammates fill the room dedicated to our study hall in the athletic building. It's like our own small library, with whiteboards and computers and tutors whenever needed. One of the many perks of being a college athlete. That and all the awesome team swag we get: shoes, jackets, bags…endless swag.

"I would've slapped her in the face. Before she put her mask back on," Katie says. I grin at how her accent brings a little extra punch to her words. She has the kind of chewy Southern accent that's inked on her tongue like a birthmark, and I'm addicted to it. Her family lives in the Atlanta suburbs now, but she grew up in Valdosta until they moved away before she started high school. Katie is the kind of girl who wears camo in earnest; there have been multiple times when I've had to turn away from her gory photos of an eight-point-buck massacre.

"Oh my God. I wanted to so badly. I just don't know how to get to her. She hates me because I'm not some hotshot recruit like Kim. And she thinks she should be captain."

Katie whips her damp chestnut hair into a topknot. "Hey, you're better than Kim. That's why you're the starter, not her. Today was the first team practice. You have time to figure it out." She pauses. "Well, it's bullshit that it's all on you. Really, I should be saying *Maya* has time to figure it out. No wonder UGA passed on her."

"I wish they hadn't so we wouldn't have to deal with her." I say it, but deep down, I don't want Maya to leave. I'm holding on to a small hope that we could be close-ish again.

"Hang in there. She may be an ice queen, but we both know what kind of pitcher she is. She's got something special."

"Yeah."

Katie is right. Regardless of her intensity, Maya is our deadliest weapon, our best player. Bettering our relationship should be my priority, but I'm feeling petty. I try to focus on my biology flashcards as Maya walks in and plops right in the one free seat next to me. I can smell the shampoo in her wet hair, the same tea tree oil shampoo the entire team uses.

She smells just like me. Just like Katie. I tell myself that I am thoroughly unaffected. But her wet hair hints at her shower, and her shower hints at—

"Hey," she says.

The goddamn nerve of this girl. I chew my lip, wanting to ignore her, wanting to lash out, but I land in the ineffectual no man's land of the two. "Hey." I keep my eyes glued to my notecard describing the traits of bivalves.

"We have that team-building thing this weekend, and we're supposed to choose partners."

I look up from my notecard and narrow my eyes. She doesn't flinch. Of course she doesn't. "Okay. So? Go ask Kim. Katie and I are already working together."

I catch something flash across her face, and it's not anger. I could swear it was hurt. Katie leans back to holler at Maya from behind my chair. "Hell, yeah. And me and Andy are going to crush y'all." She grins and slaps my shoulder.

Maya gives her a death stare that not even I have ever received. "Um, no. You're not. Andy has to be my partner. Coach Clay just gave me the *oh-so-exciting* news. You have to pick someone else."

I look at Katie in exasperation. She just shrugs and paints a little sorry on her face. "You're serious?" I ask Maya.

"Look. I want to be your partner this weekend just about as much as I wanted you to catch for me this year. But here we are." She pulls out her phone and scrolls through Instagram, paying attention to no posts in particular but slapping an amused smirk on her face as if she's finished with our conversation.

I've never met a girl like her. So brazen. "Maya."

She doesn't look up from her phone.

"Don't you want to make it to the World Series this year?" I ask.

She places her phone facedown on the table and glares at me, all surly and brooding. "That's the stupidest question I've ever heard. That's all I want. To win."

"Well, I'm your best shot at that, so just chill out. I know you wanted Kim, but Coach made the right call. I'll prove it to you. Not that I should have to."

She stares me down, then seems to give up on whatever scorching rebuttal she was cooking up. Instead, she sighs. "I have to go study for this stupid chemistry exam. Where do you want to meet on Saturday?"

"I don't know, just text me."

She stands to leave and stares down at me.

"What?" I grumble.

"I don't have your number." Maya unlocks her phone, ready for me to spill my digits.

Oh, the power. Oh, the joy.

I could just leave her hanging and embarrass her in front of Katie, but instead, my digits flow out of my mouth like Niagara Falls.

*Ugh.*

"All right, later." She sighs and walks across the room to Kim.

"Later," I mumble to my notecard.

I look to Katie for some kind of support that she just can't give me. I'm alone in this one. Well, not technically alone. It will be me and Maya.

Alone *together*.

Maybe when it's just us, she'll let go of whatever it is she has against me. Beyond me being named captain over her. Maybe she'll let go of whatever came between us last year—we haven't been alone together since then. I allow a tiny bit of foolish hope to mix with my dread of this weekend.

Emma sits on my bed with her back against the wall, a pack of ice dripping from her knee. I close my laptop and sit next to her. I like when she comes over after practice, all tired and wet-haired from the shower. I'm her "social interaction" during her season. While she hems and haws and decompresses, I muse at how possessive I feel of her in my room. In my bed. Her cool blue eyes hold mine for a moment before she breaks the connection with a wink. She's always telling me we have the same color eyes. It may be true, but while my eyes appear average against my light complexion and dull blond hair, hers pop against her darker lashes and brows. She tightens her ponytail of golden-blond hair and adjusts the ice on her knee.

I watch the water drip down her leg onto my comforter. I want to lick that ice melt off her cold skin. I want Emma. Still.

"She actually spit on you?" Rachel asks from her bed. The textbook she's trying to absorb falls against her chest, and she turns to me and Emma, her face scrunched in disgust. I like Rachel's side of the room way more than mine. She's the type of girl who is effortlessly cool, and her understated yet funky decor reflects that.

"Yeah. I mean, she spit on my cleat, but for all intensive purposes—"

Emma throws a hand on my ankle and squeezes. I hold my breath at the contact. "Andy. You're killing me. It's intents and purposes. You are the worst at phrases."

"What'd I say?"

Rachel shakes her head. "Intensive purposes."

"Well, it sounds like both phrases could work in this case," I say.

Emma is right. I am the worst at common phrases. But in my defense, I have a theory about the phenomenon. It's my hearing and maybe a lack of reading in my younger life. I would hear all these common phrases and never see them in writing, and with me rocking forty-percent hearing loss pre-hearing-aids, I heard all sorts of nonsensical phrases. "Play it by year, nip it in the butt," etc.

Emma pats my ankle. "We know, we know. It's the hearing."

"It is." I cross my arms. *It is.*

"Yeah, but I've been correcting you for years. You should know better by now." She's playing, but her condescension gnaws at me. I let it go just like I let everything go when it comes to her.

Rachel sighs. "Em, you know, old habits—"

"Die hard. I know that one," I say.

Emma scoots off my bed and glides into the bathroom, moving like a cat through my dorm room, swollen knee and all. She dumps her mostly melted ice pack in the sink and relieves herself with the door wide open. Sure, I can't see her, but still. Her confidence annoys me sometimes. It's not lost on me that it's most likely because I'm jealous of it. I cross my room and slam the door on her right as she finishes. The sink cuts off, and she opens the door.

"Rude," she says.

"People don't want to hear that."

She winks at me. "Really?"

"*Ugh.* Shut up, Em."

She plops on the bed, her grace spent on the bathroom trip. "Okay, okay. Back to Maya. What're you going to do?"

"I don't know. Coach Clayton wants me to help her, which I feel is wildly unfair. It's like she feels cheated out of something. I know she feels cheated out of being captain"—I throw two thumbs to my chest—"by this girl, but that's out of my control. I don't even want to be captain. She can have it for all I care."

I rub my hands down my face. Coach Clayton put a giant target on my back. I believe I should be the starting catcher, sure. But captain? I'm a sophomore. I'm not outspoken. I'm not a proven leader on my team. And I'm just supposed to flip a switch and lead my team to regionals? To the World Series? Clearly, this would rub Maya raw. Sure, she needs to harness her emotions and check her attitude, but it should be hers. At least, it shouldn't be mine.

And she blames me.

"Well, regardless of Maya and regardless of your title, your responsibility is to your team. All you can do is your best. Do your best to be a leader for your team," Rachel says. "And start slow with Maya. Make a small move. All you have to do is get her on your side. Everyone has the same goal."

"How are you so wise?" Emma asks.

"I'm a redshirt sophomore. Got a whole year on you babies." Rachel transferred to Alder from a D2 college in Bowling Green, Kentucky. She redshirted her first year here and has since developed into our basketball team's best player.

Emma flips her off.

"How's Melissa, by the way? Haven't seen her around in a minute," I ask.

Rachel abandons her horizontal lounging and swings her legs over the side of her bed, elbows on knees. She swats at one of the braids that dangles in front of her mouth before she bunches them into an elastic.

"Basketball has been crazy lately." She looks to Emma, who nods along. "I mean, you know how it is, Andy. Our lives are spoken for, and Melissa isn't an athlete. She just doesn't understand why I can't hang all the time. Like right now, she's mad 'cause she knows Em is here, and we're just chilling, recharging. She doesn't get why her presence would change the vibe."

Emma nudges me in the ribs. "Rach is over it."

"Shut up, dude," Rachel says.

"Are you?" I ask.

She lets out a long breath. "I don't know."

"It's okay to not know. Just don't be an asshole," Emma says.

Which I totally agree with, but it's pretty hypocritical coming from her mouth. I've spent the last five and a half years pining for Emma. I made it clear that I'm into her by always being available. Always being at her beck and call, but she just keeps me on her hook, holding my hand here, brushing her lips against my neck there. It's not like she's scared or not "out" or anything. She's not interested. She just wants my support and attention, and I give it to her.

"Yeah," I say. "Just don't lead her on." *The way you've led me on for half a decade.*

"I know. I'm trying."

Last time Rachel's family was in town, Melissa expected an invite to their family dinner. But Rachel made up some excuse about how her little brother wanted to talk to her and her parents about something personal, and she thought it'd be best to have just their family at dinner. Then, Melissa found out that me and Emma got to go to dinner with the Dunstons, and all hell broke loose. After that, I knew they wouldn't last because I knew Rachel didn't want it to last.

Emma rests her head against my shoulder and nuzzles into me. The feeling of the contact spreads into my extremities, warming me every inch of the way. I'm not totally blameless when it comes to Em. I have the power and prerogative to turn away from her, to draw a hard line between friendship and friendship with flirting and touching.

But I don't.

And deep down, I don't want her to, either.

I shower, make coffee, crack my window to let in the fresh autumn breeze, and wait. The knock on my door startles me, even though I've spent the last two hours pacing around my room waiting for it. It's as abrasive and exciting to me as the girl herself.

I open the door to let Maya in; fifteen minutes late, of course. Stray hair spills out of her messy bun, and she wears tight dark jeans with a cozy gray sweater. Her beauty annoys me at this point. I find it adds insult to injury.

She shoulders past me into my space. "Let's get this over with. I have other shit to do." Lovely entrance for a lovely girl.

It's not often that I have company. Katie will drop by on occasion to have a chat or make me watch *The Bachelor* with her, and Emma is a constant who doesn't register on my radar anymore. Being an only child and kind of a loner in high school made my personal space, well, kind of sacred.

Her gaze rakes over my desk, my bed, my closet, and I'm hit with the overwhelming urge to hide everything from her. I scan my room and will a forcefield between my life and her prying eyes. It doesn't work.

She spins in slow circles.

"What?" I ask.

She drags a finger over the top of my dresser and rubs it against her thumb. "You're, like, a neat freak or something."

"Why? Because I keep my room clean like a normal person?"

A snort bursts from her nose as she fingers the medal on my dresser, pushing it into the middle of the empty space. It looks awkward and naked there all alone. It's not where it belongs at all. My fingers wiggle with the urge to run over and fix it. It's driving me insane.

"Graduated with honors, huh?"

That's it. I can't.

I step to the dresser and move the medal back in its correct position. "Please don't touch anything."

"I don't know what you are, Andy. Not yet. But I know you're not normal."

I cross my arms and instantly regret the basic move. *I'm* not normal? "And you're, what? Just some sweet normal girl who never throws her teammates under the bus or spits on their shoes?"

She smirks and moves past me to sit on my bed. I turn to maintain the daggers I hope I'm piercing her with. She sighs. "Exactly. You have me pegged there, Foster." She runs her hands down her face, pulling her eyelids down like a clown. But when they run over her mouth, they pull her plump bottom lip down, too, and it bounces back with a sexy wobble. "Are you ready to get this over with? Or do you want to talk about me all day? You're the captain, so your call."

I lick my lips and peel my eyes from her mouth. She holds up her phone as if to take a selfie and tames some of the wild hair escaping her elastic tie.

"Are you really posting right now?" I knew she was conceited, but it's common courtesy to not waste someone else's time. I may be Gen Z, but I don't understand the social media obsession of my generation.

She drops her phone on my mattress and locks eyes with me. "I was checking my hair. But for the record, since you seem to be so concerned with my social media habits, Instagram and TikTok are two of the most powerful branding and marketing tools of our generation. So yes, I utilize them. And when I graduate from"—she clears her throat—"college, not only will I have a degree in business marketing, I will have established my personal brand. A personal brand that will be an advertisement of my skills and knowledge of the marketing field. People want an intimate connection, and that equals sales." She looks me up and down. "While you're judging, I'm hustling. Any other comments or concerns?"

I shake my head and close my mouth. I'd never really thought about what motivates her, or anyone, to be so active on social media. "Hadn't really thought of it that way," I say in surrender.

"Yeah, well."

I plop into my desk chair in defeat, open my laptop, clear my throat, and read the first instructions from Coach Clayton. "All right, another scavenger hunt this year. Winners don't have to go to study hall for two days of their choice next week. The first clue should hit my inbox in…" I check my watch. "Well, now."

Last year, Katie and I spent five hours completing the scavenger hunt, so sure we were going to win, only to arrive at Coach Williams's house to find half our team already chilling in her backyard eating hotdogs. I want to win this year. It would be a good show of leadership, and to do it with Maya would be a great way to show Coach Clayton that I'm succeeding with her.

My inbox pings with the first clue.

"Okay, nobody cares, just read the clue."

But I'm clearly *not* succeeding with her. "What do you mean? No study hall is like the apex of any reward we could receive. A couple of free nights. You could actually go out with your boyfriend."

She straightens. "First of all, I see Jeremy plenty. Trust me, the night doesn't end after study hall."

"Gross." I cringe at the thought of her with him. He's fine. He's just…not good enough for her. I shake the thought out of my head, not wanting to feel protective of someone who clearly doesn't care an ounce about me.

"Second of all, some of us actually use study hall."

"Yeah, to gossip in the corner with Kim all night."

"Jealous?"

Jealous? *Hah.* I run a hand through my messy waves. I'm losing control of the situation; at this rate, we'll be strangling each other within the next five minutes. I think of what Rachel said yesterday. Do my best, one step at a time.

Focus on how the grain runs through the warm old wood of the dorm floor.

*Breathe, swerve.*

"Jealous? Maybe. I'm your catcher, not Kim. Instead of obsessing over her, can we focus on the reality of the situation? It's you and me. All season long. We need to get used to it, or our team is going to suffer because we're too petty to figure it out."

She adjusts her weight left and right on my mattress, opens her mouth to speak, but I steal the opportunity to pivot for both of us.

"You're worried about your chemistry exam?"

Maya blinks and focuses on me. "If I fail, I'll be on academic probation."

"Okay, so—"

"I care about my grades."

I close my laptop and lean toward her. Slowly. Just in case she does actually bite.

"I know you probably think I don't give a shit about anything or anyone except softball. But that's not true. School is important to me, and I'm smart. I just don't understand chemistry. Or calculus. They're like, weird nerd magic."

"I don't think that about you."

Maya raises an eyebrow. "Like I said, I'm not stupid, Andy."

"Okay, maybe I thought that about you a little bit." I wink. "When is your test?"

"Monday. I really only have one more day to study since we have to do Coach's stupid scavenger hunt today."

I take a deep breath and sit beside her on my bed. She raises her eyebrows when her gaze meets mine, as if she's shocked to have me next to her. "How about we don't waste all day on the scavenger hunt? Instead, let's lock ourselves in my room until you feel good about chemistry. Rachel will be gone all day, so it will be quiet. No distractions."

As Maya searches my face for something, I become keenly aware of her knee pressing against mine. I pretend to stretch my back and scoot away from her. "You'll help me study?"

"Yeah. I love chemistry. The way I see it, we'll still be spending time together working toward a common goal. Sounds like team-building to me, and we don't really have a shot at regionals, much less the World Series, if you're on probation."

Some flattery can't hurt. She looks at her phone, then back to me. "Okay, but I don't have any of my stuff."

"You live across the quad, May. Just go grab it. I'll wait for you here. Okay?"

She nods. "Yeah. Okay."

Before she leaves, she looks over her shoulder at me and takes a deep breath, as if she's about to concede something. "I missed," she says.

I study her. Her face is open, the slightest bit of shame tugging her gaze to her shoes. "What?"

"I would never spit on you," she says in almost a whisper, closing her eyes and shaking her head. "Or your cleat. It was just bad aim."

"But—"

She raises a hand to cut me off. "Still bitchy, yes. I just wanted you to know. I meant to spit in the dirt. I know I can be…intense."

I chuckle. "The pitcher has bad aim."

She smiles at me, the first genuine smile I've received from her since before the Mayan ice age started last year. I try to memorize it. It's so—"And Andy?"

I tear my gaze from her mouth for the second time, startled by her voice and her, even if minimal, vulnerability. "Hmm?"

"I did throw you under bus. I'm sorry. I was angry and couldn't form any words for Coach. I froze." My face heats at her admission, and I'm momentarily paralyzed, too shocked to form a response and too scared to say the wrong thing. She chuckles and shakes her head. "Wow. You really think the worst of me, don't you?"

I bite my lip. Lying is a rarity for me. "I think—"

She holds up a hand to stop me again. "You know what? I really don't want to know. Let's just call it a rhetorical question. Deal?"

I nod.

She disappears into the hallway, leaving me alone to digest our interaction while she grabs her chemistry notes. I flop onto my mattress and drape an arm over my face. I'd call that a sweet, sweet victory.

It only takes Maya fifteen minutes to return with her things. When she knocks on my door this time, I'm excited to answer, hoping we can continue to build on our last interaction. "Hey."

"Welcome back."

She walks into my room and sits on my bed again. "Okay. Chemistry." She pulls her textbook from her bag and hands me the study guide for her test. It's all about balancing chemical equations and Stoichiometry. I love this stuff. I smile as I finish skimming the guide.

When I look up from the notes, I catch her staring at me, and my stomach tightens. "Chemistry really gets you going, huh?" she asks.

I hand the paper back to her and nod. "Yeah. You could put it that way. I love science."

"Chemistry is a foreign language to me."

"Don't worry, we're going to get you where you need to be for this test. If it takes all day." I crack open the book to the chapter on balancing chemical equations. "Okay, let's start with the basics. There is one main truth to balancing a chemical reaction: the mass is always conserved. That means that the atoms on—"

"Are those your parents?" Maya points to the framed photo on my desk. I blink as my brain climbs out of chemistry mode and refocuses on her question. She grabs the photo and returns, tracing over their faces. An hour ago, I would have wanted to rip it from her hands and kick her out. But now, I don't mind her curiosity.

"Yeah. Alex and Alex. I call them Alex Squared."

Her head snaps to me. "No fucking way. They're both named Alex?"

I laugh. "Yep. Swear to God. It's really handy for when I have to play two truths and a lie."

"No kidding. Hey, why is your dad in a wheelchair?" Her question hits me like cold water in the face, and she holds up the photo to show me, as if I haven't seen it. As if I am unaware of all the metal and wheels and leather underneath him. As if it is the smallest detail one could overlook, like the basic brown of his eyes.

"He has multiple sclerosis. Most people with MS don't need a wheelchair, but my dad has progressed to the point where he uses one daily. It just takes too much out of him to try to get around without it. Not to mention that the pain and the dizziness he experiences makes walking hazardous."

"Shit, I didn't know that, Andy."

"Doubt it would have made a difference," I say automatically, and the salty words beat on my eardrum before I even consider them in my brain.

Maya stiffens.

I turn to her, desperate to get back on good terms. "I'm so sorry. I can't believe I said that."

"Well, you said it, so own it. Tell me what you mean."

I close my eyes and drop my head. Let out a sigh and curse myself for ruining this day. I clear the hesitation out of my throat. "I meant that you knowing about my dad wouldn't have made you treat me nicer. It wouldn't have made a difference in your attitude toward me. I mean, not that it should. I don't want your sympathy, and let's be real, having a sick parent isn't the end of the world. Life could obviously be so much worse." Vomit. Pure word vomit.

I touch her wrist, and she yanks away, sending the photo of Alex Squared plummeting to the ground, the glass of the frame shattering against the hardwood floor. We both stare at the mess for a moment, stuck in the quicksand of our shock.

"Fuck," she mutters, then slides to the floor and begins picking the shards from the ground. I fall to my knees and try to block her hands from the rest of the broken glass.

"Maya, stop. Please. You're going to cut yourself." Speak it, and it shall be. She recoils from a small shard of glass and sucks in a sharp breath between her teeth.

"Motherfucker." She sits with her back against my bed, examining the cut on her finger. "It's not bad." She winces and looks away from the trickle of blood. "I just really hate cuts."

"You should have thought of that before you dove headfirst into a pile of broken glass." I slide in front of her and take her hand. A bit of glass sticks out of her pointer finger like a little iceberg. She's right, it's not deep and not on her pitching hand. My fingers hover over hers, ready to snatch the little culprit, but my anxiety catches up to me. "Um, do you have any STIs or any other bloodborne diseases?"

Her eyebrows scrunch together. "No. I was just tested. Why is that relevant?"

"I don't have any tweezers or gloves, so..." I pluck the bit of glass out of her finger, her blood smearing on my hand. "I'm going to come in contact with your blood. Just want to make sure I'm safe."

I wash my hands in the bathroom and bring Maya some toilet paper, Neosporin, and a Band-Aid.

"You're safe. Thanks." She sucks her finger clean and secures the Band-Aid, a spec of blood clinging to her lip. She pulls it into her mouth before I do something stupid like run my thumb over the red spot.

As she takes a couple of deep breaths and squeezes her finger, I try to memorize this moment. I'm not happy that she cut herself, but seeing her like this only adds to her vulnerability. She let me take care of her in a small way, and that's *something*. Hopefully, it's enough to get us on track again.

❖

I lie in my bed and try to sleep while Rachel snores away on her side of the room. I close my eyes and replay the day. Studying with Maya was nice. Well, it was more than nice.

It was fun once we moved past the broken picture frame.

The way she tapped the pencil eraser against her perfect teeth while she tried to untangle a particularly hard problem was one of my favorite parts. Or the way she squeezed my arm when she got an answer right. She has never been so open or vulnerable. It was like getting to know an entirely different person. And when she left, she hugged me. Pulled me against her, against her thighs and abs and breasts. That is, until eardrum-rattling feedback made us both jump away from each other.

"What the? What the hell was that?" she asked, fingers pressed to her ear, eyes wide.

"Sorry. I, uh, guess I haven't hugged anyone in a while."

She cocked her head, and I tugged out one of my small hearing aids to show her.

"Hearing aids. They give feedback if they're covered. Normally, I lean my head away when I hug someone. I just. . ." *Got carried away.* "Forgot."

"Oh. I didn't know. They're so tiny. Wait, what about your helmet?"

"I don't wear them when I play. My hearing loss isn't major, so I can still hear most things. It's classes and cafés that are the trouble, not your loud mouth." I winked to make sure she got my joke, and she gave my shoulder a quick shove, then she was gone.

I haven't felt the need to make a huge deal about it, but I'm into girls. Exclusively. I've never dated anyone because of softball, so it hasn't manifested into any real relationships, except for the Emma stuff. But I know I'm a lesbian. And I'm pretty sure my parents know it. I wonder if Maya knows it.

I snatch my phone from my nightstand and open Maya's Instagram page.

*26,000 followers.*

I have 170 followers, most of whom are high school acquaintances, family, and old teammates. But she has complete strangers commenting on every photo. Thirsty comments. I stare at one photo of her in a little black dress—emphasis on *little*—and how the fabric hugs her body, and how she looks at the camera, at each individual follower as if she's posing just for them. In the next photo, Jeremy's arm hangs around her, both of them in their crisp Alder U uniforms. Of course she'd want someone like him, the shortstop on Alder's baseball team, her perfect complement.

A new follow request pops onto my screen.

*Maya Gonzalez is requesting to follow you.*

I fling the app closed, as if somehow, she could see me stalking her. Maya wants to see my page. My five photos. Okay.

*Accept.*

# CHAPTER THREE

Coach Clayton accepted our excuse of working together to save Maya from academic probation instead of participating in the scavenger hunt, which ended at Hyde Hill Farm. Our teammates culled the fallen apples from this harvest for our Student Activities Week this coming Thursday. We sit around the tables in the Lazy, snacking and painting the finishing touches on our bull's-eye for Maya to pitch the rotten apples into. The hope is for some epic explosions of fruit to draw a little hype for the spring season. Softball isn't the most popular sport, but it's been having a moment these last couple of years, and we want to capitalize on its growing popularity.

Ashlyn dips her sponge paintbrush into the can of gloopy red paint. "Should I widen the bull's-eye?"

Kim leans over the large janky pallet. "Yeah, definitely," she says.

Maya watches me study the target, holding whatever comments she has deep in her throat.

"Wider? No way. It's Maya. Gotta give her a little bit of a challenge," I say.

Kim crosses her arms against my opinion. "It's just a game, not a competition."

*A competition.* That's exactly what we need to draw a crowd to our booth. "True, but what if we made it one?" I point to the pallet. "This was easy to throw together. How about we make a second target and invite the baseball team's pitcher to compete against Maya? Who's the top pitcher this year, Kevin?"

Kim pushes her sleeves up to her elbows. "Yes, it's Kevin. And he's an All-American. Not sure it's the best idea to pit him against Maya."

I narrow my eyes at her, shocked that she would stand behind anyone's talent over Maya's. She is one of the best pitchers I've ever seen, and she's our *teammate*. "You're not betting against her, are you? She's the most talented pitcher I know." I surprise myself by taking a small, very aggressive step toward Kim. Ashlyn looks up from her paint and eyes the two of us.

"There's no bet. I'm just saying it's our booth. We should make ourselves look as good as possible. Let's make Jeremy do it. It'd be a cute couple competition thing. They've both got the Instagram followers, and that way, we guarantee Maya will win."

"And she was hoping for you to catch for her this year." I shake my head. "She's going to pitch against Kevin. And she's going to win."

"This is dumb. Maya, will you please tell Andy you want to pitch against Jeremy."

Maya pushes out of her chair and saunters behind Kim, dropping a hand on her shoulder. She locks eyes with me, a small smile twitching on her lips, and she winks, sending a bolt of lightning through my chest. This is the moment where all our progress together goes out the window. Our one day of progress, but still. I spoke up for her, and now she has the power to reinforce or destroy.

"Andy is your captain, ye of little faith. Instead of arguing with her, start on the second target. We'll message Kevin on IG." With a squeeze of Kim's shoulder, Maya brushes past us toward the locker room. Kim's mouth hangs open, and I scramble to follow Maya.

She zips her softball bag and grabs her chemistry book from the top shelf of her locker as I sidle up next to her and rummage for nothing in my own locker.

"Thanks for…that," I mutter, not daring to look at her.

She shoulders her backpack and turns to me, producing a stapled piece of paper from her chem book and pushing it into my hand. Her exam. She got an eighty-nine. "You invest in me, I invest in you. Plus, it fucking pisses me off that she doesn't think I can beat Kevin in a goddamn apple toss. An apple toss, Andy."

I nod at her test and make the terrible mistake of meeting her gaze. She smiles that beautiful full smile that I've been dying for since last year. "This is great. Great job."

"Yeah, well." She squeezes my arm, a friendly move that shouldn't have my brain synapses flooding with dopamine. "I'll see you at five for practice?"

"Yeah. Yes. Pitching practice. Five."

She smiles and shakes her head. "You're something, Foster."

While I have better control of the Maya situation, every time the girl smiles at me, I feel as if I'm losing a little control of something else, the butterflies in my stomach. My old crush is dusting itself off.

After Maya leaves, I pack my bag and head out into the crisp October day, my limbs pleasantly sore from our morning weight training. I try to push away the image of Maya lying at the bench press, her arms rippling with the effort of pushing the weight off her chest. Me hovering above her, my hands ready to grab the bar if necessary; her sweat beading down her temple. No, I shouldn't be thinking about it. About her damp T-shirt clinging to her curves. About her guiding me to the next station with her hand on my lower back as if I'm hers.

But thoughts are just thoughts, so I allow myself to think about Maya through my entire kinesiology class and through my entire psychology class, too. My phone buzzes in my pocket and brings me back to earth. I shake Maya out of my head. One apology, one hug from the girl, and I cave into her like a mudslide. She is beautiful, yes, but there's something about her intensity that is magnetic to me. Annoying and attractive.

Maya: *Hey. Change of plans for pitching today.*

I make sure the professor is busy at the whiteboard before I type my response in my lap. *Oh. Canceled?*

*No, we're going to do it on the field, not in the clubhouse. Ashlyn will be joining us.*

What would a pitcher, a catcher, and a shortstop be practicing together on the field?

Throw-outs.

I bristle at the idea of having this solo practice focused on me and my weakness. Alas, vulnerability is the only path to change. I shake my head at how quickly sports psychology has permeated my mind. *Running me on throw-outs?*

*Yeah. I gotta pitch anyways, so why not practice it all together?*

*Okay. I like that idea.*

Maya sends me a kissing emoji, and I shut off my phone. Girls like her end pretty much every conversation with that kissing face, but it still makes me blush. The silly emoji feels more like a ticking bomb on the verge of souring into the nauseous emoji or even worse, the one with all the expletives pouring from its mouth. I'm probably just in the eye of the storm, and I need to stay focused unless I want to get swept away in the raging winds.

I ignore the compulsion to reread everything she's sent me since the team-building day. It hasn't been much. Just a couple of schedule questions and details about practices, but I'm the one she asks now. I'm her catcher, her partner in crime.

Not Kim.

After psychology, I rush through the sea of students on the concourse to grab a banana from the dining hall, my favorite building on campus. Like in the dorms, the gray stone glows under the light of electric candles and fireplaces and is studded with oak tables and faded armchairs. It's a cozy place to enjoy a cup of coffee and kill time. If you are a person with time to kill, that is. I, on the other hand, weave through lines of students waiting for food to get to the grab n' go section.

"Hey." Katie taps my shoulder in the checkout line.

"Hey. Do you have a solo today?" I ask as we shuffle toward the payment station.

"Yep, Taylor and I have batting with Coach Clay."

We pay for our snacks and make our way across campus to the softball clubhouse. I try to be mindful and take a deep breath of the fresh fall air. Enjoy the amber smell of dead leaves and how the cool air juxtaposes the sunshine on my face. We tromp down the stairs leading from the Ag building down to the lower concourse.

"Seems like you and Maya have been working well together this week."

My ears prickle at the sound of her name. "Yeah, we have. I feel like she's finally accepted me."

"Careful, there."

Every move I make with Maya is dipped in caution. "What do you mean?" I know darn well what she means.

She grabs the sleeve of my sweatshirt and pulls me off the sidewalk. "Just because you may be on Maya's good side right now doesn't mean that she has changed at all. Her general issues are still very much a problem for the team as a whole. Also, I wouldn't get too cozy. The girl is fickle. All she cares about is winning and Instagram followers. If she's being nice to you, it's because she's found you useful for one of those things. And no offense but—"

"It's not for Instagram?"

She laughs. "It's not for the Gram."

I shake my head and pull at my sweatshirt. "Is it the clothes? My glasses? Don't laugh. I could be an influencer."

"Oh, Andy. Adorable Andy. Come on, don't want to be late."

As we continue walking to the softball field, I turn her warning over in my head. How could Maya be using me? In a sense, aren't we all using each other to win? I don't get it. Is it really using someone if it's mutually beneficial, and we all have the same goal?

I shrug. I'm finally starting to feel like I'm doing a good job. Maya's attitude toward me is just the result of that. It has to be.

I stash my softball bag in our dugout and pull on my catcher's gear.

"Hey, you." Maya melts me with a smile.

"Hey, May. I'll be ready in two minutes." I clip on my shin guards and slip into my chest protector. Chug a quick drink of water.

"No rush, Ashlyn is running a little late. But we can warm up without her."

"Sounds good. What do you want to work on today?"

"I need a slow warm-up. My arm is pretty tired from working with Coach Williams yesterday. Here." She crouches behind me and unclips my shin guards, tucking them into the catching gear cubby next to the bench. "It will be a while before you need this." Her words brush against the back of my neck, and her knuckles graze my hip, unhooking my chest protector. The reins of my guttural butterflies slip a little more from my grip.

"Thanks."

We warm up slowly. First with stretching, then regular throwing, then small distance wrist work. Ashlyn shows up when I'm finally suited back up in my gear.

"All right," I say. "Let's get this show on the road."

Ashlyn takes her position at shortstop, Maya hits the mound, and I crouch behind the plate. We start with fastballs. Maya does a couple of last-minute stretches before she falls into her pitching routine, so exact, so thorough every time. It's beautiful. With no batters, she doesn't need her mask, so I get a better view of the determination that narrows her stare, of the way her lips press together over her teeth, and how they part to let a grunt of effort escape when she releases the ball.

*Pop.*

The ball hits my mitt right on target, the impact muffling into the leather. I fall forward on my knees and toss it back. She catches it and quirks her head to one side. Walks toward me.

"Hey," she says.

"Uh, hi. Everything okay?"

"Yep. Are you a little distracted, maybe?"

"What? No. I don't think so." Maybe just a little.

"Because Ashlyn's probably going to get bored if you never run your throw-outs with her."

I give her a little chuckle and a self-deprecating nod as she walks backward away from me. She grins and winks, then turns to the mound.

Her next pitch strikes my mitt, and I cock the ball, sink a knee, and launch it to Ashlyn at second. She tags the imaginary runner and tosses the ball back to Maya.

"Perfect throw, Andy," Ashlyn yells.

"Thank you."

Maya smiles, and it hits me square in the chest. *I make her smile.* I say the words to myself through the next five pitches until my cheeks become sore from my own smiling. This is good, hopefully not too good to be true. I try to swerve out of my negative thought pattern, but the familiar walls begin to build up around me, and I feel myself peeking around corners, waiting for angry Maya to pop out at me.

Damnit, Katie.

❖

"It's too early in the year to be needing ice after practice," I say. The locker room is mostly empty, the girls trying to get to study hall as quickly as possible so they can leave study hall as quickly as possible.

"It's just a precaution. I needed to iron out some kinks this week, just getting back into it." Maya grimaces as she tries to secure the ice around her shoulder with an Ace bandage. I drop my backpack and stand in front of her.

"I can help with that. Not really a one-person job."

Maya drops her hands, allowing me access. "I'm normally pretty good at it."

I tighten the ice against her. "I bet you are. How's that?"

"*Argh.* Perfect." I can feel the hot and cold of her breath and the ice, something like the girl herself. The side of my palm skims over her pectoralis as I wrap her, and a warm buzz hums through my body, making me wish this roll of bandage would last forever. The tea tree oil in her wet hair is playing games with me. I lean an inch closer, letting the scent of the shampoo immerse me in her. And only her.

I wrap it once more, then secure it with the small metal clip and step back.

"Thanks." She pushes off the bench with a sigh and grabs her bag from her locker. Her movements are slow and pained, and it makes my heart ache to see her this way.

"Careful."

"What?"

"The season hasn't even started. Far from it, really. Don't let the coaches overwork you."

She turns away from her locker, bag hanging from her non-iced shoulder. "I'm fine, and I don't need you to be concerned over me. I don't owe you anything. I don't owe it to you to be careful or safe or whatever. Do you understand?"

"Maya, I was just—"

"Just worry about yourself. Okay?"

I stare into her dark brown eyes set against me. Her tight jaw seems to hold back more. I've crossed some line, some boundary of something. Intimacy? Was I prying? Maybe she sees my concern as trying to slow her down. I take a step backward and try to smile. "Okay." I nod and leave for study hall.

As I walk through the quiet campus, a pit grows in my stomach. Did I just ruin all our progress? It was too good to be true, just like Katie said. Regardless of my responsibility to the team, I just want Maya to like me. It felt good to be on her side.

## CHAPTER FOUR

We spend most of our next team practice scrimmaging. I step out of the batter's box and receive my signal from Coach Clayton. *Swing away.* Daniella winds up and throws me a fastball high and inside. Not for me.

"Scared to hit that?" Kim heckles from her squat behind me.

"Nope. I'm waiting for that juicy changeup she's about to throw."

The fastpitch gods smile upon me, and Daniella's next pitch is a stat-building changeup. I force myself to wait. *Hold. Hold. Cut.* No outfielders have secured the ball when I round first, and Coach waves me through second. I slide into third. Safe.

"Good hit, kid." Coach slaps a meaty paw on the back of my helmet as I dust off my practice uniform.

"Thanks, Coach." While I love catching, it feels good to shed all my gear and step into the batter's box. Hitting is like a chess match between the batter and pitcher, and having to work with Maya nonstop gives me a leg up in that battle. I'm pretty good at it, and I'm a great base runner. Nothing feels better than turning up the speed and ripping around the bases.

Ashlyn bats me home with an RBI, and I watch from the dugout as Maya hits a double. Only one out, and Katie is up to bat. She drills one down the right-field line, and Maya takes off. Her legs pump as she flies past third. I wince when I notice Taylor, the freshman on deck, fail to clear Katie's bat out of the basepath. The ball soars to home plate as Maya launches into a headfirst dive. She somehow grabs the bat and throws it out of the way with one hand and extends the other to skim the back of the plate. Safe.

I'm frozen for a moment, in awe of her athleticism, then I rush out of the dugout to meet her before she has a chance to pounce on the freshman. She brushes dirt from her arms and chest. I reach for—I'm not sure what—but Maya knocks my hand away.

"Maya," I say, like that would stop her.

She pulls off her helmet and drops it. She doesn't actually throw it, so I give her a little credit for that. She takes four quick strides to Taylor, and I follow to meet them both by the on-deck circle.

"Hey, Taylor. What, did you space out? Forget to protect your teammate?" Maya bites at the girl.

Taylor stands with her bat across her chest as if she thinks she may have to use it.

Maya shakes her head and lays into her again. "It's the on-deck player's responsibility to clear the bat out of the basepath. You could get someone seriously injured." Her voice flirts with yelling, and I tug her elbow. She obliges me this time and steps to the side, leaving Taylor to fidget in her own shame.

"Hey. Easy on her, okay? She's a freshman," I whisper.

"I don't give a shit what she is. That was just straight-up dangerous. It's serious, Andy."

"I get it. But do you really think yelling at her in front of our entire team is productive?"

Maya stares past me at the rest of our team milling about and pretending to not be paying attention to our little meeting.

I lay a hand on her crossed arms, feeling the fresh dirt bleed with the sweat on her skin. "Maya. You are a thousand-percent right. When I saw you start to slide and the bat was right there, I…" I drop my hand. "What I'm trying to say is that your message is accurate, but your delivery, while it may feel good to let it out with a shout, is statistically proven to be less effective." Maya refocuses on me, and I launch right back into my spiel. "Not to mention the detrimental effects on team morale in general. Countless studies have demonstrated that teams and individuals perform at their highest in an environment in which they feel most comfortable. Therefor—"

Maya grabs my shoulder to cut me off. "Foster."

"Yeah?"

"Stop talking. We're literally in the middle of a scrimmage. They're waiting on us." She looks over my shoulder again and brushes past me. "Well, they're waiting on *you*."

At the end of practice, Coach Clayton assigns us a mile run. Not too bad. There are still softballs scattered around the field when our team begins to pack up their personal items, and I look to Maya to see if she's going to say anything. She leans against the far wall of the dugout, arms crossed, watching me. I move through my teammates to reach her.

"They haven't cleaned up the field. It's like they're just going to pack up and leave," I say to her.

"What do you want me to do about it?"

"Well, I…"

"*Well, I*…Jesus, Andy. You're the goddamn captain." She pushes off the wall. "What? You only have a voice when you want to lecture me in front of everyone? Cool, Foster."

"Maya—"

She moves through the rest of the girls to the front of the dugout. "Hey! Why are you packing up when we haven't even cleaned up our field?" she yells. Everyone's attention turns to her. "This is completely unacceptable and not how we handle our business on this team. Everyone, stop what you're doing and pick up the field. And when we're done, we will run *two* miles to show the coaches our regret for not doing things right in the first place. Let's go." She claps her hands and starts for the outfield.

The girls follow with urgency. And I follow with shame.

I towel dry my hair and tie it in a sloppy bun while I track Maya at her locker. I need to catch her before she leaves, but my feet won't carry me out of the bathroom. I steal a glance at myself in the mirror. Pink-cheeked like a damn baby, hair a wreck.

"Maya, can we talk?"

She tucks her pitching mask in the top shelf and takes an extra second before meeting my gaze, hands gripping the sides of her locker. "I'd rather not."

"Please."

"Fine." She follows me outside to the bench behind our clubhouse, out of the way of our teammates leaving the locker room for study hall.

I want to apologize for my word vomit on the field and for not speaking up at the end of practice. I want to scold her for being such a loud and volatile presence on our team, and I want to figure out how to tame her, but instead, when I turn, I say something straight out of left field. "Why don't you like me?" I ask like a wounded child who got picked last for kickball.

She blinks in surprise. "What?"

I take a small step toward her, closing the gap between us. "Why don't you like me? You hardly acknowledged my existence last year, even though my locker is literally right next to yours. And this year, I'm your catcher. Maybe we don't agree on everything, but you're just so darn hotheaded."

"Is that all?" she asks, looking bored.

"No." I feel the control over my anger slipping. "When you're so loud and angry all the time, you don't notice other people. You don't notice your teammates or how they're feeling or what they need. It's no wonder you're not the captain." I step back when I hear myself say the last sentence.

She drops her arms and glares at me. "That's rich. I don't know why I'm not the captain, but at least I'm not afraid to address my team *like a captain*. You want to know why I don't like you, Andy?"

I stare at her.

She gathers a deep breath and exhales. "I don't like you because you'd rather sit there in silence and judge everyone instead of getting up, being part of the conversation, and being a part of our team. You walk around me like I'm fucking contagious, and you are the most condescending person I've ever met. I'm trying to go places in my life, and yes, that means I have passion. *Passion*, Andy. Have you heard of it? You just stand in the shadows and tug on my sleeve when you think I'm getting too carried away, and that earned you the title of captain." She chuckles into the dark. "Well, guess what? If you think being a captain means watching from the sidelines, then you're going to fail. And if you think making connections is just helping someone study and trying to control them, then you're going to be alone."

Like a bucket of ice water in the face. I feel tears welling in my eyes.

"You're so contained in your stupid little box. Spill it, Andy. Come on." She pokes me in the shoulder with a sharp pointer finger, egging me on. "Get angry. Overflow, Foster!" Another jab of her finger.

I knock her hand away. "Don't touch me. I may be quiet sometimes, but it's because I notice other people. I pay attention. I'm in tune. You? You just steamroll everyone and everything. It's all about *Maya*. I don't want to spill all over everyone else the way you do. It's selfish. *You* are selfish and arrogant. Everyone just tiptoes around you, waiting for your next tantrum to erupt."

Her sharp laughter blinds me in the night. "You think *I'm* arrogant? To think you're the only one feeling deeply, that you're the only one noticing or observing because you just can't bear to open your mouth and be vulnerable…that doesn't make you special, Andy. That makes you weak. I have no idea why Coach named you captain. It was clearly a mistake. At least I try."

I take a step back. Away from her. The backs of my knees hit the bench, and I lower myself onto it, exhausted from our vitriol. I've never fought like this with anyone in my entire life. What just happened? "I don't even want to be captain. I didn't ask for this."

"Well, you are captain. So you should probably stop acting like a child and start acting like a leader." She holds out her arms. "I mean, this is just ridiculous."

I wipe at the stupid tear trickling down my cheek. "You're hurting me, May. Please. Stop."

She's quiet for a beat, then shakes her head as if she's waking up. Her mouth drops open, and she slides onto the bench next to me. "Andrea, I'm sorry. I—"

"Don't." I hold up my hands in defeat and try to will my tears to stop their constant slow stream down my face. I can't believe I'm crying in front of her. I'm crying because I believe her. I believe everything she said about me.

Her breathing slows. "I shouldn't have said all that."

"I know it already. You think I don't know this already?"

"I got so worked up, so angry, because"—she runs a hand down her face—"I care what you think about me."

"Stop, Maya. You don't have to try to explain it away. Everything you said about me is true."

She shakes her head. "It's not. I think the reason I snapped at you is because you're a person I respect, and it can feel like you hate me sometimes. I know you're trying to help, but it's constant, you know? It overwhelms me." Her gaze falls in her lap, and moonlight plays with her hair. "Do you hate me?"

I sniffle, confused. "What? I don't hate you."

"I know I can be intense. But it's not because I don't care about other people. I care so much it literally drives me crazy. I care about Taylor. I care that she does a good job and learns how to be a teammate who protects all of us. I care about our team and about reaching our potential. I care when they disrespect us and our coaches. That attitude isn't going to take us where we need to go." She looks into the night sky. "I know how good we could be." She shakes her head, then looks at me again. "And I care about you."

The hot and cold of this girl gives me whiplash, but her last sentence burrows into my chest and ignites, leaving me warm. We're bonded somehow. We're a push and pull, opposites headed in the same direction. All we have to do is get out of each other's way and move some mass.

"You have a funny way of showing it."

"Yeah. I need to work on that." She nods. "Why didn't you speak up today when they didn't clean up the field? You're the captain, Andy. We need you to step up in those moments."

She's right. Deep breath. "I'm not used to being in the spotlight. And you're totally right about being vulnerable. I don't like to be vulnerable. I was afraid that if I tried to command them, they'd ignore me." The truth tastes bitter.

"I would've had your back. I've got your back."

It's a strange thing to believe of this girl. But I think I do. "I know. I'm sorry."

She grabs my hand, her eyes searching mine. My gut tightens around every confusing feeling I have for her. "I was completely out of line. I know I have things to work on, and I promise, I will try to do better. I hope you can forgive me."

I squeeze her hand and drop it. Wipe under my eyes one more time. "I don't know why you're not the captain. You're the soul of the team. I'm not trying to extinguish you. You're meant to be fierce, May. I hope some of that will rub off on me." I examine my hands in the night. "It should've been you."

Maya sighs and examines the dark woods in front of us. "I guess there's a reason for everything. Coach Clay may not have a lot of hair, but he has a lot of experience." She pauses. "When UGA passed on me, I was shocked, broken, completely shattered. But something about him earned my trust. He knows something. He knows you need to be our captain, and we both need to start trusting in that. It's just, I don't know what it's like with your parents and having a sick dad, but you're not doing anyone any favors by shrinking. You sell yourself short, but you also sell the rest of us short, too." She pulls me off the bench with her. "Let's try again. I think this all started with you asking why I don't like you."

I nod, a little bit of shame tickling my cheeks when I hear my childish question out loud again.

"I like you a lot more than you think. Clearly." She grins.

"That much, huh?" I chuckle, a tingle forming in my stomach from how the words sound.

Her eyes stay glued to mine. "I guess time will tell."

A breeze pushes through the woods to meet my skin, freezing my wet hair to ice, and I shiver, realizing I forgot my hoodie inside. She runs a hand up and down my forearm as if trying to warm me. I'm not sure if it's the wind or her touch, but goose bumps take over my body.

"Look at you," she says. Her teeth are bright white in the night, her canines sharp and long. The one dimple in her right cheek deepens as she grins at me. Her hand stops at my elbow, then drops to my waist, her fingers tugging gently at the hem of my shirt, and for a moment, I think she's going to slip her hand underneath. The thought of her fingers skimming across the skin of my stomach makes me twitch, makes me shudder. "You're freezing." She tugs my shirt as she turns and walks to the front of the clubhouse. "Come on, Foster. Let's get you inside."

I follow on my short leash until she releases me. I feel the disconnect in my entire being, missing her hand in my shirt and her knuckles brushing against my waist. I want to keep her close.

When we get back to the locker room, everyone else has left. I throw away bits and pieces of pre-wrap and tape and Gatorade cups, not even annoyed that our team left the locker room looking so sloppy. Not annoyed at all that we could've been punished with an extra study hall or morning conditioning for leaving our clubhouse in such a mess.

"You don't have to do that, you know. It's the freshmen's job," Maya says, shouldering her bag.

I walk over to our lockers and grab my bag. "Yeah, I guess I should talk to them tomorrow."

"You should. I would do it for you, but word on the street is that I'm scary, and I wouldn't want anyone to feel uncomfortable," she says, trailing off into baby talk.

"Shut up." I laugh and punch her in the arm. She grabs my wrist and pulls me into her, her chest knocking the air out of mine. Her arms wrap around my waist in a hard embrace, and her eyes crinkle with mischief. "Maya…"

She breaks into a giant grin and tackles me to the ground. We roll around on the AstroTurf, letting it nip at our skin as we struggle against each other for dominance. Maya has a couple inches on me and is stronger than I am, but I don't think I mind when she bests me, her body pressing mine into the fake grass, her fingers squeezed around my wrists. I buck like I want her to get off, but really, I just want her to keep pushing into me. I want her breath to blanket my face, her strength to dominate me.

She rolls off and blows out a deep breath. "Whew. Good effort, Foster."

We stare at the ceiling like we're staring at the stars, the sides of our bodies pressed together, our hands squeezed together between our hips. I can't find words to respond.

After a moment, she fills the silence again. "I'm sorry, Andy. Sometimes, there's a whole storm of things." Her palm moves in circles over her chest. "And the way I anchor is to grab on to something. Something I can turn the storm toward."

I blink against the recessed lighting of the ceiling. "You swerve."

"Swerve?"

"Yeah, like when you feel the storm start to take you over, it sounds like you try to *swerve* it into something."

Maya takes a moment, then nods. "Yeah, I swerve. But you know, turns out people don't like to be yelled at." She sighs.

"Yeah. So weird."

She pushes herself up, leaving me cold, and reaches out a hand. "Come on, walk with me."

We wave at Coach Williams through her office window and walk out of the clubhouse. The night hums with a static chill. I match Maya's pace, brushing against her arm every so often. "Sounds like," I start, a little surprised at the sound of my voice against the quiet night, "you could try to swerve just a little more, and maybe you'd end up outside of the storm instead of just redirecting it."

"Maybe. I don't know, sometimes it feels like I'm the only one who really cares."

"That's not—"

"I know it's not true. I'm just telling you how I feel."

I stay quiet this time and wait for her to continue.

We walk up the alley next to the physics building and hang a right. The athletics building comes into view, and Maya stops. "I know we all care. And we all want to win. But I have everything to lose."

I stare at her mouth as she speaks. Her face shifts from completely open to surprised to hidden. "Wait, what do you have to lose?"

She shuffles her feet. "Nothing, I didn't really mean it like that."

"I mean, we all want to win, but Alder has only made it to Super Regionals once. We've never even made it to the World Series."

"I know, I know. I didn't mean anything concrete. Just—"

"But we will." If that's what she wants, if that's what would bring this girl peace, I'll do anything in my power. "We're going to the World Series this year."

"We're going to *win* the World Series this year."

"Well, if we're going to do that, you need to get your butt in study hall and crack open that chemistry book."

"Oh God, not chemistry."

As Maya chuckles and walks next me, I allow myself to feel optimistic. I feel optimistic for our team and the possibility of making it further in the postseason than we ever have. I feel optimistic for myself and my capabilities as captain.

And I feel optimistic for us.

## CHAPTER FIVE

Student Activities Week always feels something like an office party carnival where none of the booths have any fun rides, but you can spin a colorful wheel for the chance to win a roll of Smarties, and all it costs is *your soul* in the form of your email address. Regardless, the Friday night of activities week has an electricity to it. Like, if I didn't look directly at what was going on around me, I could be on Coney Island.

I pass the women's basketball booth, which is raffling off a fifty-dollar concession gift card to anyone who can beat Nicky in a vertical jump. So far, they only have two names in the raffle jar. I say a quick hi to Rachel and Emma, who are looking damn good in their team swag, and continue to our booth, closer to the end of the concourse. But on the way, a booth on my right catches my attention with their bright rainbow banner: *Alder Queer Fellowship.*

"Hi. Can I offer you some literature?"

I snap my attention to the group of people behind the table, realizing they're talking to me.

A girl behind the booth with honey gold hair chuckles at herself. "Sorry, I really love saying that."

"Oh. I, um, I think I'm okay."

"I don't blame you. This one can be pretty intimidating," a girl with dark brown hair says, throwing a thumb over her shoulder at the first girl. "I'm Bailey. And I know you may not identify as queer, but we're always looking for allies. Either way, AQF is a space for all of us."

The first girl whose name tag reads *Noelle* steps next to Bailey and snakes an arm around her waist, offering me a warm smile that compels me toward their table.

I pick up the pen attached to their sign-up sheet and write my Alder email address in slow, neat print. This may be the first time I've officially "come out." Growing up with Alex Squared never made me feel like being gay was an issue. So much so that I didn't even feel coming out was necessary. I kind of just assumed I'd bring home a girlfriend one day and confirm what they already know. There have been a handful of times on campus when I second-guessed being out, Alder being a Catholic college and all, but my parents being so open and progressive has always made me feel secure in my sexuality. Some yelling religious assholes and a university that's stuck in the past can't change that.

"I do." I lay down the pen. "Well, I am. Gay. But I'm on the softball team. Doesn't leave me much spare time for other activities."

A huge smile breaks across Noelle's face. "That's fantastic. Come whenever you can. No pressure. We mostly eat snacks and play games. But when we're not doing that, we like to lobby the school for protections and try to change the world," Bailey says.

Noelle tightens her grip on Bailey. It's clear that she's proud of her—who I assume to be—girlfriend. A pang strikes me low in my belly as I watch them. They're adorable.

And I'm jealous.

I want to touch a woman like that. I want to be touched like that. I break out of my trance and look at Bailey, waving the pamphlet I just grabbed. "Thanks. I'll do my best to make it to a meeting."

"We are so excited to have you," Noelle blurts. Bailey winks at me, and I continue down the concourse to our fastpitch booth, the Alder Queer Fellowship pamphlet feeling warm in my back pocket.

Jeremy finishes drilling the two targets to their wooden bases as I walk up. "Thanks, babe," Maya says. "Oh, did you grab your jacket? The lion's pride one that matches ours? Because I need you looking cute for the Gram today."

Jeremy packs his drill into a Black and Decker bag and stands to stretch his back. "God, woman. You could have texted me."

I busy myself helping Katie and Ashlyn set up our table with our schedule, some swag, and other fastpitch paraphernalia. Maya brushes by me and whispers something to Jeremy, her hand on his arm. For a second, I forgot about him. That she has a boyfriend. That I'll never be that person for her. Not that I've ever used a drill in my life, but who cares? Lots of men have never used a drill in their lives, and lots of women have. I could be a suitable—

"Andy, can you grab the rest of the game photos and just kinda scatter them over the table?" Katie asks.

I shake my head out of my crazy thoughts. When did these feelings for Maya sneak up on me again? I thought that fire was out, extinguished, but apparently, the embers are still very much alive. And these last couple of days with Maya have been the bellow of wind that ignited it all back to life. "Of course." I place the photos in the perfect spaces so it doesn't look like clutter but like a clean collage. I look up. "Wait, we definitely need a trash can."

She turns in a small circle. "Um, I see like five within thirty feet of us."

"Mm-hmm, mm-hmm. I see this now. A broom and dustpan, at least. It's going to be a mess of rotting apple bits once they get started." A mess that will no doubt reflect my feelings for Maya. A mess that will be impossible to clean up once the first apple hits the target. Once I take a step that's just a little *too far*.

The air smells like warm apple cider and sweat, and the sun dips lower on the horizon as I zip my coat and tuck my hands in my pockets. I tiptoe through the sludge of broken apple cores to a no-spray zone after being hit by sticky shrapnel one too many times in my spot, but the rest of the student body is all about it. A huge group of students has gathered around, hooting and hollering for Maya, for Kevin, for smashing apples and the spectacle of it all. We've created a true carnival at our booth. All we need is deep-fried Oreos and funnel cake.

"Oh shit. Maya pulls ahead of Kevin with another bull's-eye. Only two apples left for each of them. Who will be dubbed apple pitcher of the year, folks?" Jeremy yells through a megaphone.

"Wow. This is a wild success," Ashlyn yells in my ear, the vanilla-mint haze of her vape circling around our heads.

I nod and give her a thumbs-up.

Kim flirts with the freshmen on the baseball team, stealing their hats and play fighting, while Katie bobs her head to the music streaming from the Bose speaker that Jeremy set up for us. Maya snags her last apple from the bucket at her feet. If she hits a bull's-eye, she wins.

"Maya is going for the kill. Watch out, Kev," Jeremy yells.

She spins the apple in her hand like it's a softball while she scans the crowd to her right. Her eyes catch mine, and I smile. "Get him, May," I cheer, and she winks, sending my flames higher and higher for her.

Maya dips, shifts her weight, and rockets the apple from her hand. It *thunks* hard into the wet plywood and explodes against the bull's-eye. Students cheer as apple chunks splatter into the air.

"Oh my God, she's done it. Maya knocks off Kevin, the All-American," the megaphone booms.

The boys grab an undershirt that has Sharpied chicken scratch all over the front and scribble one more word on it.

"That's my girlfriend, everyone." More applause. "I know. Sorry, guys, all mine. Okay, Maya, I officially name you champion apple pitcher of the year. It is my honor to offer you the most coveted trophy of all"—he grabs the undershirt from the table—"Corey's undershirt, only twice worn. Don't worry."

Maya smiles and holds up the T-shirt. I squint to read the words scribbled across it: *Winner of the apple wars. Maya G.*

She pulls out her phone and snaps a selfie of her and Jeremy. Then in a quick move, she yanks off her jacket and pulls the hem of her shirt up and over her head. Her skin is only bare for a second, her bra is only bared for a second, until she shimmies into her new championship shirt. I look at the mass of people that just got to witness that, but I know they didn't see what I saw. It was too brief for them to notice how the fading light dripped down her curves, how the shadows pooled in the definition of her muscles, or that she's wearing her favorite purple bra, the one with the frayed lace under her left armpit.

I unglue my eyes from her as she kisses Jeremy and snaps another selfie. I'm sure she'll get thousands of likes for that one.

❖

"Hey, girl," Rachel says as I walk into our dorm. She collapses into bed and turns off her lamp. "Y'all crushed it at your booth tonight." She gives a tired chuckle at her pun.

"Yeah, people seemed to really like it, but will the hype translate into ticket sales next spring? That's the question." I never understood why people prefer to watch baseball over softball. Softball is faster, with more intricacies of game play, while still maintaining the thrill of crushing home runs.

"I bet it will. I think you may have a star on your team. I don't want to piss you off, but people are obsessed with Maya. Especially if she keeps taking off her shirt. She's hot as hell. Folks will go to the games just to see that girl in uniform."

I wince as I trade my shirt for pj's. It gives me anxiety to find a girl attractive who the entire world finds attractive. Even if she was single, even if she was into girls, I'd be one in a million other people in line trying to be close to her. I don't like crowds. "Yeah, have you seen her Instagram? I don't know exactly what qualifies someone as an influencer, but she has, like, twenty-thousand followers," I say.

"Sounds about right."

"Also, she's been pretty chill lately. We had kind of a blowout fight the other day, but
since then, she's been great."

"That's good to hear. Hopefully, it continues that way." Rachel shifts in her bed and tugs the covers over her shoulder.

"Fingers crossed. What's up in basketball land?"

"Misery."

I tuck myself under my covers and switch off my lamp.

"And I broke up with Melissa."

"What?" I switch my lamp back on and cross our small room to her bed, somehow shocked by the breakup that we all knew was coming. I perch on the edge of her mattress, her knees at my lower back. "Are you okay?"

She rolls over and wipes her eyes with the back of her hand. She's not crying, just seems exhausted. "I'm good. I don't want to be with her, but it's really hard to hurt someone. Feels inherently bad, you know? Even though it's the right thing to do, and it's a hard thing to do, the other person still gets to be angry and hate you and say dumb shit to you."

"Not everyone handles breakups well. She's just sad. It can't be easy to lose a Rachel Dunston." It's true. Rachel is smart, sexy, athletic, and cool. How many gorgeous D1 starters are also premed? Poor Melissa.

"Yeah. Thanks, Andy." She pushes up to lean on her elbow. "Well, since we're getting all mushy and intimate, can I ask you something?"

"Yeah. Shoot."

"When are you going to give up the Emma thing? I mean, don't get me wrong. I love her, she's incredibly gifted, and I guess she's cute. But damn, Andy. She ain't into you like that. Even though the girl cannot turn it off around you. Or anyone, really."

I rub my hands down my thighs and bob my head. *Emma.* Emma is not the person taking up space in my brain right now. The dull ache that I usually feel for her is barely there, if it's even there at all. It's filled with a fresh want. "I know. I've known she's not into me since sophomore year of high school. But it's all good. I honestly haven't been thinking of her that way lately. Haven't been thinking about her much at all, actually."

"That's good. 'Cause you're a catch." She waves over my general being. "Don't waste all of this on Em. Don't waste it on someone who won't appreciate it."

My cheeks warm under her words as I stand to turn off my lamp. I catch a glimpse of my arm, vascular and strong under the golden glow, before the darkness steals my vision. I've never thought much of my looks, but I think Rachel is right. I'm a catch. I'm smart, athletic, and cute enough.

"I saw you blushing. Just own it. You're awesome."

My cheeks burn. "Thanks, Rach. You're awesome, too, by the way. Pretty much my favorite person to share a room with."

"I'm the only roommate you've ever had. Low bar."

I smile against my sheets. "You got lifting in the morning?"

"Yep."

"Cool, well I'll probably see you in the morning, then. Night, Rachel."

"Night."

I turn away from her and open Maya's Instagram. Just out of curiosity. To see how our booth was received tonight. The photo of her and Jeremy pushing their lips together stares at me from my phone. *Ugh.* He's a nice enough guy, I guess. But how did he get *her?* His eyes are squeezed shut, but somehow, Maya keeps hers on the camera. Interesting. Kind of disturbing but it gives me a little hope.

*Hope? Jesus, she's my teammate. And don't forget,* straight.

I toss my phone on my desk in disgust and let the darkness of the night flood me. Flood Maya out of me. It was literally a couple weeks ago that the girl spit on me. She hated me. And it's not like she's changed. That's who she is, a hotheaded diva.

My phone vibrates against the wood of my desk, and I snatch it so it doesn't disturb Rachel's sleep.

Maya: *Okay, so tonight was fucking awesome.*

Oh geez. Well, why wouldn't I be friendly? There's no point in ignoring her, so I type, *Yeah. I was so excited when you won. Like, how can apple toss feel so important?*

*Because you did such a great job putting it together. That's why everyone was hyped. Great idea, Andy.*

*Well, I can't take all the credit. Your boy was clutch with the megaphone.*

Sure, I only referenced Jeremy because I'm petty and jealous. I'm not sure what kind of response I'm hoping for as I stare at the bouncing dots on my phone. It's not as if she's going to tell me she randomly dumped him tonight. Bounce, bounce, disappear. Don't text her, don't text her. Be cool. The bouncing dots return, and a small exhale of relief escapes me.

Maya: *What are you doing right now?*

I grin. *Just lying in bed. About to go to sleep. I hope you are, too. I don't want my spotter dropping the bench press bar on my face because she didn't get enough sleep.* I add a winky face to make it clear that I'm joking. Kinda. I'm *kinda* joking.

*Same. I just can't fall asleep. Jeremy is like the Hulk when he snores.*

My gut twists in on itself, trying to wring that boy's name out of me. She's in his bed. Or worse, he's in hers. I wonder if she knows that she just slashed me open. I pound my fist on my forehead. Keep it cool, Andy.

I type, *I don't snore*...I move my thumb to the little 'x' to delete my silly text. It just felt good to write, but I would never actually send—*shit*! My finger misses the backspace button and instead hits send. I stare at my catastrophe for what feels like eternity before Maya responds.

*How do you know? I guess I'll have to verify that one day. Sleep tight, Foster.*

Oh my God.

*Night*, I type.

My eyes stay fixed on her last text, on the kissy face after my name. She liked it, my blatantly flirty and line-crossing text. My body responds to her words. I close my eyes and imagine Maya's body is pressing me into my mattress instead of my weighted blanket. I slip my hand to the waistband of my boxers. Rachel snorts in her sleep and rolls over to her stomach. I wrench my hand from myself and wake up from my stupidity.

I have a thing for Maya Gonzalez.

Scratch that.

Everyone has a thing for Maya Gonzalez. But I'm the one person who really, *really* shouldn't.

❖

The bath of warm air hugs me as I walk into the Lion Athletic Center and shut the cold out behind me. I take slow sips of coffee from my travel mug and walk down the sleepy maroon hallway toward the faint sound of clanking weights. With every blink, my eyelids feel heavier and heavier; I am not ready for this morning. Deep breath. I push open the doors to the weight room, and the familiar smell of stale sweat, musty mats, and commercial cleaner wafts into my nostrils and makes me want to gag.

Maya and Coach Williams are the only ones here so far. We never plan it, but Maya or I are always here first. On a day when she's not early, I happen to be. And just like today, when I'm not early, she happens to be. Maya wipes down a barbell, and Coach Williams pats her on the shoulder.

"Good work, May. I'm going to grab a refill." Coach Williams shakes her empty coffee mug. "Be right back. Morning, Andy. Your partner's all warmed up and ready for you."

I swallow my nerves and try to block out the image of myself from last night. I was "all warmed up and ready" for my partner, and as a result, I couldn't fall asleep. The last time I remember seeing on my phone is three twenty-five.

"Great." I smile at Coach Williams as she walks past me to the hallway.

I start toward the locker room and try not to stare at Maya drinking from her water bottle, a stream of liquid running down her neck. "Good morning," I say as I walk past.

"Is it? You look like shit, Foster."

I turn back to her with my hand pressed against my chest. "Ouch."

She wipes her mouth and takes a step toward me. Grins. "Did you, uh, not sleep very well last night?"

My stomach crunches on acid from my coffee. She tightens her ponytail and pins me with her gaze. "I slept well once I fell asleep."

"Mm-hmm. And when was that?"

I drop my eyes to my shoes. "Late."

"I don't want my spotter dropping a weight on me because she stayed up too late last night." She winks.

The direct reference to our texts makes my stomach drop in a good way. In a bad way.

A couple of sleepy teammates shuffle in from the cold and exchange quiet hellos and lazy fist bumps with us as they drift toward the locker room.

"You know I got you." I blink in surprise at my audacity with this girl. Maya grins, taking it in stride.

She plants a hand on my chest and pushes me away. "I know, now go get ready or someone else will 'got me.'"

*Someone else already has.*

When I make it back to the weight room after changing, Maya sits on the mat waiting for me, one leg extended in a deep stretch. I drop my water bottle and let gravity take me to the ground next to her like the zombie I am. I lie flat on my back and throw one leg over the other, twisting my hips, getting a good stretch in my glutes; they've been giving me a hard time lately. My eyes drift shut as I focus on how good the stretch feels. They fly open when Maya leans into me, hand on my thigh, deepening the stretch.

"Too much?"

I let my head drop back to the ground. "No, it's good. Thanks."
*Too good.*

She pushes a little more. "So why couldn't you fall asleep?" She drops my leg and motions for me to switch to my left. Pushes against me.

My mind pulls up an image of me, my hand in my waistband, my teammate on my mind. "I stress on the small things sometimes. Does it matter?"

"It might. Matter, I mean. Depending on what you were stressing about." She releases me and helps me up.

I grunt and haul my deadweight off the ground. "I just got stuck in a loop. It's all good."

"You should text me next time you can't sleep. I have a trick."

"Can you just tell me now?"

She shakes her head as she leads us to the bench press. "Nah, it doesn't really work like that."

"Um, okay."

"You first, Foster."

I lie on the bench as Maya piles weights on the bar for me.

"Ready? I added ten today. You got this."

The shaking in my arms and the pounding in my head makes me feel like I really don't "got this." The bar lowers to my chest, and I struggle to push it back up through the ten reps. On the last rep, I completely flail, my arms shaking like jelly.

"You can do it, Andy. Breathe. And up."

I push against the bar as hard as I can, my hips bucking off the bench and my vision blurring. The bar stalls above my quivering arms until Maya's hands tighten around it and guide it to its resting place. I grab my water and wipe at the instant sweat gathering at my brow. "Phew," I breathe. "There's no way I was going to get that alone. Generous spot, May."

"You were ready." She squeezes my sweaty bicep. "I have to get out of here early today. Got a presentation in public speaking. Kill me. Anyway, I'll see you at practice."

"Yeah. Good Luck."

When lifting comes to an end, I gather my now less sleepy teammates around for a quick chat. I'm a little nervous, but it's my job to address things like leaving trash in our locker room after practice. I deliver my message in a firm, clear tone, and to my surprise, they nod along. No riot commences at my words. Just a little more respect in my pocket.

"Which Mass do y'all wanna go to this Sunday? I'm trying to meet a friend for lunch, so I need to know," Daniella says.

I sneak out as they discuss among themselves. I'm one of the only girls who isn't religious, preferring to not attend Mass until the season starts. Then I attend out of solidarity. Coaches don't care what we do. They lead us in a short prayer before games, but I'm not even sure if they're Catholic. I think they may be contractually obligated to pray with us.

I have forty-five minutes to kill before my eight-a.m. class starts, so I take a quick shower and buy a coffee from the Starbucks on campus and sit at an empty bench. I sink into the coffee, the bench, the November morning air. I try to find a meditative place of calm, but Maya keeps popping my peaceful bubble.

*Focus on anything else.*

Students flow by on the concourse in a constant wave of humming energy, one big kinetic crest. *The trees.* The oaks hold on to some of their green, only the slowest creep of brown has begun, while the maples strike brilliant poses of red and orange. Sip. Breathe.

Maya wants me to text her next time I can't sleep.

"Screw it," I mumble to myself and pull out my phone. I've owed my parents a call for a while now. I try to talk to them once a week, but it's pushing two at this point, and I know they're already awake.

There's the familiar dull ring, then my dad's voice. "Hello? Is this my long-lost daughter?" There's the slightest tremble in his words, a symptom of his pain shaking everything up.

"Come off it. Hey, Dad. How are you feeling today?"

"Oh, you know, fresh as a newborn baby. How are things? Wait, hang on, let me get your mother on the phone so she can hear, too." *How are things?* If I answered his question honestly, we'd be on this call for hours. But just because I'm going to withhold almost everything that's going on in my life doesn't mean that hearing my parents' voices won't help. They're always centering for me. A comfort.

"Andrea. You missed last week's call. I'm not mad, but I definitely didn't love that," my mom yells into the speakerphone.

"Hey, Mom. Sorry, you know how crazy things can get with my schedule."

"It's not even season, yet. Don't try to pull a 'fastball' on me." She interrupts herself to laugh at her own joke. "Once a week. That's all we ask of our only daughter after feeding, clothing, and housing her for—"

"I'm sorry, Mom. I promise, it won't happen again."

"Mm-hmm."

My dad whispers something unintelligible to my mom, probably talking her down. "Andy Pandy, how are things at Alder? Softball going well? We're dying to get up there for a game in the spring. And how's Rachel? She's just such a lovely girl. And our Emma?"

"Oh, she is. She is. What a sweet girl. And our Emma. We miss her," my mom chimes in.

I cringe at the mention of Emma. "Our" Emma. I know my parents have always wanted to see us together. Or at least, for my crush to be reciprocated. They've witnessed Emma and I flirt enough times to know the score, but it feels like they think I'm the one dragging my feet and not Emma.

"Your mother has been working on our Lion fan gear. Just wait until you see it."

I shake my head in amusement and try to stifle a chuckle. "That was a lot of questions, guys. You know, you can just ask one, and we can go from there. But Alder is good. The trees are starting to change color, my classes are going well, I joined a club. Softball is going well, too. I'm still figuring out how to be a captain—"

"So proud," my mom interjects.

"So, so proud, dear."

"And I think the last question was about Rachel and Emma. They're good. Really busy right now. They have their first game next week, so Rachel is never home. And I can only imagine what kind of fan gear you've whipped up." I imagine a wild lion's mane made of quilting scraps. That is exactly the kind of thing my mom would make.

"Good for them. We'll have to make it up for a weekend that you both have a game," my dad says.

"Yeah, come in March."

"And what club did you join?" my mom asks.

They know. I know they know, hence their whole wanting me and Emma to be together vibe. Also, I know that they won't bat an eye. My parents are giant nerds, have hearts of gold, and wouldn't see me being a lesbian as even a blip on their radar. "It's called the Alder Queer Fellowship. Well, it's not actually a school sanctified club yet, but that's a major part of their agenda. Haven't been to a meeting, but I plan to when I can find the time."

"That's fantastic. A lot of these private colleges have big strides they need to take when it comes to equity and diversity. We're very proud of you, Andrea."

"Thanks, guys."

"You know, I always thought Rachel was very pretty…"

I laugh into my phone. At least it's not Emma they're drooling over this time. "My God, Mother. Subtlety is a virtue. Rachel is gorgeous, you're absolutely right. She also just went through a messy breakup, and I don't really see her in that way, you know, because she's my roommate."

"What about Emma? She's gay, and you guys have always been close," my dad suggests.

*There it is.* "You know, it's so weird. Being queer is not the only thing I look for in a woman," I say, trying to avoid the topic of Emma at all costs.

"Okay, okay. Are you interested in anyone else?"

*Yes.* "No. Not much time for that, I'm afraid."

"You know, Andrea, life will always be hectic and busy. Some things are worth making time for."

"I know, Dad."

"Don't forget to put yourself out there. You are lovely."

"Thanks, Mom. Listen, I love you guys, but I have to head to class."

"Promise to call us on Sunday," my mom says.

"I promise."

"And tell the girls we say hi and good luck at their first game," my dad says.

"Alex, we should send them a package," I hear my mom say to my dad.

"We're going to send them a package," he shouts into the phone.

"Okay guys. I love you. Gotta go."

"Love you," they yell in unison.

I tuck my phone away and draw in a deep breath of fresh air. I feel stronger now. Settled. My parents know me. They *know* me, and they believe in me through and through. I need to believe in myself. What could stop me, then?

## CHAPTER SIX

I open my door to Katie in the hallway holding up a bag of Tostitos and a jar of salsa. "What's up girl? You ready?" she asks.

"For bad reality TV *and* bad snacks? Yeah, let's do this. Come on in."

She sets the chips and salsa on the floor and leans pillows against my bed with my laptop a couple feet in front of them.

"If you give me a virus with all your sketchy streaming websites, I'm going to kill you."

She slinks to the ground and types on my keyboard hunt-and-peck style. "Relax, Andy. It's not like I'm downloading porn. Just streaming a show that makes so much money, they won't miss out on two people's viewership."

I grab my water bottle and join her on the floor.

"Okay, this is the best season. The dude proposes to this one girl, then like a week later, changes his mind, dumps her on live television, and gets with the other girl instead," Katie explains through a mouthful of chips.

"That sounds terrible."

"Oh, it is. It's the best. Don't act like you don't love watching reruns of this show with me."

"We could pick a better show…"

"Blasphemy. Your phone buzzed."

"Oh, thanks." I shimmy to my knees and snatch my phone off my desk, then settle back in next to Katie.

"I didn't know I had competition." She raises an eyebrow and nudges me with her shoulder.

"If you're referring to being my only friend, then don't worry. You're still the *one*." I flutter my eyelashes and clutch at my heart. "You know, besides all my basketball friends."

"*All* your basketball friends?" She laughs through her crunching.

I unlock my phone and feel my lips tug into an involuntary smile. "It's just Maya."

"Maya? What does she want? Tell her to leave you alone. You're off the clock."

Maya: *How was the rest of lifting? You miss me?*

I put my phone on the floor next to me, waiting for the show to start and Katie's attention to fall elsewhere before I respond. "She's not that bad."

"You're just saying that because you happen to be in her good graces right now."

Am I? I know we've had our ups and downs, but under every interaction we've had, good or bad, there has always been *something* pulling us together. I'd like to believe that even in the worst moments between us, we still gravitate toward each other. "No, I mean it. We had this huge fight outside the locker room after practice last week. I basically confronted her and told her how I thought her attitude was detrimental to the team." I look at the golden planks of wood underneath me. "I said it was no wonder Coach didn't want her to be captain."

"Holy shit. Are you serious?"

"Yeah. And that was after I asked her why she hates me."

"Whoa. What'd she say? What happened?"

"She basically said I never engage with anyone and that I'm too timid to be captain. That I can't speak up and be a leader when I need to be."

"What a bitch. I mean, seriously. You stand up to that girl all the time."

"No, she was right. Everything she said was spot-on. I need to learn to open my darn mouth and speak. Not just pull her aside every practice to chastise her, but, like, I need to be a captain. I need to correct freshmen instead of always leaving it to her. I don't know. She apologized after, and I feel like she really tried to open up to me."

Katie shakes her head. "Whatever is going on between you guys is so weird."

"What do you mean going on? There's nothing going on between us." My heart races at the implication. Does she even know what she's implying? It would be really bad for the team if any rumors started about us, or more accurately, me.

She shrugs and pops another chip in her mouth. "I'm just saying, the girl is used to having the world wrapped around her finger. She has goals and people in her life to help her achieve them. You're just a stepping-stone."

I shove a chip in my mouth so I don't blurt something stupid. Something that would give me away. "Just start the show, already."

"So salty," she mutters.

"You better be talking about the chips." She's right—I am salty. Every time she tries to warn me about Maya, I'm forced to see the situation for what it is. I'm forced to remember that I have a crush on a teammate who has a boyfriend. Forced to remember that Maya could flip a switch on me any second and take us back to square one.

Once the main character has made out with four different women and Katie is drawn deep into the murky waters of reality TV drama, I hold my phone in my lap and open Maya's text. I start to reply. Something short, with no response necessary: *You know it.*

My phone buzzes right after I send my response. *Well, don't worry, I nailed my presentation.*

I grin. *I wasn't worried.*

Maya: *Hmm. Confidence or apathy?*

Me: *I'm wounded that you even have to ask.*

Maya: *You're not the easiest to read sometimes, Foster.*

"Are you paying attention over there? That chick just totally threw her best friend under the bus."

I peel my eyes from my phone and refocus on the laptop for a couple of minutes. Feign some amusement when tears start streaming down one woman's cheeks. "What even is this show? Like, how is this still entertaining when the same exact things happen over and over every season?"

"That's the genius of it. It's like the changing of the seasons. The same thing every year, just a little different each time. This show is equal parts reliable, comfortable, and funny. It's not really supposed to be serious."

Maya: *See? You got me checking my phone for you.*

Me: *Confidence. Always.*

The bouncing dots, here and then gone. I hate those dots.

Maya: *What are you doing? Do you want to come over? I have to study for my chemistry final next week. Could use your help if you're willing.*

I move the mouse around on the computer screen to see how much time is left in the show. An hour. Christ, how do people watch this crap for so long?

"What, you got somewhere to be?" Katie asks.

"I, uh, just realized I forgot to outline a chapter for Microbiology. Sorry, Katie...finals in a couple weeks, and with our schedule... well, you know, gotta stay on top of things."

She stares at me. "Seriously?"

"What?"

She rolls up the bag of chips and tightens the lid of the salsa. "Nothing. I guess I'll see you later."

"I'm sorry, Katie."

"It's chill. See ya tomorrow." She leaves me on the floor with my laptop.

That was shitty of me. That was, like, epically shitty. I shouldn't have kicked her out like that. But what's done is done, and my shame is quickly replaced with anticipation. I grab my phone and fall into bed.

Me: *Katie just left. I could come over if you want.*

Maya: *Cool. I'm room 217 in Carter.*

Me: *Be there in twenty.*

❖

"Hey. Thanks for coming."

"No worries." I walk into her room, and when the door closes behind us, my stomach churns. A few articles of clothing are scattered about her side of the room, but it's still pretty clean. A family photo that must be part of the same series as the one from her locker stands on her desk...next to Jeremy's hoodie.

"Is Jeremy not good with chemistry?"

"Um, I don't know. Fine, I guess. Why?" She sits on the edge of her bed and pats the space next to her. I try not to look at where her boxers have ridden up her thighs. Try not to smell the fresh detergent on her T-shirt or the warm skin underneath it.

"Nothing, just wondering."

She grabs her notebook from the desk and opens it across her lap. Looks at me. "So Katie, is she like...your friend?"

"Katie? Yeah. She's my friend." I cock my head.

"Do you guys...is she gay?"

I stare at her, trying to discern any other motive than the very clear one staring me in the face. I guess Maya didn't know I'm a lesbian. I suppose it makes sense. I can be quiet, and since I haven't dated anyone, there's really been nothing to share with my teammates in the realm of sexuality or dating, even though I assumed everyone just knew.

"What? No. She's still dating her high school boyfriend. He goes to Auburn."

"Oh. Okay cool. I thought maybe you two..." She waves a finger to encompass me and an invisible Katie.

"Not at all."

She bites at a dry spot on her lip and shakes her head. "But would you?"

"No. I mean, don't get me wrong. I love Katie, but she's just my friend. No desire there."

"I haven't heard you mention a boyfriend."

"That's because I don't have one." *Unlike you.* The annoyance is followed by a sharp pang and a dizzying realization that she wants me to be single. She wants me to be single *and* into women.

She slaps an open palm on her notebook. "Okay. Chemistry." Her black hair curls around her ear in a perfect wave, and she sucks in the corner of her bottom lip. Does she really think I'm just going to let her get away with this super gay interrogation without calling her out? Having a boyfriend can only shield her for so long.

I clear my throat to get her attention back on me. "You know, for someone as confrontational as you are, you sure have a roundabout way of asking me if I'm into girls."

Her blush is immediate and only bolsters me.

"I am," I say.

"That's cool. So you're not dating anyone?"

"No. I mean there's this girl, Emma—"

She snaps her head up from her notebook. "Emma Wilson?" I nod. "Like, basketball Emma Wilson? You're involved with her?"

"Um, not exactly. We're friends from high school and have had...some moments." Maya's focus is intense, and I'm suddenly annoyed at her prying. At her having a boyfriend. I lean into my Emma explanation. "Things never quite worked out for us, but I think I've been holding an anvil for her all these years."

Maya shakes her head. "I'm sorry, what? You've been holding an 'anvil' for her?"

"Oh no. Is that not how the phrase goes? To hold an anvil for someone?"

To her credit, Maya doesn't laugh at me. Not even a chuckle. "I've never heard of that one. I think it's 'candle.' You hold a candle for someone. For Emma, I guess." She shrugs.

I smile. "That sounds easier than an anvil."

"Do you miss phrases like that a lot? Because of your hearing?" Her eyes flit to my hearing aids. I only have them in from watching *The Bachelor*. I can never hear what they're saying on television shows, especially when we watch on a laptop. But now, alone in a room with Maya, so close to her mouth, I wouldn't miss a single word she said.

"Yeah. This is a new one, though."

"Emma's bad news."

I lean away from her. "Excuse me?"

She stares at her chemistry notebook and shakes her head. "I've just heard she's kind of a player. Likes to sample around, you know?"

"That's her prerogative as a single woman in this world. It's not bad to be open to multiple people. It's not like she lies about it."

"I didn't mean—"

"She's my best friend."

"I'm sorry. I didn't mean it like that. It's just hard to hear you explain your long-held feelings for her when everyone knows how she is." Her gaze finds mine. "You deserve a lot."

In another context, these words would melt me into a pile of mushy flesh. But right now, they just agitate me. If I'm *so great* and *deserve so much*, why does no one want me? Maya doesn't get to make me melt when she has a boyfriend.

"So this final." She pulls out a worksheet. "It's all going to be like this. 'Calculate the rate constant for the reaction between pheno… pheno-something and the hydroxide ion if the instantaneous rate of reaction is this"—she points to the number on her worksheet— "mole per liter per second when the concentration of blah-blah-blah is *this* molar.' Like, what does that even mean?"

My attention is immediately sucked into chemistry land. "Nice, you're into kinetics. This will probably require a whiteboard, though. Should we head to the library?"

"*Ugh*, you're right. No, I was going to try to get to sleep in an hour or two. Maybe you can help me in study hall tomorrow?"

"Yeah. Definitely." I stand to leave, but she grabs my wrist.

"You just got here. Don't leave. We can just hang out for a minute. We don't have to study."

"Okay." I let her tug me down to her bed, and I'm an awkward middle-schooler now that the reason for being in Maya's room has vanished. I look around, trying to find something to hang on to. My eyes land on the Gonzalez family photo, and I nod to it. "Is it hard being part of such a competitive family?"

She grabs the frame and considers it. Hands it to me. I stare at it just like she stared at the photo of Alex Squared when she was in my room. "I wouldn't call it hard. It's just who we are."

"Athletic?"

"Driven is probably a better word. My dad came to the US from Mexico when he was thirteen, and my mom was eight. Together, they had this attitude that they were going to take over the world, and no one could stop them." She smiles at the photo. "They grinded their way through, and now they own a bunch of apartment complexes throughout the Southeast. Tech bros are their average renter."

She points to her parents, her fingers brushing mine. I hold my breath, and her eyes flash to mine before she fixes her gaze back to the photo. "Edgardo and Gloria," she says.

"I don't remember them from last season, but I'm excited to meet them in the spring."

She smiles. "I want you to."

I hand her the photo and clear my throat. "And you and your brothers? Do you think you're similar to your parents in that way? Is that why you all manifested into a family of athletes?"

"I guess so. My parents have always taught us to be unapologetic." She moves a hand to encompass an imaginary landscape in front of us. "Be bold and brave and whatever we want for ourselves will happen," she says in her best wizard voice. "They expect a lot from us. Like, they gave us this 'gift,' and they want to see us be as successful as they are. They have that immigrant mentality, you know? My dad is always saying that to be an immigrant is to be an entrepreneur of life."

"Are they hard to please or something like that?"

She tilts her head back and forth as if calculating something before she breaks into laughter. "Yes, absolutely. One-thousand-percent. They can be hard on me, and I know it's because they care, but it can be pretty intense. I'm expected to be this perfect, smart, athletic princess, and there's not a lot of space for failure in their eyes. They expect the same from my brothers, but because I'm a girl, there is this weird added pressure to be, like, desirable, too." She cringes.

"Sounds like a tall order."

"Yeah, it is. But I'm doing all right so far. We gotta win a championship, then maybe I could even achieve Miguel and Robbie levels of approval."

I pop an eyebrow. "Miguel and Robbie levels?" I shake my head. "They should be hoping to be on *your* level. You crush everything you do."

Her face shifts. Eyes drop to her lap. She places the photo back on her desk and flops backward on her mattress.

I lie on my side to face her. "What's wrong?" I ask.

She takes a deep breath and turns on her side, her face landing close enough for me to feel her words on my lips. "Sometimes, I'm jealous of them, Miguel and Robbie. They wanted to be athletes, and they're succeeding."

"*You're* succeeding."

"Yeah, but they have an attainable dream, you know?"

I shake my head. "What do you mean?"

"Miguel is going to be in the NFL, and Robbie is probably going to the majors. They have clear next steps to continue their careers." She plucks at her comforter, and I stay quiet. "When I was little, I wasn't thinking about a career path. I just *loved* softball. But then I realized that I wasn't like Robbie, who has a shot at the MLB. A softball career rarely continues past college. I chose the wrong fucking sport." She scrapes her lip between her teeth. "And even if I were in the WNBA or something, I'd still have to work twice as hard as my brothers because I'm a woman. For money and for respect. Did you know the average salary for a WNBA player is one-hundred and twenty thousand dollars?"

"Oh wow. That's actually way up. A couple years ago, it was seventy-five thousand." I know this because I wrote an essay about professional women's sports for my sociology class in high school.

"That's not the point. The average NBA salary is over twelve million."

"Ah."

"Yeah. And it makes total sense. You know why?" I shake my head. "Because men don't respect women. Hell, women don't respect women. It's the perfect manifestation of what we value in our world: men. And I'm fucking sick of it. There is no six-figure salary waiting for me out there as a softball player. As much as I wish there was, I can't bank on that. I just want to play and be valued for my skill. Like my brothers. So I work hard to build myself into a different kind of product. I'm not just selling my talent, I'm selling me." She swallows. "And I might not be enough."

My hand reaches for her, loses all of its courage, and crash lands on the bed next to her knee. "How could you ever not be enough? I would choose you on my team over the whole Alder baseball team. Shoot, over the entire major leagues. I know respect is important to you but, like, *fuck them*? Whether you end up playing softball at the next level or end up as a badass marketing executive, you will be uniquely and wildly successful in a way that no man could be. In a way that no other person could be except for Maya Gonzalez."

She arches her left brow, and a smile breaks the tension in her lips. "Wow."

A nervous chuckle boils in my chest and erupts through my mouth. For a moment, I forgot that Maya can struggle with being vulnerable, and that my words could easily offend her. "Wow what?"

"I think that's the first time I've ever heard you curse."

"Yeah, that makes sense. I curse in my head, but I try not to out loud."

She pops her chin in her palm and studies me, seemingly entertained by this fact. By me. "Is this part of your *take up no space, work from the shadows* schtick?"

"It's not a schtick. I like to be in control, and cursing is a small act of losing control. Also, it draws attention. But not just attention, it draws other people's energy down." I shrug. "It's a sum negative action."

Her grin widens, and she reaches out, running her hand down the length of my arm. I freeze while the chemicals in my body synthesize into a heady drug. "To avoid cursing because you feel like it taxes others…is not normal." My blood drug chills in my veins. *I don't know what you are, but you're not normal.* She said that to me in my room not too long ago. And here, now, again. "That is *exceptional*. I've never met anyone who cares so much about other people."

Blood burns my cheeks. "I'm not—"

"How do you do it, anyway? Or why? Most people are ass—" She smothers her mouth before the rest of the profanity can make it out.

I laugh. This girl deals in curse words, and I like it for some reason. What you see is what you get with her. I pull her by the wrist, tugging her hand away from her mouth and onto the mattress. I hold it there, and she lets me. "First of all, *you* can curse all you want. I actually kind of like it when you do." Her cheeks turn an elegant rosewood color, while when I blush, I turn into a hot pink paint splotch. "As long as it's not directed at me or our team. But to answer your question, I think growing up with a sick parent taught me how to be a good support system. And so much of that is just being a person who doesn't need much from other people and who doesn't drain other people."

"Don't you feel like sometimes, people want you to drain them?" She scrunches her nose and tilts her head. "That sounded oddly dirty. What I mean is, how deep can your relationships really go if you don't share all of you? Your fears and needs and profanities. Sounds like it could get a little lonely."

I stare at my fingers curled around her wrist. "That's a good question. But I feel pretty open and vulnerable right now. I guess that means I'm draining you."

Maya's eyebrows lift, and she lays her other hand on my hip. Every cell of my skin catches on fire. "No. That was poor word choice. It's the opposite. You're giving to me right now, not taking. It's a gift," she says.

That gorgeous color in her cheeks makes my stomach ache, and my fingers tighten around her wrist without my permission. Her stare bores into me, and the room blurs in my peripherals.

"Andrea…" My name pulls my gaze to her lips, and my instinct is to lean in and kiss Maya Gonzalez.

Maya Gonzalez who has a boyfriend.

I push myself off her bed. "I'm sorry. It's getting late, and I forgot I have to outline a chapter for Microbiology." I grab my jacket from the back of her desk chair. "Finals coming up…"

"Wait, you don't have to go."

"Yeah. I think I do."

"Well, thanks for coming over. Even though we didn't study, it was nice." She pulls the front of my jacket around itself, tightening me up in it. I get woozy at the sight of her fists tangled in my fabric. "Can I hug you?" she asks.

I nod.

She uses her grip on my jacket to pull me into her. My feet stumble toward her. I try not to breathe her in, try not to feel her curves under her one layer of clothing, try to tilt my head away from her until she releases me.

"No feedback," she says.

I give her a thumbs-up. "Yeah. No feedback. I was a little more cognizant this time."

As I walk through the halls of Carter and back into the night, I replay every second of our time together and realize I'm dangerously close to losing control of my feelings for her. *Christ, I almost kissed her.* It was a toss-up, kissing her or not. I blow out a breath, relieved I stopped myself this time.

When I get back from Maya's, I sit at my desk and open my micro book to bring a little truth to my lies. I don't need to study, though. I need to process and compartmentalize my feelings for Maya. She has a boyfriend, for God's sake. Why does it feel like she doesn't? I may not have the most experience when it comes to matters of romance, but I could swear she's into me. At least a tiny bit. She speaks to me as if I'm the only one who matters to her, her eye contact is crazy, and she seeks me out.

But none of it matters because Maya is my teammate. Is it even allowed to date your teammate? I imagine Coach Clayton's red face, his constant adjusting of his ball cap. I shut my book and get ready for bed. Only, as is happening too often lately, I can't sleep.

I pull up my conversation with Maya on my phone. She's the one in the relationship. If brakes need to be pumped, it's her job to pump them. I'm single.

Me: *So what's the trick?*

Maya: *Turn it off and back on again? Did you try blowing in it? What are we talking about?*

Me: *Sleep. We're talking about sleep. I desperately need it. But my body refuses.*

Maya: *Oh...that trick.*

Me: *Unless you're already sleeping.*

Maya: *I'm texting you, not sleeping. You ready for this? It's a little weird, but it always works for me.*

Me: *At this point, I'm willing to try anything. What do I do?*

Maya: *Get in whatever position you naturally sleep in.*

I roll onto my side and shove the pillow tight into the crook of my neck. Check.

Maya: *I can't believe I'm going to do this with you.*

Me: *Do what with me? You're the one who told me to text you if I couldn't sleep.*

Maya: *I know. I meant it. Okay...You need to pick a person to undress. Pick someone you're attracted to. Your mind needs to be invested in it, or it'll just keep wandering.*

I pick you. Okay. I have someone.

Maya: *What? Who?*

Me: *What do you mean 'what'? You just told me to pick someone I'm attracted to. I'm not telling you who I'm about to mentally undress.*

Maya: *Is it Emma?*

Me: *Are you going to help me or what?*

Maya: *Okay, okay. First, just so we're all at maximum enjoyment, ask for consent from your imaginary subject.*

Me: *Really?*

Maya: *Yes. It makes it better. I promise.*

Me: *Okay. She said yes.*

Maya: *She, huh?*

Me: *Did we not just go over this in your room earlier?*

Maya: *Lol. I'm going to do one, too. I'll walk you through mine so you can get an idea of how it works. Then you do it. You don't have to text me, and hopefully, you'll just fall asleep.*

Me: *Okay. I'm ready.*

Maya: *I start by pulling the elastic tie from her hair and unpinning that side wispy that's always escaping. I run both of my hands through the soft blond locks until they fall out of their braids and onto her shoulders.*

Everything is hazy. I reach for that side wispy and tuck it behind my ear with a trembling hand. It's me. She's undressing *me.* As I'm taking in Maya's text, a second one pops up on my phone: *I can stop at any time.*

My skin is molten, and my fingers shake as they hit the small keys on my phone. *Keep going.*

I reread, reread, reread the text before last while the dots after Maya's name bounce, promising me more.

Maya: *I unbutton her shirt from the top down. It falls open as I work lower and lower. Until I can part it and ease it off her shoulders. Freckles kiss her shoulders, and she has the creamiest skin. That white bra...*

My blood is kinetic, my body feverish. Those freckles on my shoulders itch.

Maya: *This is my favorite part. Because she refuses to wear sweats, I get the pleasure of taking off her jeans. I use her hips for balance as I sink to my knees in front of her. I tuck a finger into the fabric where her hip bones dip into it, drag it along the waistband to the button.*

This is doing the opposite of putting me to sleep. The heat continues to build lower and lower. I feel my cheeks burn, my mouth dry. Suddenly, I'm in a desert.

Maya: *Should I stop?*

I scoff to my empty dorm room. Can anyone stop halfway to frenzied? *No.*

Maya: *I pull down the tongue of her zipper. Each metal tooth plucks away from its partner until I can see your matching underwear. I tug down your jeans until there is only skin and lace in front of me.*

I can't. I don't know where Rachel is. Don't care. I run my hand down my stomach, slip it into my shorts.

Maya: *I think I should probably leave it at that for now. I'm guessing you probably get the idea. Just go slow and enjoy yourself. Sleep tight, Andy.*

My back arches off my bed, and a calm dissipates through me.

❖

Every time Maya tries to catch my eye at practice the next day, it's like my entire body revolts. I immediately break eye contact, and my palms begin to sweat. I have no idea how to be around her now that we have very clearly crossed a line. *I think* we crossed a line. I keep second-guessing what actually occurred between us while Maya seems to be totally unfazed. She seeks me out even more, if anything.

I sigh as I watch her step into the batter's box. After I touched myself to the thought of touching her, I spiraled through a million outcomes of us. Over. And over. And over. I'm just here stalling out. What the hell is happening?

## Chapter Seven

As finals arrive, the coaches ease up on us; practices are called early, study halls are made optional so it's easier to visit our professors' office hours, and lifting has been canceled. Coach Clay says there's no point in being in shape if we wind up on academic probation, therefore, we take it upon ourselves to stay fit the best we can while studying and preparing for the end of the semester.

Finals is the time I feel most like a regular student at Alder. Though I'm exhausted most days, the rest of the student body seems to reach college athlete levels of tired during finals; welcome to the party, everybody. We move as one mass from the library to our dorms and to the dining hall, all bleary-eyes and aching heads. Coats are drawn tight across chests and scarves around necks against the growing cold of campus.

I leave the library to grab dinner at the dining hall. My Microbiology final is tomorrow, and I have at least another four hours of studying to do. It's mostly just reviewing at this point, but my stack of flashcards is a couple inches thick. I serve myself a large piece of lasagna and scoop some broccoli into the open space on my plate, then sit at the farthest table by only one other student, who turns out to be Katie.

"Hey. I thought that was you," she says.

I sit on the bench next to her and push my backpack under the table. "How are your finals going so far?"

She swallows a bite of chicken. "Good. I've only had one, but I think it went well. I have chem tomorrow and history on Thursday. I don't know…It'll be fine. How about you?"

"I've only had kinesiology. Got micro tomorrow, but I feel pretty good about it."

"Nice."

I nod and take another bite. "Maybe we can meet up in Atlanta and throw around the ball or something during break. I'm close," I say.

"Yeah, that'd be cool." She stands and gathers her trash. "I gotta run. Catch ya at the party on Friday?"

One of the guys on the baseball team is throwing an end-of-semester party at his house, and our whole team is going. These parties happen a handful of times throughout the year, and I dread every single one of them. The baseball team is nice enough, so I'm not sure why, but I really hate being around them.

"You know it." I poke at my lasagna as she walks to the trash. "Hey, Katie?"

She turns back to me. "What's up?"

"I'm really sorry about ditching you while we were watching *The Bachelor*. That was lame. Maybe we can finish the episode over break?"

A grin breaks across her face, and she nods. "I knew you secretly love that show. Yeah, let's make it happen."

❖

Corey's house is what you'd expect a college guy's house to look like. Most of the scuffed wall space is covered with Atlanta Braves paraphernalia and half-naked women, and empty beer cans litter every surface: the faded brown plaid couch and all the chipped black IKEA furniture. Does Corey not have a recycle bin or something?

"Oh, hey, uh, Mandy, right?" Corey welcomes me, his Hawaiian shirt hanging unbuttoned to his navel, golden chest hair and muscles on display under the dim light of the two lamps in either corner of the living room. I guess the beer keeps him warm.

"Andy. Thanks for having us over." I slink out of my coat and place it as neatly as I can on top of an already crumbling mountain of coats on the kitchen chair next to the front door.

"Yeah, yeah, sure. Beers are in the kiddie pool out back. Help yourself." He shuffles past me to a group of bros who try to chat up some of the freshmen on my team, Kim being one of them. She bounces around the boys like a caffeinated Ping-Pong ball. I cringe. Her eagerness is off-putting.

I consider grabbing a beer. Finals' week was a little more grueling than I had anticipated, and my discomfort level at this party is growing exponentially, but I don't really drink. I scan the house. There is one reason I came to this thing. Well, two reasons. Solidarity for the team.

And her.

Maya laughs at a joke Kevin just told and takes a small sip of beer. Jeremy stands next to her, of course, arm snaked around her waist, but I barely notice him. I only notice Maya in her tiny, very low-cut, black dress and her strappy high heels. *Jesus, her legs.* The last time we really talked, she was undressing me. I've done my best to avoid conversations with her since then. My whole body warms under the thought of those texts.

I want to run to her, but I don't. I'm way too jumbled, so I join a small circle of guys chatting. I ask about their finals, if they're going home for break, their hopes for the upcoming season, but I can tell they aren't interested in talking to me. That is, until the one with the greasy black hair and the bloodshot eyes changes the topic.

He holds up his beer to me as if to make a toast, then looks me up and down. I look me up and down, too. I look fine, I think. I wore my fitted jeans, my nice brown boots, and a gray sweater. I even tried to curl my hair.

"You," he slurs, and it's clear he has frequented the kiddie pool. "You'd be fucking hot if you weren't a dyke."

I feel the blood drain from my face, and his friends stifle a chuckle like they're trying to be polite, but really, on so many levels, that is the meanest thing anyone has ever said to me. As the chemicals in my body react to his words, to the pure hate and ignorance in them, the other boys close into a smaller circle without me in it.

Sometimes, even when I'm not being verbally accosted, I feel weird hanging around the baseball team. Like, I'd rather not. Being a lesbian, there's not much they want from me, and since we're all in college, they don't seem to be interested in any other kind of social contract besides a sexual one. As that asshole just made plain. Being surrounded by women all day, I sometimes forget the sting of feeling like I don't belong. The sting of ignorant men.

I sit on the couch while my chest pounds and watch my teammates try. Watch them try so damn hard to catch a boy's eye. I hate it. They change from how they are with each other, from how they are on the field. They shrink in the worst ways and expand in the loudest.

"You came. Wow, you look incredible."

Not all of them, though. Not Maya. She is incapable of shrinking for anybody. It's what I love most about her. Her voice melts some of the ice in me, and her tentative smile melts the rest. I look at her as she sits next to me, but I still can't untangle the right words to say to her.

She drops her gaze to the stained carpet. Drops her voice, too. "I knew I shouldn't have." She stares at a blank space of wall across the living room. Gathers something there. "I'm sorry if I crossed the line. You're clearly uncomfortable. It was silly, you know, it was just a—"

"Don't."

She looks at me, eyes searching. I need to say more words.

"Don't say what I think you're going to say. It wasn't silly. And God, I hope it wasn't…a joke?"

She lets a breath coast out of her lips, and I feel its warmth. Feel her scoot just a bit closer to me. My fingers itch to touch her. Her perfume wraps around me, and I hope it tangles in my fabric, in my hair, anywhere it could linger. "No. It wasn't silly, and it wasn't a joke. I was just scared that I creeped you out," she whispers. She looks over her shoulder before her eyes meet mine again, and the pure vulnerability in them guts me. "There's something...here. Right?" Her pointer finger bounces between us like a pendulum.

I nod, but my mouth refuses to produce any more affirmation. What can I say? I feel like a deer caught in headlights, completely at a loss as to which way to step. I feel like I'll get crushed either way.

"Do you want to get out of here?" she asks, concern in her voice.

The anger creeps up my throat. What does she expect? Does she just want me to ignore the giant guy with the beard in the kitchen, the guy who is her *boyfriend*? Just have no problem at all with our flirting and assume it's harmless? "Do you mean with you?"

She looks over her shoulder at Jeremy leaning against the kitchen counter and back to me with a piece of her lip trapped under her incisor.

Well, that makes it pretty clear to me. I release all of my indecision in one long breath. "Yeah, I don't know what I was expecting. I'm going to go. I'll see you in the spring, Maya."

The whole pile of coats topples to the ground when I try to grab mine. I almost leave them scattered about the floor but let out a huff and drop to my knees to gather them. Maya squats next to me, legs clamped together, trying not to flash me while she scoops up the fallen coats and piles them on the chair.

"Thanks." I pull open the door to leave.

"Wait. Andy. Can I walk you to your car?"

I look back at her. And does my breath catch a little at the sight? Yeah. 'Cause the thing about Maya Gonzalez is that she's the most beautiful woman I've ever seen, but the other thing about Maya Gonzalez is that she's not mine. Not even close. Not even a little bit. She pulled on that tight dress for *Jeremy*. She's going home with *Jeremy*. She'll probably fuck him tonight.

"No. Thanks. I can manage."

The hope slides off her face into a puddle around her heels. I try not to care. About her. But I remember my team, Coach Clayton, and my responsibilities as a captain. I pull her into a quick hug.

"Have a Merry Christmas," I say and drop my arms when she tries to hug me back.

"You, too."

And I'm gone. Away from the stupid baseball team and away from Maya fucking Gonzalez. I need to get out of here. I need to go home where she can't reach me. Can't affect me. And when I come back to Alder after break, I'll be ready. It will be strictly business between us.

I wipe the tear running down my cheek. I'm done with this.

## CHAPTER EIGHT

Campus is still sleeping when I arrive on Saturday. A light dusting of snow covers the pines, and everything at once feels a bit colder and a bit warmer. I take the couple days I have off before the new semester starts on Monday to try to center myself; that means warm cups of coffee and slow walks around Alder. A quiet to capture a calm. Because I have no idea what Monday brings besides the guarantee of change: new classes, the start of softball season, and Maya.

I turn into the arboretum to admire all the different trees in their new snowy attire.

*Maya.*

I pause in front of a particularly goofy-looking tree and bend to read the little placard next to its trunk. "False Cypress." Its fuzzy gumdrop demeanor takes my mind back to where it's supposed to be before she pops right back onto center stage. Fine, but just for five minutes. I set a timer on my phone and sit on the bench closest to the squat cypress that I love.

And start.

I didn't hear from Maya once over break. Which could mean, oh, I don't know, *a million different things.* She could hate me, I could show up to our softball meeting on Monday and find that Maya and I are right back where we started, or even scarier, we are right back where we left it. Because where the hell did we leave it? All I know is that I drove home to Atlanta the day after Corey's party with a hollow ache in my gut because Maya Gonzalez saw me, liked me, made me feel special and accounted for...then made me feel like garbage.

Or maybe I was reading too much into all our little moments, but that feels highly unlikely. Friends don't mentally undress friends. I mean, maybe I do with Emma sometimes, but wait, that's the point. I want to be more than friends with Emma. *Wanted?* Maybe Maya wants to be more than friends with me.

*Argh.*

Maybe that intimacy is what we needed to solidify a functional and appropriate bond before the season starts, and everything will be perfectly fine, and we'll win every game, and I'll be the best damn captain the Lions have ever had.

I startle at my alarm blaring in my pocket and rush to turn it off. Shit.

*Breathe. Swerve.*

❖

Arms wrap around my waist from behind as I wait in line in the dining hall. I jump and tense the muscles in my stomach because my hands are otherwise occupied carrying my dinner tray, and it's the only reaction I have.

"Damn, Andy, you're cut as hell under here." Emma prods at my abs before tightening me against her hard body and pressing a, "Merry Christmas," somewhere between my ear and my hoodie.

Yeah, *her hard body.* This person is not off-limits, and this person, all of her faults aside, cares for me. I push back into her, the only way I can somewhat return her hug, and it feels good. Familiar. Her dad has never changed their brand of laundry detergent, so she smells the same as she did in middle school when we first met. I clear Maya out of the desire chamber in my brain and place Emma back where she's always been because she isn't my teammate, and she isn't dating the shortstop on the baseball team. My feelings for her are way safer. Harmless.

She squeezes one more time and walks in front of me.

"How was your break?" I ask.

We both chuckle. "Yeah, not much of a break, as you can imagine. I mean, I got to go home for Christmas Eve and Christmas, then we had to be back on campus for training. We had a team meeting this morning, but we get the rest of today and tomorrow off, so I'll take that." She wraps an arm around my shoulder as I wait to pay. "Thanks for meeting us for dinner. Rachel got us that table by the fireplace." She nods in the general direction.

I hand the cashier my lion card and follow Emma to our table. "Hey, Rach."

"Yay, my beloved roommate has arrived. How was your break? Tell us everything so that we may live vicariously through you."

I fill them in. There isn't much to tell, really. I hung out with Alex Squared, which was actually incredibly helpful. They could tell I was stressed by something, but instead of telling them the whole truth—Maya—I told them I was concerned with my ability to be a good captain. To which they both had great insight from their experience leading civil engineering projects. After that rather teary conversation, we watched all the sappy Lifetime movies together. We cooked a lot of food and baked a lot of cookies. Even my dad seemed to be feeling okay, as if his MS took a little holiday, too.

I hung out with Katie a handful of times. We worked out together, and yes, finished that episode of *The Bachelor*. She asked me about Maya and offered another thinly veiled warning, which I leave out of my detailed description.

"Are you guys ready for Monday?" I ask. "I mean, you're really getting into the meat of your season."

They both nod. The basketball team didn't have the smoothest start, but I know they're going to pull it together. Maybe the little reset of winter break was all they needed.

Emma swallows a bite of dinner roll. "Yeah. No more fucking around. We're ready."

"Well, I think the team is coming to watch you guys play Olson next weekend. I'm excited."

"She just wants to see us get all sweaty on the court," Emma says.

Rachel shakes her head. "Dude, you are so gross sometimes. Andy is not interested in what you're selling."

Emma smirks at her tray because she knows I am.

I blush because I know I am, too. But there's no stress in that fact. Me wanting Emma is as comfortable to me as the worn-in hoodie I'm wearing. It's a secure little bottle that I can tuck all my desire into because lately, I've felt like I'm losing control over it. But with Emma, it's safe.

❖

Our clubhouse is empty except for the coaches huddled in the office and going over their notes for our meeting. I take inventory of my locker to make sure everything is in order for the new semester, for softball season, and more immediately, for practice after class today. I avoid looking to my right at Maya's locker as I spin to take in the rest of our locker room. It's peaceful here this early in the morning. I snag my travel mug off the bench and clear out before the chaos of my teammates descends upon the place and before one particular teammate arrives.

All morning, I tried to ignore the anxious flutter in my stomach, the knowledge that I will soon see Maya brews and bubbles within me. I sit in the front of the Lazy, trying my best to tackle my team responsibilities head-on. Fresh semester, fresh start for me as captain. Katie and Taylor shuffle in, bundled up and bleary-eyed. I try to take slow deliberate breaths to counteract the spike in my blood pressure.

She'll walk through that door any second.

"Morning, Andy." Katie gives my shoulder a lazy pat as she sinks into the chair on my left. There's still one spot next to me for Maya, if she wants it.

"Someone didn't stick to their morning routine over break," I say to her with a grin.

She yawns as if to prove my point. "Don't tell me you actually did that shit. I mean, I know you did because you're Andrea Foster, but come on. You know it only takes a week to get back on the early morning train."

I catch a glimpse of Maya's thick ponytail whipping past the window, and every nerve in my body prickles, making me shiver in my chair.

It's not like I didn't expect my body to react like a volcano. No, I knew this was coming. It is my total inability to control myself that is freaking me out. Maya walks into the Lazy and hesitates for a split second, her eyes on me, but I can't decipher the look on her face. She's either tired, upset, sad, or some combination of all of them. She takes the seat closest to the door, next to none other than Kim. Blood wooshes in my ears, and the slow drip of panic swells into a wave. I haven't had a full-blown panic attack since high school when I was driving home from a softball tournament and was convinced I was dying of a heart attack. I pulled into a fire station and made them take my blood pressure. I'll never forget the woman looking me in the eye and telling me it was just a panic attack.

*Breathe. Swerve.*

"All right, everyone, settle in. Happy New Year. We hope you all had a wonderful break, but now it's time to get back to business," Coach Clayton says, and I anchor to his words. Pull myself out of my hot pool of nerves. Everything is okay. Normal, even.

After the meeting, the girls shuffle into the locker room to gather their things for class. Before anyone leaves, I mentally count to three. Deep breath. Do it.

"Hey, everybody," I start, but the girls continue to rummage through lockers and chat to each other. My voice drowned out by the mundane. I feel the flint of my skin strike into a spark and adrenaline pool into my bloodstream. Seriously, fuck public speaking.

*Breathe. Swerve.*

"Hey, guys," I shout. Everyone stops what they're doing and turns to me, confusion on their faces. My control hangs in this moment. I'll say what I need to say, and they will choose to respect me or ignore me, and I don't even know if I have Maya in my corner anymore.

"We have a fresh start to a new semester, our first game is just around the corner, and there are a few things from last semester that I want us to work on." I scan the room. Haven't lost anyone yet. Maya's face remains unreadable. "We weren't required to have weekly team activities last semester, but I am reinstating that now. Every weekend. Our first team activity will be supporting our fellow athletes at the basketball game against Olson this weekend, and someone else can choose what we do next week."

Mumbles of acceptance fill the locker room, and I sense the antsy, wandering eyes of girls ready to get the heck out of here. Backpacks are strapped on shoulders, and water bottles are in hand.

"I'm not finished," I say. And the hint of a smile on Katie's lips keeps my confidence afloat long enough to maintain control. "How we train, how we treat each other, and how we care for our facility are all reflected in how we play. This will be the last time we leave an ounce of trash on the ground in this locker room or in the Lazy. Every ball will be picked up off the field before a single person leaves. The only way to win is to work hard together. To work hard for each other. We have one of the most talented teams Alder has ever seen. Let get this done. Bring it in."

While I don't imagine I gained instant respect from every team member, all the girls throw a fist into the huddle.

"One, two, three," I shout.

"Lions," they reply in unison. And it feels pretty damn good. Even if I know Kim is going to walk right out of here and start talking shit with Maya.

Though Maya has basically ignored me this last week, she chooses to sit right next to me at the basketball game that I'm still shocked my whole team actually showed up to. I play it cool when she sinks into the seat on my left, not daring to make eye contact quite yet. I focus on Emma running down the court and pivoting into a backpedal as the other team presses forward. She steals a sloppy pass from the opposing point guard and breezes down the court to score an effortless layup.

"There's your girl," Maya says. I turn to her, then. Her eyes are on Emma, appraising her.

"My friend. Sure." I could give her more, but I'm just not willing to comment on this when Maya hasn't given me anything but some wet boxers and confusion. She doesn't get to feel protective or possessive over me.

Refocus on Em. Focus on the compression shorts peeking out of her uniform.

"You did really great at the team meeting. Did you go to a leadership conference over break or something?" She chuckles, and I let it die in the air between us.

I bore my eyes into Emma as she tugs her jersey out of her shorts to wipe the sweat off her face, showing off an impressive stack of muscle down her sweaty, heated torso. This is not news to me, though. I've seen this girl next to naked a thousand times.

But that nagging hits me, again—my responsibilities. I try not to audibly groan at it. I push away the hurt that she caused me last semester and focus on being the captain that Coach Clay needs me to be. The captain that has a productive relationship with Maya.

"Sorry, May. What did you say?"

"I just want to make sure we're good, you know? The season is about to start, and we have a lot of work to do. Can we just be good? Like, I'm sorry. Okay? Whatever happened last semester"—she looks out over the court and shakes her head—"it won't happen again."

"Sure. Yeah, we're good."

I present all the outward signs of being entranced by the game. I whoop and holler, my eyes track the ball through every pass, and I yell at all the appropriate times. I should feel good about what Maya just said to me. This is what I wanted, a simple, respectful relationship with my teammate. But the truth is that I want that something to happen again. I want to cross that line with Maya again, and I'm realizing that what I wanted the most from winter break was for Maya to choose me.

❖

Alder's chapel is gorgeous. It doesn't try too hard, which feels fitting for a place to worship a selfless and humble God. I mean, I totally get the whole "glory" to God thing, but come on. He's gotta look down at some of those gaudy giant churches and think, *oh Jesus, that's not how you should've spent the money*. But Alder's is the perfect subtle beauty. A small stained-glass window kisses the stone walls with a watery rainbow of light that dances along the cool gray of the classic campus stone, and giant oak beams cut an earthy warmth across the undomed ceiling toward the altar.

I join my team in the far-right corner of the church and slide into the pew next to Katie. Most of my team is religious. The amount of Bible verses these girls scribble everywhere is exorbitant. Mathew peeks out of gloves, Corinthians holds down a line in everyone's Instagram bio, and Romans sneaks around with the Philippians on bathroom stalls, bumper stickers, and the inside of girls' wrists. They get around. Unless these girls truly cannot make it to Mass, the team is here every Wednesday or Sunday, schedule dependent. We do our own thing with Mass during the off-season but make sure to sit together during the season. Which means, now that it's spring, I attend Mass with them.

Religion doesn't bother me. I hold no deep wounds from it. Though I could never understand why all these people trust a random man up there in the pulpit, especially after the Catholic church has been exposed on such a fundamental level. I think inertia is quite real with religion. My parents never went to Mass, though they were both raised Catholic, so I never went to Mass, and slowly, over time, I imagine fewer and fewer people will be a part of any organized religion. For better or worse.

I prefer to do my centering within. But whatever, it's my duty to be here for my team.

Maya isn't a Bible verse kind of girl, though, and I appreciate that about her. Instead, her outward sign of faith is a saint medallion that hangs on a gold chain around her neck. Not a dainty chain, either. The thicker gauge and deep gold of the chain is radiant against her dark skin.

As Father Kyle drones on in his homily, I think about how my team would take it if Maya and I ever…*stop it.*

I'm pretty sure the whole team just kind of knows that I'm gay. "Coming out" doesn't feel necessary because I don't think I'm closeted, but dating a teammate, not that it's on the table *at all*, would surely cross a line of comfort for them.

The people in the pew closest to the front stand and shuffle into the aisles. Phew, almost done. My mind wanders, and I reflect on my first week of new classes. Hard to say, but I think I have two professors whom I really like and a promising course load. Katie stands next to me, so I take my cue to get up, too, and go do the thing. I let the stale little wafer dissolve on my tongue and sigh when I sit back down. Katie smiles at me, silently encouraging me to make it through the end of Mass. She knows how I feel about being here, but my sigh wasn't about making it through the last ten minutes of church. It was about Maya and how gorgeous she looks in her Sunday best.

# CHAPTER NINE

The day has finally come. I slip out the emergency exit of the locker room to steal a quiet moment while the rest of my team does their hair and makeup—softball players are notoriously made-up for games—films TikToks, and falls into individual routines of superstition. I run my hands down the front of my crisp maroon uniform. Tighten my belt. Breathe. Visualize success. Close my eyes to the sun and harvest its warmth for just a second longer.

Season opener time.

Maya is, of course, the starting pitcher for our first game against Pullman. We quietly make our way to the bullpen while the rest of our team warms up on the field with throwing, catching, and grounders. It's hard not to admire the girl. They way her uniform hugs her body...women really do wear it better. Her hair sits in a low ponytail, no braid. Her makeup is simple and light.

She pitches to me with intent and a bit of frustration, like always. A sheen of sweat covers her arms and neck. The bullpen is quiet save the sound of leather smacking leather and soft, effortful grunts.

Coach Williams pops her head over the gate. "All right, ladies, let's finish this up. It's go time."

"Be right there," I say. I shake out my legs and begin to take off my helmet.

"One more," Maya demands from the rubber.

"Yeah, sure." I pull my helmet back on and squat, giving her a target. She bows, a small piece of hair falling in front of her eyes, and launches into the pitch. The ball smacks hard against the leather of my mitt. God, I love that sound.

We gather our gear and water bottles as we make our way out of the bullpen and onto the field for the anthem, starting lineups, and bat checks. I tug Maya's elbow to get her attention while we're still in the foul territory of right field. At the beginning of last semester, I could've only dreamed of Maya acting how she is now. Reserved, focused, controlled, if not a little passionless. But knowing her better, she seems off.

"Hey. You okay?"

"Of course I'm okay. Been waiting for this day for forever."

"We're going to crush this game. We got this."

"Yeah. I know." She pulls her arm from my touch. Not in a mean way, just in a, "let's get this show on the road," kind of way.

After all of the season opener fanfare and pregame responsibilities, Pullman's first batter steps up to the plate, and our decent-sized audience roars to life. Activities week seems to have paid off. Maya stretches her arms and pulls on her facemask. We both look at Coach Williams, who sits on a ball bucket at the mouth of our dugout with a black clipboard in hand. She holds up three different numbers with her fingers.

1-0-2

We look to our wristbands and find the right play call on the grid. A curve ball inside. Everyone gets in position, the batter sways with anticipation, and Maya delivers a fastball straight down the middle of the plate. She either gravely missed her target or missed Coach's play call because there was no curve to that pitch at all. It was a strike, regardless. I think the entire audience would have bet on the batter taking the first pitch. But still.

The next pitch is what I thought was supposed to be a changeup but didn't look like one from Maya's delivery and is hit for a single. I brush it off and focus on the next batter and the next pitch, a rise ball. Maya fires a drop ball that makes the girl swing for a strike, but the ball dives into the dirt and escapes to the backstop. I launch out of my squat to grab it, but the base runner is safe at second.

"Time, sir," I ask the ump, and he holds up his arms to pause gameplay. I pull off my mask and can already feel that my hair has turned wild against its braids. Maya looks guarded against my approach.

"May, what's going on? What was that?"

"What are you doing back there, Andy? You look totally lost. You have to stop that ball."

All eyes are on us, and déjà vu hits me like a Mack truck. Is she really trying to pull this shit again? *No.* Not even Maya would go against her coach's call in a game. She glares at me.

"That was a wild pitch," I say.

"That was a perfect pitch. Dipped right at the perfect time, and it was a strike, if you didn't notice."

"It might've been a strike, but it was about four feet off target for a rise ball, and now they have a runner in scoring position because of it." I know I'm letting exasperation creep into my tone, but I just can't with her anymore. We're on the second batter of the season, and she's already pulling this weird power stuff.

"Wait. Did you say *rise ball?*" She grabs my wrist and yanks me toward her. I stumble in the divot her dragging toes have already formed in front of the pitching rubber and collide against her. "Easy, will ya? I'm trying to see…" She pulls at me until my wristband is in front of her face. "Oh." She drops my arm like it's a discarded lead pipe and motions for Coach Williams to join us.

"What on earth is going on out here?" she asks.

"One of our wristbands doesn't have the right call cards in it. I think it's Andy's."

Coach Williams grabs my wrist like Maya and yanks me to her. She pulls her call card from her back pocket and compares them.

"Yep, this is all wrong." She sighs. "Okay. One second." She jogs to the dugout and returns with a backup wristband for me. "Remind me to talk to Dave after the game." I tug on the new call card. "All right. That should do it. Back to business."

Coach leaves us alone on the mound with all of our tension humming between us. I look at Maya. She looks at me and shrugs.

At least she didn't spit on me this time. Though I'd be lying if I said I didn't miss her passion, even if it did land her saliva on my shoe.

"Let's play ball," the ump calls from behind home.

❖

After the game, I slip into the farthest shower stall. I don't mean to hog it, but I like to mentally retrace the game before the details escape me. It was an easy win, Pullman being the worst team in our conference and all, the perfect matchup for our first series, and we played really well. Minus the first batter, Maya kept the bases clear the rest of the game. And minus me having the wrong call card, we had minimal errors on and off the field. I even had a double for an RBI and a walk. Not too shabby for our first day back.

But as I scrub at some dirt on my forearm, I can't shake the feeling that Maya is back to hating me. Every word from her mouth is forced, and I can tell it grates on her when we speak. And she's back to hanging out with Kim. I should be happy that her fire on the field seems mostly tamed, but really, I'm just worried. It's fine for Pullman, but the truth is, we *need* Maya to be Maya. We need her to be fired up.

I wrap my towel around myself and slip out of the stall as Maya walks toward the showers, brows drawn down in annoyance, fist clutching her towel around her body. I can smell the earthiness of the dirt mixing with her sweat. She smells like a thunderstorm in a forest, ozone and mud. Her presence overwhelms my senses, and my body sputters and stalls out in the hallway.

"Took you long enough, Foster."

"Sorry. It's all yours." I catch her glance down my body as she brushes by me, and my mouth goes dry. "Maya?"

She pauses midway to the shower and looks back at me. "Not the best time for one of your lectures." She disappears, and I hear the spray of water splash against tile.

"Good game," I mutter to no one.

❖

I keep my head down the next week. Just try to focus on my classes so I can get ahead now that our season has begun. I won't even hang out with Emma in the spare seconds of her schedule. We swept Pullman, so my "captain duties" have been minimal. I'm in and out of practice, the locker room, and study hall. Besides, it's not softball that will pay my bills after Alder; it's my education. I outline future chapters in my spare time, read *The Champion's Mind*, and try to make it to all my professor's office hours.

I'm doing me, and Maya's salty attitude can't change that.

Unfortunately, it's Saturday night, and we don't have a game, which means it's Katie's turn to organize our team activity for the week, and she picked *The Bachelor*, of course. Coach Clay gave me the keys to the clubhouse when he made me captain, so I asked for permission to use the Lazy for our *Bachelor* viewing pleasure. I buy the student store out of microwave popcorn and stop by Katie's dorm to walk with her to the clubhouse.

"What's in the backpack?" she asks.

"Let's see." I tilt my head to the stars while I do the simple arithmetic. "Twenty-four bags of popcorn and my laptop."

"You're the best captain ever."

I press my hand over my heart and spin in an exorbitant circle. "Oh, me? Really?"

She grabs my backpack and yanks me along. "It's just because you bribed me with my favorite show and popcorn."

I unlock the clubhouse and take a second to revel in the peaceful quietness of it. It feels like a sanctuary without the constant sound of metal bats thwacking balls in the batting cages or music blaring from the speaker in the locker room.

"Whoa, I like it like this," Katie whispers.

"I was just thinking the same thing. Come on, let's get set up."

Katie pushes some tables and chairs out of the way of the two old couches in the back and throws a bunch of blankets on the ground for the overflow. With just the corner lamp on, a cozy glow warms up our Lazy. I connect my laptop to the projector and load the show. We are popping our fourth bag of popcorn when our team begins to trickle in.

Ashlyn snags a bag and plops down in the middle of the bigger couch. "Dang, y'all. This is perfect."

"Yeah, thanks for setting this up, guys," Taylor says.

"There are more bags of popcorn, so feel free to pop them while people keep showing up. Otherwise, get cozy. We have some trashy TV to watch," Katie announces.

I wait for everyone to make their popcorn and settle in before I hit play and turn off the lamp. Half the girls squish together on the couches, and half sit on the floor, backs against someone's legs or the little bit of accessible couch. I duck under the screen and join the viewing party. There's only one spot with back support, and it's on the floor against the arm of the couch. Of course, Maya is sitting on that couch, half her body draped over the arm.

Screw it. Everything is fine. Everything is normal, and it would be weird for me to avoid sitting near her. That would definitely *not* be normal. I slink to the floor next to Taylor and rest my back against the arm of the couch next to Maya's legs. As I settle in, her knee brushes my shoulder. It only lingers for a moment before I hear her sigh and shift away from me. I do my best to avoid touching her as well, but after the tenth accidental contact, she huffs and pushes off the couch. I try to wait a minute or two before I follow her into the locker room.

Maya sits on the bench in front of our lockers, scrolling on her phone.

"What are you doing?" I ask.

She looks up and rolls her eyes. And we're right back where we started. "It's cramped in there. I'm just taking a break."

"Okay." I sit next to her on the bench. I'd be lying if I said I didn't miss being close to her. Or miss seeing her smile. "How are your classes going?"

"Fine."

I can feel her lean away, and it's driving me crazy. I can't tell if I want to yell at her or push her up against a wall and kiss her. "Maya, I—"

"I need some space. Okay? I know I have to be here for the team activity or whatever, and I'm here. But I need some space from them. And I need some space from you. So do you mind?" She nods toward the door.

A twisted fuzziness settles in my stomach. I run my hands down my jeans and stand. "I can ask Coach Clayton if I can do weights with Katie on Monday. If you want. Give you a break from me."

She looks up from her phone and shakes her head. "Don't try to guilt me. I don't care about being your weight partner or your partner for every damn thing we have to do." She takes a deep breath. I'm annoying the hell out of this girl. "Please leave me alone."

There's no arguing with a request like that.

I nod and leave.

Instead of sitting on the ground, I sit in a chair by the projector. The girls hem and haw at all the crazy women fighting and crying and trying to get the attention of the guy, but I can't get past the interaction I just had with Maya. A sticky sick feeling settles in my gut, like I made a mistake. Maybe I made a mistake somewhere along our relationship last semester, and now it's all shit.

After another ten minutes, Maya walks past me to her spot on the couch. She doesn't watch the show, just stares at her phone. Mine buzzes in my pocket, and I nearly rip a hole through my jeans trying to get it out. Trying to see if it's her.

Katie: *What's up with M? All good?*

I try not to let the disappointment show on my face. *Yeah. I think so. You know how she can be.*

Katie: *Don't say I didn't warn you.*

My eyes are bleary as I walk into the athletic center on Monday morning. Coach Williams is the first one there, and she greets me with a coffee-breath hello and side hug.

"Morning, Andy."

"Morning, Coach."

"While I have you here, can we have a quick chat? Before the others start rolling in?"

I shift my weight from one foot to the other and back again. "Of course. What's up?"

"Look, Andy, you've been doing an excellent job this year. We have really noticed you rising to meet your captain responsibilities and how you try to lift up your team. And you and Maya seemed to have solidified a beneficial relationship, even a friendship, on and off the field last semester. But I can't help noticing things may be a little off between the two of you lately." Coach Williams takes another sip of coffee and taps her lid. She doesn't make eye contact with me, so I wait for her to continue.

"With the season just starting, we're hoping that you can find your way back to solidarity soon. I think it really helps Maya to have a partner in you. Makes her a better pitcher and teammate. Do you understand?"

And I am again casually tasked with the job that is Maya.

I startle out of my sleepy concentration when the weight room door cracks open, and Katie mutters drowsy hellos to Coach and me on her way to the locker room.

"I understand."

Coach Williams pats my shoulder. "Great. That's great. Thank you. You can go ahead." She nods toward the locker room.

I relish the last second of my own body heat before I peel off my sweatshirt and let the AC tickle my sleeping skin. I toss my bag and the rest of my stuff in a vacant locker and return to the weight room. The gravity of Monday pulls my body onto the mats for stretching. Tries to pull my eyelids down, too, but I fight it. I'm still in the middle of my half-awake stretching when Maya appears on the mat next to me, silently falling into her morning routine.

"Hey, May."

She ignores my greeting for a moment as she finishes a deep back stretch and sighs as she rolls out her neck. "Morning."

Well, that's something. I decide not to push the matter. She did ask for space, after all, and regardless of my "team duties" or whatever, I care about Maya, and I want to respect her needs and boundaries. Besides, you can never really know someone completely. I have no idea exactly what Maya is going through or how she feels. I can only control my side of things.

"I failed my Econ test," she says. And she says it so off-handedly that it takes me a moment to reacquaint myself with where I am in the universe and who is speaking to me. And where in the mess of our friendship we stand. "Well, I didn't exactly fail. But I got a seventy-two. Anyway, can you help me? You had to take Econ, right?"

It's hard for me to register her tone. What is this? She drops an ounce of annoyance from her cadence when she needs my help? I guess it's irrelevant if it helps get us back on track even a little. I spin on my butt to face her. Do a little butterfly stretch.

"Yeah, I took Econ. Want me to come over sometime?"

"No. Study hall is fine." She picks herself off the ground but doesn't extend her usual hand to help me up.

Maya and I are quiet throughout weight training. Just metal clanking on metal, heavy breaths, Maya's sweat mixed with her body wash, and a whole bunch of silence. Coach Williams is right—this isn't working. What I thought would be an ideal place for me and Maya is ending up to be a dispassionate hellscape that isn't helping our team. I'm running out of forms our relationship can take.

I walk into study hall and find Maya in the far corner hunched over a book. We had a good practice today, even though it was as distant and quiet as weight training was this morning. But everyone played solidly, and we're prepared for our first away game on Friday.

"Can I sit?" I ask Maya.

She looks up at me as if that was the stupidest question in the world. "Well, yeah." She pulls out the plastic chair next to her, and I slink into it.

I push my backpack under the small table and angle myself toward her. "All right. What do we have going on?" I ask.

"A bunch of bullshit."

I can't help but crack a smile as she pushes her book to me, and I scan the chapter she's reading. "Okay, so it looks like we're doing cost minimization graphing?"

She nods.

"Is there an assignment you're working on, or do you just want to talk through these problems in the textbook?"

She sighs and slides the book away. "My professor hates me. I went to his office hours for help, and he was annoyed that I had to leave early for practice. It's bullshit. I know I can do this stuff. He's just refuses to help me."

"Maybe you should ask for a tutor. I'm happy to help, I just—"

"Fine."

Maya flings her textbook shut and shoves it into her bag. Before I have a chance to react, she's halfway to Coach Clayton. I guess I'm off the hook for Econ, but I'm definitely not off the hook with Maya.

Tomorrow is our first away game against Covington, and my goal is to get my team out of practice a little early tonight so everyone can rest up for the trip. The beginning of the season can be taxing when it comes to sleep and energy levels, and I want us to be fresh for tomorrow.

Clouds darken the sky as we run through our defensive plays for when runners are on first and third. I love how the trees sound right before it rains, like they're warning us. Or celebrating.

"Andy. Are you even listening to me?" Maya stares through my catcher's helmet as if she's trying to find me, but I've done a pretty good job at disassociating around her lately. I can only take so much. I'm not listening to her. I'm listening to the trees and the dull drum of cleats against the dirt as our teammates jog to the dugout for a water break.

"Yeah. What'd you say?"

She drops the ball at her feet, glove raised in frustration. "The answer is clearly, *no*, you weren't listening to me. Whatever. Look, I hate the cutoff option of this play. It's chaotic and is more likely to result in an error and a run than it is an out. I'd rather have the runner advance to second than risk it."

This I can follow. I nod. "I agree. I'll talk to Coach Clay after practice." She's right. I also hate the cutoff version of this play, the one where I throw the ball like I'm trying to throw out the runner advancing to second base, but Maya cuts off my throw to then throw out the runner on third, who is probably advancing to home at that point. It's messy and not worth it.

Like Maya.

She tucks her glove under her arm and wipes down her face. She looks tired. Which is exactly why I want to get this practice wrapped up. "Okay," she says.

"All right, ladies. Good practice. Let's end with five poles. Don't forget, no study hall tonight, and be at the clubhouse by one tomorrow," Coach Williams shouts. While the rest of the team packs and groans over the minimal amount of poles we have to run, I thank the softball gods for giving us an early night. "Andy, come chat with me in my office while they wrap up," Coach Williams says.

"The poles?"

"Don't worry about it. I gotta go pick up my daughter. Come on."

I zip my bag and follow Coach Williams's heels, wanting it to be clear that I am not skipping sprints by choice.

"Long story short, tomorrow will be the first game of the season that Maya isn't pitching. I wanted to touch base with you about Daniella and how you can best support her during the game."

We walk into the clubhouse, the air still pungent with our sweat. "Of course, let me just ditch my stuff, and I'll meet you in your office." It might be a nice break for me and Maya, but I'm anxious to have someone else on the mound. Winning every game possible is essential to making it to regionals, but as good as Daniella is, she's no Maya. Regardless, a championship team needs a world-class pitching staff, not just a single superstar who they pray doesn't get injured. Not at this level. So we need to invest in Daniella.

Coach Williams and I chat about her strengths and weaknesses, what the pitch calling strategy will be, and where she'll need the most support from me, her catcher. We talk for about twenty minutes before Coach releases me back into the wild. The locker room is empty. I spin in a circle, taking in the absence of my team. They should have been done with poles by now. Five poles does not take longer than twenty minutes to run. I walk back outside.

Everyone is still running. A thick gray drizzle that seems to match the mood of my teammates falls. As I approach, I can see the exhaustion on their faces, in their bodies, in their limbs. Instead of sprinting across the outfield to the opposite foul pole and jogging back along the fence, the girls run their poles in one trudging jog, too tired to even run them properly. I walk out to left field and wait for Maya to loop back around to me.

"Maya," I call, waving her over.

She wipes the rain and sweat off her face, only to have it instantly wet again. Her eyes are dark and narrowed. "What?"

"What is going on out here? Why are you all still running?"

Girls jog by in a huffing and puffing wave of negative energy. This is terrible.

"What's going on is they still haven't learned to clean up after themselves. After you and Coach left, I stepped in someone's chewed gum. Just on the ground. Like someone was too lazy to throw it in the trash."

"Gum on your shoe? That's what this is about?" I push past her, knocking her shoulder on my way to center field. The cold rain goose bumps my skin. "Everyone, stop running. Bring it in."

The girls walk to me, cleats dragging, hands on hips, breathing heavy. I try to ignore their glances at left field, where Maya continues with her poles alone, refusing to stop running her own punishment.

I focus on my team. "Good practice today. Let's wrap this up and get some rest for Covington tomorrow. On three." Every girl piles her wet hand in the middle of the circle and yells, "Lions," on my count. Low grumbles and mumbles roll like thunder as the girls leave the field.

Katie snags my arm as Maya sprints past again. "This is fucking ridiculous, Andy. Fix it. Please." She lets me go and walks away, not giving me a chance to respond.

When the last of our teammates is gone, I run. It doesn't take long to catch up to Maya. I still have gas in my tank. The grass begins to squish underfoot as the rain picks up. I run two poles with her to show at least a sliver of solidarity, but she struggles to make it across the outfield in a slow-motion jog, the wet grass not helping.

"Maya, stop. Just stop." I put my hand on her shoulder to slow her negligible momentum.

"Everyone else can be a quitter, but I'm finishing these poles." I pull her back. It's too much for her to power through, and she grinds to a stop where we started, the left foul pole. I give her a moment to catch her breath and recenter. Our practice uniforms are glued to our bodies from the rain, but I'm not looking at how hers hugs her curves. I'm frustrated and concerned. This is bullshit.

"What the hell was that, Andy?"

I stare her in the eye. My breathing is slow and even compared to hers; it makes me feel more in control. "I was going to ask you the exact same thing. You stepped in gum, so what? So you make our team run a thousand poles in the rain when they're already more than exhausted, and we have our first away game tomorrow? Because running on empty wasn't enough, you needed to completely destroy their morale, too? What were you thinking?"

She takes a step toward me, landing uncomfortably close, our faces only a couple inches apart. "My apologies. I thought we were a championship team with a championship attitude, not a fucking junior varsity squad full of whining preteens."

I step away, not willing to stoop so low as to posture like men about to fight. Not willing to be as weak as that. "Jesus, Maya. What is going on with you? You know running them ragged like that isn't helpful."

"What's going on with me?" She jams two fingers into her chest and laughs. "What's going on with me? Andrea Foster wants to know what's going on with me." Her sarcastic laugh burrows into my ear canal and flips a switch in my brain. Every profanity I know races through my brain. My tongue itches to be released, begs to lash out.

"Do it," she says, stepping back into my space. She shoves my shoulder. It's a light shove, but it triggers every fight response in my body, just like when she egged me on outside the clubhouse. "Come on, Foster." I can't catch a deep breath in this damn rain, and she shoves me again. My body hums with adrenaline as I bounce on my toes, ready to spring, about to tackle her to the soaked earth. But anger doesn't stand out against anger. *I need to swerve.* I focus on her face. She wants me to lash out at her, wants me to start a fight. She's asking for my attention.

"I miss you," I say.

It's true. And I'm tired of this. I'm tired of the fact that when things go a little off between us, we revert to this old habit of being "enemies." We are not enemies. We are partners. And under this stupid act of Maya's is a person who cares about me. Under her furrowed brows are eyes that see me and know me better than anyone.

She looks down and twists her cleat into the mud. "Don't," she says.

"I miss you, Maya. You know it's true." Her chin falls against her chest in a half nod. A half acknowledgement of what we actually have between us. "What's going on?" I ask.

She drops her arms to her sides, palms up, shaking her head at the clouds. "I can't."

Some cheesy teenage lyric about the rain hiding tears dances through my head as I watch her, wondering if this rain is hiding hers. Or at least her watering eyes. My feet squish into the earth as I step toward her. No one sees this girl for who she really is. She is out here in left field, probably crying because she literally overflows with passion. A passion to be the best. A passion for our team to be the best. But as I look at her face, I can see another torment.

"I'm right here. Tell me." I slide my hand down her slippery arm, past her wrist, until her hooked fingers save mine from running off the end of the Slip 'N Slide.

She drops my hand and wipes her face again. "Coach Clay talked to me today. In between drills." I stare at a bead of water hanging from her long dark lashes. "He said my kind of passion is misplaced, that it's too much, and he wants me to curb it for the sake of the team." She shakes her head and wipes the raindrop from her lashes. "And all I could think about is Kevin erupting with pure competitiveness when he plays and the swagger and energy that these men have on the field or the court or whatever. I wonder if their coaches are tugging their sleeves, whispering for them to 'tone it down.' If Kevin's coach thinks he's 'too passionate' or if he just smacks him on the ass and says good job."

I shrug. "I don't know, May."

"And it's not just with sports. My marketing professor has the opposite criticism. I'm not loud enough. I'm not aggressive enough in closing negotiations. Why can't I work the room like Charles, and you know what, Andy? I have a fucking higher grade than Charles and made more sales in our mock marketing campaign. 'Loud' isn't a sales strategy. Listening and responding to the market data is." She sighs. "What does the world want from me?"

I shake my head. There's no answer here.

"It's like, no matter how tough I am or how forgiving I am, how strong or fierce, or strong and gentle, I'll never be taken as seriously as a man. Will never be respected like one or valued like one. I will always be found wanting. And it's just out of my control," she says.

"You may be right. I guess that means you should just be the purest form of yourself. And screw them if they don't like it."

"And yet, look at how you treat me." She stares me down, taking in my whole body. I think I'm found wanting as well. "You're a sleeve-tugger. I guess women share the same male bias." She walks away from me as I wrap my head around her words.

"Maya."

She looks back over her shoulder. "You know, Andy," she calls through the rain. "I'm fucking fierce. Don't try to dim me."

## CHAPTER TEN

I don't expect Maya to sit next to me on our two-hour bus ride to Chattanooga, but it would be a good show of solidarity for the team. Instead, she flows past me to the back of the bus, and I don't even have to turn to know who she's sitting with. Katie plops down in the open seat next to me, pulls an AirPod from her right ear, and hands it to me. I pop it in without question.

"I missed these bus rides," she says.

"Me, too. You aren't going to make me watch *The Bachelor*, are you?"

She shakes her head as she opens the YouTube app on her phone. I usually love watching music videos with Katie, but some quiet time to reflect would be nice, too. I spent the entire night thinking about my conversation with Maya. She may be right about the role I've played in our relationship and how it aligns with the "patriarchy's agenda," but I also have a different leadership style. And I am the captain, not Maya. There has to be a way to reconcile these truths.

"You play two videos, I play two. That's it. I kinda want to focus on our game. Get in the zone," I say.

"Yeah, yeah, I know."

Most of the trips to away games are beautiful because we live in a beautiful place. Chattanooga is just across the Tennessee border, and the majority of our drive is through the North Georgia mountains. Covington University's field is much like ours, tucked into a private grove of trees with no roads in sight, save the small one connected to the back parking lot behind the third-base dugout. Just like Alder.

I hate playing in city parks. I'll be batting, trying my best to focus, and a car will zoom by the field blaring its horn. Not at Alder and not at Covington. Every building, field, and sidewalk in these places feels like it was carved out of forest. So when we play, we play with the sway of the trees, not the distractions of a city.

I watch the peaceful landscape flow past my window, wishing my relationship with Maya could be even half as tranquil.

Maya is not pitching today, which means our defense has a little more responsibility this game. It's nice to warm up with Daniella, someone who actually talks to me. She's having a slow start to the game but finds a little more of her footing with each at bat. It's the bottom of the fifth, and she has walked two batters and allowed two hits.

The next batter approaches the box, and I turn to Coach Williams for our pitch call. The sun just set, and the softball field is bathed in the best kind of golden glow as all the park lights switch on. The runner on first crouches and prepares to take her lead. Daniella winds up; she has a totally different pitching motion than Maya. Her arm starts at a right angle, and she boasts more extraneous movement while Maya's form is more clean and powerful. The ball launches out of Daniella's hand, and the Covington batter smashes it to right field.

Our outfielder takes a bad angle to the escaped ball but quickly recovers as the runner approaches third. I step in front of home plate and prepare to receive a rocket to tag this girl out. Our right fielder makes the perfect throw to Katie, the second-base cutoff, who beams it home right on the money. The second the ball hits my mitt, I slide on my knee into the basepath to put the tag on—

Maya is yelling. She's always angry with me.

I crack my eyelids and spot her behind Coach Williams.

"Thank God. She's awake," Maya says in a huff, and Coach Williams pulls her away.

"Give her some space," I hear her say.

Everyone looks so big as they peer down at me. There's Coach Clayton, Dr. Eddie, the ump, and a couple strangers. My head feels like it's disconnected from my body, and a little bit of panic starts to creep into my floating consciousness.

Dr. Eddie, our sports medicine professional, bends closer to my face. "Hi, Andrea. Everything is okay. You've been hit pretty hard, but we're taking care of you."

Coach Clayton walks over to Coach Williams. "Get Kim warmed up and sub her in," he says.

My mouth opens, and it feels like I'm choking on a giant cobweb. "*Argh.*" The sound is equal parts groan of pain and groan of disgust. Everyone's attention turns back to me. "Kim is the worst." I groan again. I catch Coach Williams smiling at me, and for some reason, I'm flooded with such triumph, I want to cry. I wiggle my fingers and take charge of my right arm. I can feel my blood slowly coloring my body as I lift my arm to point at her. "You know. She knows what I'm talking about." Their quiet chuckles of relief roll over me.

"Careful there, Ms. Foster. We're going to go through this nice and slow. Easy peasy," Dr. Eddie says. He has me wiggle everything for him like I'm an earthworm in the dirt, but I feel more like a root. I'm not sure I can get up. "Don't worry about that," he says. "You're doing great."

"Do you know where you are, sweetheart?" one of the strangers asks.

"Don't call me sweetheart. Patriarchy," I mumble and point at Maya, who is too far away to hear me.

The stranger coughs out of discomfort, I hope, then poses the same question. *Where am I?* I take a moment to ponder this very challenging question. "Not home," I answer.

"That's very good. You are not home. Can you name a couple of your classes?"

This question scares the shit out of me because I should know this. I can see myself sitting in a classroom, listening to a lecture. I know the room; I know the professor; I know the photo of the beach in Hawaii that's pinned to the chalkboard. But I'm drawing blanks.

"I don't know." I begin to cry. Not like a gross sob, but I can feel the tears on my cheeks because they start nice and warm, then dry cold and prickly.

"That's okay, Andy. That's totally normal." Coach Clayton's big paw rests on my shoulder.

"I think I'm ready to sit up."

Dr. Eddie and a stranger ease me to a sitting position, and I hear clapping from everyone.

"Okay, Ms. Foster, we are going to escort you to our medical facility for the remainder of the game, just to give you a quiet, safe place to recover. We'll also have to do an examination to rule out possible brain injury. Sounds scarier than it is, I promise," the stranger says. And I'm eased to my feet with his help, my arms over his and Dr. Eddie's shoulders. I've never been drunk, but I imagine this is what it's like. Emotional and wobbly.

Relief cools my anxiety as I realize that I am, in fact, okay. I can walk, my jaw hurts like hell, but my head doesn't. I don't even have a headache. We walk slowly together off the field and onto a golf cart, which takes me to the medical facility.

Katie falls into the bus seat next to me and offers up an AirPod. I kick my bag out of the way of my feet and lean into her. A side effect of being knocked out cold, apparently, is being highly emotional. No matter how many times they assured me I was okay, a constant slow drip of tears fell from my eyes like a leaky faucet while the medical crew examined me. But it wasn't even about my injury. I'm just so in my feelings tonight. Even though sticking a hard little piece of loud plastic in my head sounds about as nice as kissing a cactus, I'm flooded with affection for my friend.

I wave off the earbud and rest my head on her shoulder. "I don't think I can handle music right now."

"Aw. Okay. I'm just glad you're alive, honestly. You should have seen—"

"Hey."

Katie and I both startle at the monotone greeting.

"Hey, Maya," Katie says.

I straighten, careful with my movements. Slow. Steady. Maya looks a little off. In a way that I can't point to one specific thing that is lacking or out of place. Maybe she's just a little foggy like me. She grips the seat back in front of us and hikes her bag up her shoulder.

She clears her throat. "Coach wanted me to sit with Andy on the way home and go over next week's schedule. Make sure we're on the same page with concussion protocol and all that. You know, 'cause of…" She fumbles for a moment and points at me, then herself. Decides at least one word of clarification is necessary. "Pitching."

In another world, Katie might question her, might challenge her directive. But tonight, I guess she doesn't want to rock the boat. "Oh. Okay. Just let me grab my stuff." She pockets her phone and slides her AirPods into their little white case, then snags her bag off the ground and looks at me. "Ya good with this?"

I nod.

Hell yeah, I'm good with this. Even though Maya has been in Maya mode, I've been dying to get a moment like this with her. One without the distraction of competition and teammates and anger. One like when we study together. Regardless of my hopes, I brace myself for another difficult interaction with the girl. Because I know I hurt her.

Maya takes Katie's place. Her eyes stay far away from me as she settles in and tucks her bag under the seat. I watch her. Careful. She's giving me all the potential energy of a spring-loaded trap.

Finally, she turns to me. "You scared the shit out of me, Andy." Her voice is strained, in a whisper-yell kind of way, stuck in a vocal purgatory. This is not what I was expecting to come out of her mouth.

"Um. I'm sorry? I'm not sure—"

"That sound." She shakes her head as if she could shake the memory from her brain. "God, it was horrible. Like a shotgun. And your helmet…" Another shake of her head and some flailing arms. "It just flew off. And everyone knew you were out."

I angle my body toward her, a little more confident that she won't bite. At least not tonight. "I'm okay. I promise. They ran all these tests on my head, and they said I'm clear. I don't even have a headache, May. Just a sore jaw and a woozy body. I mean, I obviously have a concussion, but I'm okay."

She nods along with my affirmations and takes a moment before responding. Her eyes find mine, and I realize just how concerned she is about me. She wasn't yelling on the field because she was mad at me. She was scared for me. Obviously. The fog in my brain is heavy, still, but it starts to evaporate when Maya reaches for my face. Her knuckles brush over the bruise on my jaw. It's so tender, bruise and otherwise.

"I'm so happy you're okay." She drops her hand in her lap. "*Ugh*, I wanted to kill that bitch. Coach Williams basically had to hold me back."

I blame my concussion for the way her intensity over my accident makes me want to curl into her. Make her hold me. "Do you mind telling me what happened? I mean, I've heard bits and pieces, but mostly, the medical staff didn't see it, and the coaches had to, you know, coach. That is, if you can tell me without bursting into flames of anger." I nudge her shoulder and am rewarded with a sharp smile.

"Don't make fun of me. I can't help it, okay? It's like I care about you or something." The words come with light chuckles but knead deep into me.

"I care about you, too," I say with no chuckle, no smile. I want it naked for her.

She stares at me. One slow nod. "The baserunner, Bremmer, blew through her call to hold at third and decided to try to take home. But she was so late, and Katie's throw was perfect. And you, you were perfect. You caught the ball and immediately dropped a knee and slid into the basepath to put down the tag, but she was so late that she kinda flailed. Like, she didn't full-on slide headfirst because you were already there, but I guess she still had all this momentum and kind of half slid. Which really just amounted to lowering her shoulder and smashing you right on your jaw. Your helmet flew off, and your back hit the dirt."

She releases a heavy sigh, then continues. "My stomach just dropped. I knew you were unconscious. I ran onto the field. And you were. You were out but, like, moaning a little. And twitching. Well, only half your body was twitching. The other half was dead still. It was fucking terrifying. For like three entire minutes, you were gone." She takes a deep breath. "Then you cracked open your eyes, and I just exploded with relief. Coach Williams pulled me away, but I still got to hear your little ramblings." She grins like she knows a secret.

"Oh, man, all I remember is calling Kim the worst. Which I completely stand by. What else did I say?"

"You said, 'my head is floating,' and some nonsense about how pretty the trees are."

I laugh. "Did I say anything else embarrassing?"

The busload of students and staff finishes settling in for the ride home. The driver starts the engine and cuts the blue and yellow lights, leaving us in darkness save a few emergency lights.

"You said something about me."

My whole body drops through my seat. The millions of times I've thought about kissing Maya, touching Maya, about Maya naked rush through my mind. *Oh my God.* What did I let slip?

"Relax, Andy. You look like I just told you that you peed your pants in front of everyone."

It's not unheard of for a person to urinate while knocked unconscious. That would have been way better than all the things I'm thinking of. "What did I say, May?"

"You said, 'Maya. So pretty. So mean.'"

*Phew.* Could've been way, way worse. I shake my head. "Oh God, I'm sorry. My brain is basically a pile of goo right now. I can't be held responsible for anything I said out there."

She leans into me, her head bowed next to mine. "What if I want to hold you responsible?" she whispers.

I can feel the tendrils of her hair tickle my cheek and the warmth of her words on my skin. The darkness of the bus and the night outside our window holds us in our own private world. We sit in our silence for a moment longer. "I only stand by half of what I said."

"Which half?" she asks.

I lean a little closer. "You know which half."

"I'm not that mean, you know."

My head feels impossibly heavy, and Maya smells impossibly good. Like earth and spice and home. And maybe it's the courage found in the dark, or maybe it's the fact that I can blame anything I say or do tonight on my concussion, but I close my eyes and lay my head against her shoulder. I focus on how her breath pulls deeper from her chest now, as if she's meditating on something.

"But you're that pretty," I whisper.

Her nose and mouth skim over me, her lips dragging a sigh across my hair, sending hot and cold shivers down my body. Her hand comes to rest next to my knee, and I pray she finds the courage to touch me, too, because it's just me and her tonight. All of the pressure, the intensity, and the boyfriend...they don't exist right now. I want to keep talking. And as I sort through all the words I have for Maya, shapely words and possessive words, I feel my eyes begin to water. This concussion is quite the tearjerker, but maybe a gift, too.

"Yesterday, when I said I missed you, I meant it. I miss you so much," I say.

She takes a moment, her pinky twitching against my knee. "I miss you, too."

"I don't want to be a sleeve-tugger. Your fire and passion are my favorite things about you. I promise to never dim you."

She clears her throat. "Thank you."

"But I'm the captain. You gotta let me do my thing, too. Stop stepping on my toes and let me do my job."

I feel the gentle chuckle against my hair. "Yes, ma'am."

"How are you so compliant right now? You hated me yesterday. And, like, so many other days, too." I nuzzle into her shoulder, mumbling my words into the fabric of her sweatshirt.

She takes a deep breath. "Because I don't hate you at all. I like you. I like you...a lot." I don't ask her to clarify. I take those words to mean exactly what I want them to mean. "I hated how last semester ended. It left me feeling so weird and insecure," she says.

I lift my head from her shoulder and look at her, wrapping my fingers around her forearm and rubbing my thumb over the muscle. She continues. "I told you I needed space, but the truth is that I thought *you* needed space after those texts." She looks at my hand holding her arm and swallows. "Um, so I tried to do that and was being dumb and in my feelings. But that was yesterday, and today, I watched you almost die. Or it felt like it, at least. So I want to be honest about how I feel. I don't want space from you, ever. I want the opposite of space."

I can't help but smile. "The opposite of space? That would be a black hole."

"Andrea."

In a bold move, I brush my thumb over her cheek and cuddle back into her shoulder. "I know, I'm just being silly. I don't want space, either."

The bus ride home is the kind of two hours that feels infinite. Like the beginning of a movie when the end feels like it may never come. Her finger brushes the fabric of my jeans, and when I snake an arm through hers and tug it to my chest like I'm cuddling a teddy bear, she spreads her palm over my knee and squeezes. We hit a bump in the mountain road, and her hand slides to the inside of my thigh. She leaves it there the rest of the ride.

When I get back to my dorm room, the high of my concussion and the bus ride with Maya has morphed into a gaping pit of exhaustion. The guys in Chattanooga warned me it would happen. Especially after sitting for so long on the bus. The moment I stood, I could feel every hinge in my body seizing up; Maya had to basically carry me off the bus. And to top it off, Katie insisted on walking me home. Maya tried to play the "coaches expect this of me" card, but Katie already gave me to Maya once that night, and she probably thought she was saving me or something.

I open my door to find Emma lying on Rachel's bed watching something on her phone. She swings her legs over the edge and stands to help me with my bag.

"Andy. How are you feeling? You okay?"

I all but collapse on my bed. "Yeah, yeah. I'm good. What are you doing here, Em? I thought Rachel was my nighttime concussion buddy. And you know, my roommate."

"She sent me in her stead. She's 'busy' tonight." Emma uses air quotes.

"*Ugh*, no. With Melissa? Please tell me she's not still hooking up with her."

"I mean…"

"Oh geez."

"Hey, no judgment. We're all just weird humans, living our weird lives, doing our weird things. And if you were Rachel, living Rachel's weird life, well, guess what, love?" Emma lifts me off my bed.

"I'd be hooking up with Melissa, too?"

"Ding, ding, ding. Winner. Now, let's get you ready for bed."

I follow her into the bathroom and let her do all the things for me. She squirts toothpaste on my toothbrush, brings me my pj's, makes sure I set an alarm so I have enough time to grab breakfast before our team meeting, and sets hers for every couple of hours. She lies with me in my bed as I recount my epic story of the evening. Getting knocked out, not the Maya part. She rubs the lank muscles in my forearm as I speak, and it feels incredible. But only in my arm. The warmth doesn't spread tonight. When my eyelids refuse to slide back open, and it feels like speaking words is a mountain I just can't summit, Emma slides out of my bed.

I wake in the morning with the stiffest neck I have ever experienced. Emma helps me with every little thing she can; she packs my bag with everything I ask her to, she literally ties my shoes for me, and now, I stand in front of her in my jeans, a bra, and those freshly tied shoes. I notice her eyes scan over my bare torso. It makes me feel a little sexy and powerful but without the weight of possibility. Nothing will happen here.

She grabs an Alder Softball tee from my dresser and pulls it over my head as gently as possible. We startle at a knock on my door.

Expecting Rachel, I holler, "Come in."

Maya opens my door with a greasy paper bag and two hot coffees. She stops when she sees me and Emma. Em's hands are fisted in the shirt that is currently bunched on top of my shoulders, my best bra and my bare stomach exposed. And yeah, we see each other in the locker room, blah blah blah. But that's different. It's the least intimate place in the world, and you're really just focusing on yourself in there. But here, in my dorm room, I stand exposed in front of none other than Emma Wilson and Maya Gonzalez, and for a moment, we are all frozen in frame.

"Oh. Emma," Maya says, and we all snap back into action.

I bat Emma's hands off my shirt and pull it the rest of the way down my body.

"Maya. What are you doing here?" I regret my word choice when her features fall even more.

"I thought I'd knock one thing off your to-do list this morning." She looks at the food and coffee and shrugs. "And walk you to the meeting."

I look back at Emma, who stands idle in the middle of my room. Then back to Maya. "That's so sweet, May. And whatever's in that bag smells amazing. Can I meet you in the lobby in, like, five minutes?"

"Um. Sure."

I close the door behind her and turn to find Emma's face scrunched in amusement.

"What. The fuck. Was that? Are y'all, like, friends now? I thought you hated each other."

I switch off the bathroom light and pull my jacket from the back of my desk chair. Careful but determined, I sneak one arm in. Emma grabs the other side and holds it open for me. "I got it." I pull out of her grip like a petulant child. "Maya and I are figuring it out. We have to for the team. And last night was scary. She's just glad I'm okay, and she's trying to help. Just like you, okay?"

Emma raises her hands in surrender. "Okay. You got it."

I sigh and grab my bag. "I'm sorry. I'm all weird and concussed and cranky and stiff. Can we just get going?"

"It's all good. Yeah, let's roll."

When we get to the lobby, I thank Emma for her help and send her on her way. Then it's just me and Maya looking at each other, waiting for someone to speak.

"Sorry to interrupt…that," she says.

I wave her off. "You didn't interrupt anything. Not a thing. She stayed over to help and to check on me through the night because Rachel couldn't."

"You don't owe me an explanation, Andy. I don't care about whatever's going on between you and Emma Wilson."

I reach across the space that separates us and touch her wrist. She can't do much but let me because her hands are full with coffee. I take a small step toward her and give a gentle squeeze. "Don't do that. Let's just not do that. Okay?" I say it gently. Wonder if she can hear the pleading in my voice. I'm begging. I just got her back to whatever this is, and I don't want to lose her again.

She huffs and shakes her head but doesn't try to wriggle out of my grip. "I hate that girl," she grumbles.

I windshield-wipe my thumb over her skin. "Maya. Breathe."

She ditches her scowl and looks at me. I'm not even angry at her hypocrisy. Not even angry that she feels some kind of unearned possessiveness over me while she's somebody else's girlfriend. For now, I really don't give a shit. I just want a couple more days of this. I just want a little more time in my pretty little delusion.

"That's it." I continue to rub her wrist, and the faintest little smile appears on her lips. "Breathe. And swerve."

"Swerve. You've said that to me before. Is that, like, your thing?"

I take one of the coffees, and she reaches for my bag. "You don't have to carry my bag. I'm fine."

"I insist." She slides the strap off my shoulder without letting any of its weight hang on me.

"It's my thing, I guess. When I feel overwhelmed or need a change in attitude. It's just a quick little phrase that triggers my brain to pivot. Like a step in a dance or something."

"A step in a dance?"

We walk out into the morning, the coolness of it softened by a touch of humidity in the air. Flowers are beginning to bloom, and everything is cracking open its eyes. "Yeah, it's muscle memory at this point. When I say those words to myself, my brain just knows to either chill out or redirect or whatever I need."

Maya stops at a bench in the quad and sheds our bags. "We're early, and it's so nice out. Wanna eat?"

"Yeah."

She pulls the food from her bag and hands me a small to-go box. "I hope you like bagel and egg sandwiches."

"I wasn't aware that there was a segment of the population who didn't."

We eat in quiet comfort. Every other bite, I catch the sun illuminating strands of her black hair, bleaching them platinum white for a split second. Her cheek works around its little dimple while she chews, and her leg bounces up and down. Up and down.

"I'm sorry," she says, breaking my trance.

"For what?"

"I said it in *a way*, but you really don't owe me an explanation about you and Emma. You really don't owe me anything. We're just friends and teammates, and I know that. I just wanted to check on you because I was up half the night worrying. So I was a little tired and then a lot shocked when I opened the door, and Emma was, like, looking at your body or whatever."

I nod along, trying to ignore how the phrase "just friends" feels like knives spelunking down my ear canals.

"It doesn't matter," she continues. "I don't care. I just don't trust that girl. And she was looking at you like a fucking wolf."

"Emma was literally just there to help. We've been friends since middle school, and if I'm being honest with you, Em knows she could've had me whenever she wanted me. And she never wanted me. So it's kind of a mute point. And yeah, she can be flirty sometimes, but she is with everyone. It's just her personality."

I feel Maya stiffen. She thrums her fingers over the lid of her coffee and stares straight ahead at a crooked oak tree. "It's 'moot point,' just so you know. M-O-O-T, moot. I think you said mute point." She says it delicately, and it's appreciated.

I shake my head and chuckle at myself. "Thanks. I'll add it to my collection of proper phrases."

"Could she still? Have you?"

This is a very good question. My turn to stare at the crooked oak. Could Emma still have me? I don't know if I want to date her anymore. She sprints through life, and I just can't match her pace. Don't want to. But could she have me for a night? I imagine her in my bed. The slow drip of her ice pack...yeah, maybe. "I don't know the answer to that."

Do her features fall a little? Yes. But we both know she can't say anything about it because I'm giving her the grace of avoiding the topic of her very real boyfriend. I have no idea what we have going on between us, but at the end of the day, I know two things. Maya Gonzalez has a boyfriend, and me and Maya are just friends. Sure, there's the pesky third thing—my giant crush. But for now, it's harmless. And for now, we're good.

"I think that's what I hate the most about Emma. She could've had you. And she just *didn't*."

I can think of another girl who can have me and just *hasn't*. The wind blows a dead leaf off my Adidas, and I sip my coffee. If Maya hates Emma for passing me up, I wonder how she feels about herself right now. How much longer can she hold me here in this gray area? I want her to choose me.

## CHAPTER ELEVEN

I love taking tests. Sure, I'm skilled at note-taking and organization and am, generally speaking, a "good student." But tests are where I really shine. My pen cuts across the stapled paper as I finish my short answer on behavioral phenomena and sensory processes. Done. As a rule, and I'm sure this is a very unpopular one, I never double-check anything. Not one answer. I always go with the first thing to pop into my head. Studies have shown that your gut is usually right.

While the rest of the class hunches over their papers, I pack up quietly and bring my test to Dr. Phillips. "First one to finish, again. How'd you do?" she whispers.

"Hoping for a triple-digit score." I give her a thumbs-up and a smile as I move toward the door. I'm meeting up with Katie in the dining hall for a quick bite before my next class.

"Well, that would be a first."

"See ya Friday, Dr. Phillips."

My feet thud against the linoleum of the empty hallway, and I push through the door into the early spring afternoon. Free…for a moment. I cut across the lower quad and admire the return of green on the trees and the contrast of the colors with the gray stone of the buildings. Katie sits on a bench outside of the dining hall just across the concourse.

She waves when she sees me walking up. "You're done already?"

I hold up finger guns and blow imaginary smoke from the barrels. "Fastest in the south."

"Come on, nerd. I'm starving."

We grab our lunch and sit next to the fireplace in a pair of cozy old armchairs. This spot is always taken, and I can see why; it isn't hard to imagine lounging here in the warmth of fire and leather and friends for a couple of hours.

"So you're officially cleared?" Katie asks.

"Yep. I'm cleared to resume any and all activities. That means Kim gets to reacquaint herself with the bench, and I finally get to play again."

Katie wipes some crumbs from her sweatshirt. "Oh, come on, it was one week. You flew through protocol."

"I didn't 'fly' through it. That implies that we didn't take it seriously. I just got lucky."

She raises an eyebrow. "You're positive you're okay to come back?"

"I know it seems fast, given the drama of the hit and me passing out—"

"Getting knocked out. Big difference."

"Knocked out. Yes. But honestly, I just wasn't affected very much after a day or two. Good as new."

Another brow rises.

"I promise," I say.

I take the opportunity to down a couple of bites of lasagna while Katie contemplates my ability to play. The dining hall prepares some surprisingly delicious meals, a luxury I know many colleges don't have.

"Okay," Katie finally says. "I believe you."

"Good."

"How are things with you and Maya?"

I shrug. "You know how they are."

She leans forward, elbows on knees, and rubs her hands in front of the fire. "Do you like her, Andy?"

The question doesn't shock me. It perturbs me, exposes me. Makes me realize my left butt cheek is numb. I place my plate on the side table and shift my weight. Pins and needles. "Yeah, I like her. She's just a little misunderstood, and she's had a great beginning of the season. Pitching-wise and teammate-wise."

Katie shifts, too. Not because her butt cheek is numb but probably because I'm forcing her to clarify. "I mean, do you have feelings for her? Don't be offended, I just think she goes out of her way to be around you, and I feel like you do the same thing."

I feel bad for lying to Katie. I do. But this just can't happen. Maya and I have literally done nothing, and having any kind of locker-room rumors about us is too risky. Mid-season drama like that can be weirdly deadly.

"I've developed a lot of love for her. As a *friend*. We've reached a good comfort level between us, but I regret to say that I'm still holding out for Emma." Half lie. Half truth.

"Really? Still?"

"We had this moment the morning after my accident. She was helping me get dressed, and it felt really intimate." Okay, this is mostly a lie, but Maya did say she saw Emma looking at my body, so...

"She's a slippery one. But I know you guys go way back. Maybe it'll work out for you."

"Yeah. Maybe." I'm a terrible actor, but I sell the wistfulness in my voice. Because I'm really hoping it does work out, just not with Emma.

We've been lucky with the way our schedule has panned out this year. We were able to iron out some kinks early on against less challenging teams. Today, though, we play Wilkerson, one of our biggest rivals and our biggest competition. For a team so low on the radar in D1, games like these are vital in order for us to have a shot at a postseason. No one is going to look twice at Alder if we have the same record as UGA because UGA's strength of schedule is so much higher. We can only afford to lose a couple of games.

After our team finishes a light meal together, we warm up in the clubhouse while the wave of anticipation builds among us. We laugh and joke, but we're focused during this time. Maya feeds me balls through the pitching machine, and I crack line drives into the netting, envisioning I'm on the field hitting against Wilkerson's pitcher.

The energy cranks up a notch when we all get together in the locker room. It's a party. The speaker is cranked to its highest volume, and girls dance between doing their hair and makeup and putting on their uniforms. I tuck my hearing aids in their little case, safe and sound, and pull off my T-shirt. A hand on the bare skin of my back startles me, and Maya appears next to me at her locker. She says something, but with the flood of music and laughing, I miss it. She smiles and takes her hand from me, then examines the uniform hanging in her locker.

I step right into her bubble, my abs pressed against the side of her arm. She stares at the plane of contact while I'm mesmerized by the gold chain draped over her smooth collarbone. Before I accidentally find out what her chain tastes like, I refocus on her eyes, which are still glued to my torso.

"I couldn't hear what you said before." I motion to the chaos surrounding us.

She looks around, then leans into me, her lips close enough to tickle my ear. "I said, I'm glad you get to play today. I wouldn't want anyone else to be my partner on the field tonight. Only you."

She breaks from me and tugs her shirt over her head, then folds it and places it on the top shelf of her locker. I stare for one second longer before I turn back to my own locker, the baby hairs on my neck tickled by her breath.

When everyone is dressed and made-up, I gather our team in a huddle. We always have a quick talk, just players, before every game. With heads leaned in and arms weaved over and under backs, we create a tight circle of pregame hype. Maya and I reiterate the important bits of advice we gathered from watching film on Wilkerson and end the huddle with a building song of confidence until the whole team yells, "Lion strong!"

We grab our softball bags and take the field. It's the perfect day for a ball game; the sun is warm, not hot, the trees sway with anticipation in the slight breeze, and fans have already filled most of the stands. The baseball team comes to watch our games on the rare occasion they have the time, and vice versa. They holler at us from behind the first-base dugout. Jeremy yells for Maya, and she waves. And I rot...rot on the spot. It's easy to forget about a six-foot-three hunk of Alabama muscle when you haven't seen the guy in weeks. But when he's right there, cheering for the girl you like, he's pretty damn hard to miss. I guess I needed a reminder.

Rachel and Emma cheer behind our dugout with a sign that has my name and number written in what looks like finger paint. Now that basketball season is over, they have all the free time to pursue their artistic endeavors. I wave and smile at them as Maya and I walk to the bullpen. How many times have I used Emma to push Maya off center stage? Hopefully, it will work soon.

We finish warming up early and take the quiet time in the bullpen to watch the rest of our team warm up on the field. We cross our arms and lean against the fence, side by side.

"What's wrong? You got quiet after we hit the field," she asks.

Our left fielder rockets a ball to Katie. I can't imagine the point in my life when I won't have this anymore. Will I ever be able to fill the void that the lack of softball will leave?

"Nothing. I'm just feeling a little nostalgic." It's not a lie if it's the truth.

"For what?"

I nod toward the field. "For this." And as I speak it, so it shall be. A pang strikes me in the chest, then drops and dulls into my gut. I only have two more years of this. Just two years left of the thing that makes me happiest in the world. Then, I'll just be another middle-aged person looking back on their "glory days" or whatever crap.

Maya knocks me with her shoulder. "You got two more years. Don't miss it because you're already missing it. Ya know?"

I nod. Maybe talking about Jeremy would have been easier, after all. "How's Jeremy's season going?"

She pauses for a moment while she adjusts to me breaking an unspoken rule. One not enforced by anyone but built out of habit. She turns her gaze back to the field as she speaks. "All right, I guess. We obviously don't see much of each other during season, but he stopped by last night. Says the freshmen are too cocky, and the seniors are too lazy. Par for the course."

"Yeah."

"I bet Emma is relieved that the season is over. Seemed like a tough one."

I face her and wait until we have eye contact. "She is. And so is Rachel. They did well, though. Made it further than last year. But yeah, now we have more time to hang out."

I'm not sure I could push Maya back into ice-queen status when it comes to our relationship at this point, and I don't want to. But right now, I can't help but push, push, push.

I'm fucking jealous.

"Right."

"Yeah. Shall we?" I walk out of the bullpen alone, Maya a minute behind me.

It's selfish of me to play this game against Wilkerson with any kind of tension between us, but here we are, not speaking. Not, like, silent treatment not speaking, just awkward. Neither of us knows what to say, and it's not like I'm feeling very lighthearted and jokey. Therefore, the beginning of the game is a bit serious between us.

I thank the softball gods that Maya is on her A game, so there is little interaction required today. I haven't had to make a single visit to the mound, and it's already the bottom of the fifth inning. We have the lead by one run.

I guess Coach wants to mix up the lineup and try some different strategies because he has Kim as our DP tonight, which means she's batting for Maya. It's not typical for a pitcher at this level to also be a great hitter, but Maya is. I can't see the value of taking her out of the lineup, except for the small amount of rest she gets.

Kim takes her first pitch, and with it, her first strike. Normal.

Second pitch, ball outside.

Third pitch, Kim cracks the ball through the 4-6 gap. Well done. I've been neglecting Kim for a while now, even though her attitude hasn't been as heinous lately. I hop onto the dugout fence and cheer for her so loud, I may lose my voice tomorrow. She smiles under the cage of her helmet and gives our dugout a quick wave.

For all of Kim's effort, we leave her stranded on first at the end of the inning with a strikeout and a fly to right field. We still hold on to our lead by one as we head into the sixth inning.

Wilkerson's bottom of the lineup comes at us swinging. The leadoff gets her first home run of the season off a rise ball that didn't quite hit its target, which is a rarity for Maya. I hope the girl enjoys the feeling of jogging around the bases. At least it's just one run. The next batter takes her first pitch just past Ashlyn, into the outfield. I'm on high alert as the next player steps into the box. I know the girl on first is going to steal. She looks fast, and now is the time to be aggressive. As Maya begins her pitch, I sense the base runner getting ready to launch off the bag. When the ball leaves Maya's hand, the girl is already one pace off. The ball hits my mitt, and I launch it to second. My throw is late, and she slides safely in.

I turn to the home-plate umpire. "She left early, sir. She was already leading off when the ball left her hand."

"Time," the ump calls. "You know my eyes are on the pitcher."

"Can you please check with the field ump? I just want to be sure it doesn't happen again."

He huffs, then chats with the first-base ump. I try to make out what they're saying, but end up kicking some dirt around until he returns.

"She didn't leave early," he grumbles.

"Okay."

"But she says she'll keep her eye out."

"Thanks."

The next batter takes Maya to a full count and battles off four pitches that she doesn't like. She pokes the last pitch into left field, leaving a runner at first and third. And we're tied at two.

"Time, sir."

"Time!"

I walk out to the mound, and as I near, I see the fury in her eyes. The beads of sweat along her collar become visible. Her medal hangs on the outside of her jersey. A jersey—a uniform—that no one will ever fill out the way she does. I get close enough to smell the sweetness of her sweat and hold my mitt in front of our faces to block our words from the other team.

"I always assumed your medal was St. Anthony or St. Christopher. Who is she?" I nod to her chest, surprised I've never noticed who hung on the end of her gold chain, who gets to be in constant contact with this girl.

She looks annoyed at first, then touches her medal. "St. Rita."

"Patron saint of?"

"Patron saint of the impossible."

"I expect way more information about this later because I love it."

"Okay…" She peeks at me from under those insanely long lashes.

It's time to wrap up this get-together, or the ump will be even more irritated with me. "Hey, May?"

"Yeah?"

"Let's swerve."

The corner of her mouth twitches up. "Hey, Foster?"

"Yeah?"

"Get out of here." She knocks my glove with hers and grins at me as I backpedal away.

She strikes out the next batter like it's nothing, leaving us with one out and runners on first and third.

The next batter approaches, and I get a creeping feeling that Wilkerson has something up their sleeve. I drag my fingers in the dirt while I wait for our pitch call. Maya finds her grip on the ball and bows, driving herself off the mound.

Everything happens at once. The batter shows bunt, the third-base runner charges down the line toward home, Maya's pitch hits the dirt in front of home plate, and the batter flails, trying to make contact with the ball.

And I miss it.

I sprint to the backstop, grab the ball, and turn to flick it to Maya, who is now covering home, but there's no point. The third-base runner scores. I keep my arm cocked in case the girl who is now on second gets greedy. When the play stalls, time is called, and my stomach drops. I just lost our lead because I couldn't handle a textbook wild pitch. It bounced right in front of me.

After something like this happens, it's hard to be what you're supposed to be. Calm, cool, and confident. Instead, I want to throw myself on the cross. Instead, I can't shake the feeling that I let down my entire team.

Maya secures the last two outs in a blur. The cheers from the crowd barely reach my ears as I float into the dugout. Teammates try to pat my back as I pass, but the best I can give them right now is stoicism. I tuck my helmet in my cubby but leave my gear on since I'm not up to bat for a while. I perch against the dugout fence and stare at the field. Try to keep my brain from spinning out. *Shit.*

Maya flies into the dugout, her cleats pounding like an army marching against the concrete. I'd be mad at me, too. Kim tries to stop her halfway through. "Dude, mistakes happen. Leave her be," she says to Maya. I mentally note that Kim had my back as Maya shrugs her off and weaves through the rest of our team to me. I stare forward, prepared for whatever barrage of punishment she has for me.

Her hand slips under the center backstrap of my chest protector, and she pulls me back into her. I'm surrounded by her sweat, her warmth, her curves. She ducks her head to my ear. Here it comes.

"Breathe," she whispers.

"May—"

She tugs me firmer against her. "Just breathe."

I do as she commands.

"It wasn't your fault. I knew they were going for the suicide squeeze, and I let it fuck me up. I got in my head and threw a wild pitch at the worst moment. There was no way you could've stopped that ball with the batter in the way."

With every word, I give in. Melt into her as much as I can get away with in our dugout, amongst our team. Her chest heaves against my shoulder blades. A little, "Mm-hmm," dips down the back of my neck.

"I'm right here. Swerve into me," she says.

❖

Wilkerson was a difficult loss. But more than the bitter taste of letting the lead slip through our fingers, the thought of Maya yanking me against her to not yell at me but support me? Well, that thought has lingered.

"I can't stop thinking about it." Katie sighs.

I close my textbook. The library isn't my most productive spot to study if I'm not alone, and my focus is anywhere but school right now. I pretend that it's Katie distracting me and not the patron saint of the impossible.

"Yeah. It's like it wriggled into my brain somehow, and I can't get it out," I say.

"It wasn't your fault, you know. It was like the worst pitch she could've thrown in that moment."

"It's no one's fault. And I should have stopped the ball regardless." And now I'm thinking about the loss. My limbs twitch with the need to fix something that's impossible to fix, too late to fix. "*Ugh*. Can we not revisit that game? Please. It's too fresh."

"At least we don't have to wait long for the next one."

"True."

Our next game is tomorrow against Pine Grove, which is a four-hour drive from Alder. It will be the first time this season that we stay in a hotel as a team. I have been thinking a lot about our next game, specifically the part where I sleep in the same room as Maya. Maybe. I guess she could want to room with someone else, but I doubt it at this point.

Katie closes her textbook and gathers her things.

"Well, I'm going to get back to the dorm and make sure I'm packed and ready for tomorrow," she says.

"Okay, cool. I think I'll do the same. Not much studying is happening for me tonight."

"See you in the morning, Foster."

When I get back to my dorm room, Rachel and Emma sit on Rachel's bed, watching videos on her laptop, mid-belly-laugh.

I dump my backpack on the ground by my bed and collapse onto the mattress. "I don't even want to know," I say.

"Oh of course you want to know," Emma says.

One minute I'm safe, and the next minute, Emma and Rachel fly across the room and attack me with tickles. I laugh and pinch and wiggle underneath them. There's no hope for me. "Stop. Please." My begging is breathless and playful.

They finally relent, and we all catch our breath together in a hamster pile on my bed.

"This is exactly what guys think girls do in college," Rachel says.

"What?" Emma asks.

"Tickle fights."

Emma's fingers find my hair in the mess of limbs and clothes. They run through my locks in slow pulls, like the drag of a cigarette. Why does someone else playing with my hair feel so amazing? I close my eyes.

"If a tree falls in a forest," I mutter.

"Huh?" I feel the exhale of Emma's question.

"You know, 'cause we're behind closed doors. If three women get in a tickle fight, but no men are around to see it, do the women really enjoy themselves at all?" I twist to look at Em's face. "Yes. The answer is yes, obviously."

"You're a nerd," she says.

Rachel shakes her head and pats my ankle. "My girl's just jealous that you have a new number one. And now she's gotta ride the bench."

"What?"

Emma kicks Rachel in the thigh. "She's talking about Maya."

"You're both the literal worst. Maya and I are just friends." I excavate myself from the pile of bones on my bed. "I have to pack for tomorrow."

"Boo," Emma whines.

"Some of us are still in season, slackers." I throw a pillow at them.

"Yeah, get out of here, Em. Respect the season. This dorm room still has an early bedtime," Rachel says.

Emma picks herself up off my bed and grabs her phone from Rachel's desk. "Season respected." She takes a deep bow and reaches for the door. "Bye, losers."

Emma is perceptive, and I know she's jealous of whatever is going on between me and Maya. Not because she actually wants to date me, but because what would our friendship look like if I just *didn't* like her in that way anymore? What kind of dynamic would we be left with without my unrequited crush?

I'm not sure.

## CHAPTER TWELVE

Pine Grove's visiting locker room doesn't have showers, so we pack onto the bus in a smelly, muddy, grass-stained heap. No one's too upset about it because we obliterated Pine Grove seven to two, and the bus ride to the hotel is only ten minutes.

"All right, ladies, settle down, settle down." Coach Clayton's voice fills the bus. "Like I said on the field, excellent recovery from Wilkerson. I'm proud of our performance tonight. Now, let's get to that hotel and rest up. We will stay focused, go to bed early, and respect the other patrons of the Best Western. Am I understood?"

We reply with our standard chorus of, "Yes, sir."

"Excellent. Coach Williams will check us in and distribute room keys when we get there. Roommates have already been assigned, so please do not hassle her about wanting to switch. The answer is no."

Maya and I turn to each other in our seat. It's hard to know how she feels about the assigned roommates. Her brows pinch in a way that tells me she's concerned. I'm concerned, too. What if we're not roommates? What if we are roommates? I guess we'll leave it up to fate.

"This is bullshit. It's not that hard to let us pick who we share a room with. Then Coach Williams can write it in her special notebook, or whatever, and make it official," Maya says. Her arm brushes gritty dirt against mine as the bus bounces over a speed bump.

"Who do you want to room with?"

"Foster, are you trying to be coy?"

"What? No. I just don't want to assume that you want to spend every minute together. I don't know. You could be sick of me."

Another bump in the road knocks our knees together.

"How could I be sick of one of the best catchers Alder has ever seen? That slide into home during the game"—she claps her hands once and rubs them together—"wow. That was quite the show. Only matched by you trying to shake all that dirt out of your uniform."

"It went straight into my pants. It's like a garden bed in there." I clear my throat. "I want to room with you, too, by the way."

My phone dings from the seat pocket. An Instagram notification tells me I have a new message from Trinity Bremmer, the girl who knocked me out sliding into home.

"Oh wow," I say.

"What?"

"Trinity just DM'd me."

Maya leans against me to look at my phone. "What's she got to say? She'd better step carefully, or I'll drive to Covington myself and—"

I put my hand on her knee. "Look. She's really nice. Read it." I hand her my phone.

*Hi, Andrea. I'm sure you already know that I'm the Covington player who knocked you out. It makes me want to throw up just thinking about it. I wanted to message you and apologize. I still can't believe that happened. It's like my brain froze, and I didn't quite slide. Well, you know that. Because you had me out by a mile.*

*Anyway, there's no excuse. I just hope you know it eats me alive. I pray to God that you're okay. I think about you every day. You're an excellent player, by the way.*

*Xoxo Trinity*

Maya hands my phone back to me. "Is she trying to apologize or ask you out?"

I roll my eyes. "Come on, it's nice. I had it in my head that she didn't care." I glance at her profile. She's cute. And likes to post pictures of herself in bikinis at the lake. I send her a quick response.

*Hi, Trinity. I'm happy to report that I am as good as new. Thank you for your concern. I don't hold it against you at all. Things happen. Good luck with the rest of your season.*

I end it with a smiley face.

"Why don't you tell her to learn how to respect the third-base coach's call to stop? *Some* of us learn that in T-ball," Maya scoffs.

I squeeze her knee. "Running through a call to hold at third sounds a lot like someone else I know," I say, my brow raised. "You would've been safe, though."

She rewards me with a goofy grin and a nudge of her shoulder. "Damn straight."

The Best Western comes into view a couple minutes later. We file off the bus and into the parking lot while Coach Williams checks us in. She returns in twenty minutes with her list and an envelope full of key cards.

"Okay, ladies, listen up. I'm going to call out names and room numbers. When you get your key, go directly to your room. Lights out by ten. Here we go. Ashlyn and Katie, 217. Kim and Taylor, 218. Andrea and Maya, 219."

Maya smiles, and I want to pass out.

We grab our key cards and follow our other teammates toward our block of rooms. Kim and Taylor are disappearing through their door when we reach ours. 219. Maya swipes us in.

The bathroom is immediately on the right, and two queen beds sit beside each other, separated by a small nightstand. A TV perches on top of a dresser, and there is a sitting area next to the window and AC unit.

"You know Alder's mattresses are shit when these beds look like heaven." Maya chuckles, and I can't help but notice the slightly higher pitch of it. As if she's nervous, which only makes me more nervous. She drops her bag on the foot of the far bed.

The hotel room is basic. But it's ours; we get to have a sleepover. I drop my bag on the other bed, my stomach swirling like the abstract art that hangs on the taupe walls.

Maya squeezes my shoulder. "How about you hop in the shower first?"

"You sure? I don't mind waiting."

She plucks the remote from the dresser and sits on the edge of her bed, rubbing her hand down her thigh. "Positive. You're leaving a trail of dirt everywhere you walk, and I know *The Office* is playing somewhere on here."

"Okay. Be out in a minute."

I bring my entire bag into the bathroom instead of picking through my stuff in front of Maya. This is a whole new level of intimacy. What if my pj's are nerdy? What if I snore? I strip out of my uniform, and dirt falls to the ground in clumps around my feet. It's going to be a muddy shower.

I scrub at every inch of my skin until the water runs clear down my body, and the bar of soap turns brown. I rinse the conditioner out of my hair before I turn my attention back to the bar of soap, holding it under the water until the brown layer melts into the drain. While I dry off, I try to center my nervous energy, but instead of being able to focus, my brain hums in a white noise of anticipation.

The fog on the mirror hides most of my image, so I look down at myself. A crisp white T-shirt and boxers. I look clean and acceptable. I don't want to keep Maya waiting, so I grab my bag and hairbrush and vacate the bathroom.

"All yours."

Maya pulls a toiletry bag from her duffle and brushes by me. "You smell good," she says as she passes.

When the bathroom door closes behind her, I rush to plug everything in. Hearing aids, phone, laptop. Take out my contacts and run a brush through my wet hair. Set an alarm. I pull back the covers of my bed and tuck myself in. Maya was right, this mattress feels like a dream compared to the plastic ones at Alder. I wiggle my toes in the softness as I listen to the muffled sound of water splashing against tile. When I hear the shower cut off, my heart thuds against my chest.

The bathroom door creaks open, and Maya emerges with a white towel wrapped around her body. She has nothing on but her chain, and a soft pink colors her damp dark skin. The towel forms a slit with every step she takes until she reaches her bag and pulls some clothing from it.

She looks at me looking at her. "You're not going to bed yet. Are you?"

"Just testing it out. It's so comfy."

She holds up her clothes, and that dimple winks at me from her grin. "I'll be right back."

Maya returns in a faded Alder Baseball T-shirt, which I want to rip off her body and burn, and a similar pair of boxers to mine. She pulls back her covers and sits against the headboard, patting the empty space next to her.

"Wanna hang for a bit?"

She doesn't have to ask me twice. I hop out of my bed and slide into hers. My body heats from the intimacy, from the warmth of her shower radiating off her skin, from my own nervous system going bonkers. I don't know what to do with my arms, and my feet begin to sweat.

"Feels so good to be clean. I hate when we can't shower after a game," she says.

"Yeah." I'd say more, but my mind is currently focused on not combusting.

And then I see it. Something about the glow from the TV and the damp of her skin illuminates a scar on the inside of her left wrist. Actually, it's not about the lighting at all, the scar is noticeable. *I've* just never noticed it. Without thinking twice, I pull her hand into my lap and turn it over to look at the scar.

"What's this?"

"I broke my wrist senior year of high school. I was running in one of the trails by our house. Tripped on a root and boom."

I find any excuse to keep my hands on her. I don't touch the scar, but I spread her long fingers and push at her palm, as if this is all part of my observation of her past injury. "And you needed surgery?"

"This hand massage feels great." She leans toward me and looks at her wrist. "Yeah. There's a plate and a couple of screws in there somewhere. I was lucky it wasn't my pitching hand, but UGA still passed on me because of it."

I stop prodding her hand and just hold it. "They passed on you because of your injury? It's not even your pitching hand, and recovery couldn't have taken that long."

"Trust me, I know. I was so pissed. Actually, I feel like it's only recently that I've stopped being so angry. I mean, not at UGA. I don't blame them. They were just trying to make the best decision for their team, and competition for the job is tight. But still, the anger…I felt like my dream was stolen from me. I was so close."

"So you went to Alder instead."

"So I went to Alder. I'm sure you could tell that I held on to some of that anger, but I knew I'd get a lot of playing time here, and the team has potential. It could've been worse."

"I'm really glad you ended up here."

Her hand turns over, and we interlace our fingers. I stroke her thumb while my skin buzzes. I am officially holding Maya's hand.

"Me, too."

"Even if you did hate me at first," I say.

She squeezes my hand. "Enough with that. I've never hated you, Andy." She sighs. "Last year, I overheard you call me crazy to Katie after we lost to Pullman, and I just kind of dropped you from my mind. Because that was literally the day after—"

"It was the day after you walked me home from our team activity night. Ultimate frisbee. 'Cause somehow, you landed on top of me and tweaked my ankle. You felt so bad."

"Yeah, and outside your dorm, you told me I was nice. And you hugged me. Like a tight hug. I remember."

I remember that hug, too. The beginning of last season was filled with little moments of attraction between us, and that hug was like a silent promise of more. Until it wasn't, and she started dating Jeremy and stopped talking to me.

"Then I ruined it by calling you crazy. I'm sorry, Maya. That was so dumb and mean and not true."

"I mean, I don't blame you. I had a hot head that game." She looks at her lap. "I just hope you don't think that about me now."

I turn her hand over in my lap and look at her scar, my fingers brushing the tight pale tissue of it. Then I look at her. "I think a lot about you now. But I don't think that."

She holds my eye contact as she sways toward me.

My phone dings from my nightstand and breaks our trance. I ignore it.

"You should get that if you want," she says as she pulls back.

"It's just Instagram."

"Instagram, huh? I bet it's Trinity. Let's look."

Maya slides out of bed and unplugs my phone. I unlock it and tap the Instagram icon. One unread message, and Maya is right; it's from Trinity. "You're right," I say, and hand her the phone.

*Well, maybe in the off-season you'd let me make it up to you? Alder isn't too far away...*

Maya reads it out loud, her mouth in a big "O," like she just heard the juiciest bit of gossip. "Oh shit, she *is* asking you out. What do you think? Is she cute?"

I'm not sure how to respond. She's beautiful, but right now, I'm only interested in the girl who's next to me, holding my phone. But I guess we're both supposed to pretend we don't know that.

"Cute enough, I guess."

"Okay. I'm writing her back. Dear, Trinity. I'm flattered. Unfortunately, the pitcher on my team is super-hot and—"

"Maya, give that back." I stretch for my phone, but she yanks it out of reach.

"And I'd rather have her—" She waves my phone over her nightstand.

"May!"

"What? You don't like it?" she asks, holding me in place with her other arm, a bar across my chest. "I guess you'll have to do something about it, Foster."

So I do.

I knock her arm away and swing into her lap with such momentum, I almost fall past her off the bed, but I catch myself and lunge for my phone. Only, my lunge isn't very much like a lunge at all. With Maya's thigh in between mine, I have effectively humped her.

I freeze.

Everything grinds to deafening stop as we stare at each other, her eyes blazing into mine, my fingers resting at her waistband. A crooked grin spreads over her lips, and she wiggles the phone.

"I know you can try harder than that," she whispers.

I become very aware of the warmth of her body underneath me and how it feels so hard and so soft at the same time. The challenge in her eyes, in her words. How her other hand rests on my hip. I sink my weight into her and lunge again, reaching toward the nightstand as if I care an ounce about my phone or that DM.

Her lips part and release a small gasp. I think I gasp a little, too. Because one second ago, I was in control of my body, and now I'm having all the beginning signs of a panic attack. A racing heart, a fuzzy buzz in my head, an overheated body, but none of the anxiety.

Maya *thunks* my phone facedown. Her hand joins its partner on my hips, and her eyes hold mine in burning intensity. Our breathing is a little louder, a little faster. My ears ring as she tightens her grip on my hips to hold me in place while she shifts her left leg farther out from under me. We end up completely pressed into each other, and I can feel her. Can feel a damp heat between us.

Her fingertips dig into my skin, and it's all I need to be set in motion. I rock my hips into her. Slowly. Or as slow as I can, but the friction of our seams and the hot wetness sliding between us frenzies me. I bridge over her and tuck my face into her neck. And rock. Her warm breath fills my ear with her moans. When she says my name, the sound reaches deep into my core and shakes me up. Turns me up. I clench my teeth until it feels like they'll crack—it's how I keep from kissing her.

She pulls me tighter, and I grind into her harder. The bed squeaks, and I realize I'm about to have my first partnered orgasm with someone who has a boyfriend.

"Shit, I—" I swing off her and stand next to the bed, my shorts a wet mess. I cover the giant spot with my hands as I walk backward toward the bathroom. Maya adjusts herself and pulls the covers up over her body, her breathing still heavy. I look down at my shorts and back to her like an idiot. "I gotta…" I pull one hand from myself and grab my bag "I'll be right back."

I've never seen myself this color. I stare at my face, my arms, my whole body, in the bathroom mirror. I'm totally flushed. Beet red and splotchy. My hair's all fucked-up and still half-wet. My shorts are ruined for the night, and my nipples ache.

I slip off my shorts and hang them on the shower rail but decide that's dumb and try to pat them dry with a hand towel. I give up and find a spare trash bag under the sink, tie up my shorts in the plastic, and tuck them into the corner of my bag like they're evidence of a crime.

And that's my cue to slow down.

I sit on the toilet and breathe. And pee a little.

But mostly breathe. And focus. And process.

I didn't do anything wrong. That was the most incredible thing I've ever felt in my whole life, and I think Maya liked it, too. Everything felt amazing about that moment until…until what?

I tap my fingers against my temple and try to pinpoint why I feel guilty. No, not guilty. I don't feel bad for Jeremy. I think I feel bad for myself. I guess it's a dumb line to draw, but I didn't want to orgasm with her. Not like that. Not when she's not mine, and I'm not hers. That's why I couldn't kiss her, either. Even though I desperately want to.

I dry myself and wash my hands. My options for pants are underwear or jeans. I curse as I reach for my Levi's; I can't walk out in my underwear after that. The fabric of my jeans is rigid and restrictive when it normally feels worn-in and gentle. I look ridiculous, but I don't really have a choice. If only I were normal and wore sweats after games like the other girls.

I open the door to find Maya on the other side with her fist raised, about to knock. We stare at each other for a moment, and I realize her body is as flushed as mine.

"Andy. Are you okay?" Her gaze drops to my jeans, and she pinches her brows in concern. "Wait, why are you wearing—"

"I…" I cut her off because I'm dying of embarrassment, but the only thing I have to say is equally humiliating. But it's the truth, so I say it. I look down at my jeans. "They're the only thing I have to wear. My shorts...they're too wet. And my underwear didn't feel appropriate."

"Hey, hey. Look. I'm going to use the bathroom. How about you change into your underwear and slip into bed while I'm in here? I won't see anything that way, and we can do the same thing in the morning. Okay?"

I nod and let her pass. When she shuts the door, I shimmy off my jeans, relieved to not have to sleep in denim. I grab my phone, plug it back in, double-check my alarms, and slide under my covers.

"Andy, ready for me to come out?"

For a moment, I think it's impossible for my throat to produce noise, but from the cavernous depths of my embarrassment, I produce, "Yes."

Maya double-checks the lock on our door, turns out the lights, and walks to her bed, squeezing my blanket-clad foot as she passes. She gets into bed, and by the small amount of light emitted from her side of the room, I can tell she's on her phone.

Maya has been perfect tonight. For all my growth in leadership, in being loud, in taking up space, I'm allowing her to lie over there in confusion. She probably thinks I'm upset and regretting what just happened between us. I'm not. I'm trying to process. I'm getting stuck, but I'm trying. In the meantime, Maya lies in the bed next to me. Maybe trying to process, maybe texting, maybe reading. Regardless, I need to say or do something. Anything.

I roll away from Maya's side of the room and grab my phone from the nightstand to text her. *Are you okay?*

I don't hear any notification on her phone, but the bouncing dots are immediate.

Maya: *Yes. More than okay. Are you?*

Am I? I just accidentally, and then very deliberately, humped my teammate who has a boyfriend until I ruined my shorts. It feels too messy. *I think so. I'm sorry, I know this is dumb, texting you.*

Maya: *It's not dumb. I love texting you.*

Me: *Do you regret it?* I try to ignore the thought of Jeremy. I try to pretend that he's not why I'm asking her if she regrets me. But it is, isn't it? We can't do anything about being teammates, but Maya has the power to do something about Jeremy. If she wanted to. She could at least get rid of one obstacle. But she hasn't.

Maya: *No. Not for a second. I mean, you were there, too. Couldn't you feel it?*

Yes. And I can feel it now. Just the words on my screen are slaying me. *Yes.*

Maya: *It's getting pretty late. We should probably get to sleep. I'm happy to talk about this anytime with you.*

Me: *Okay. Good night, May.*

I hear her crawl out of bed, and a second later, I feel her slip into mine. Her lips brush against the back of my neck, and her hand rests on my hip just below where my underwear ends.

"Good night, Andy," she whispers.

She rolls over and doesn't touch me the rest of the night but sleeps peacefully next to me. I smile against my pillow, thighs clenched. I am so unsatisfied and satiated at the same time. It takes all of my willpower not to roll over and finish what we started. Just knowing—really, truly knowing for a fact—that Maya wants me in a sweet way, and a very dirty way, is enough for tonight.

## CHAPTER THIRTEEN

The next couple of weeks pull more flowers from the earth. With every bloom, the Alder air becomes a little heavier, a little sweeter. I have a break before I need to be at the clubhouse for pregame warm-ups, so I sit on a bench and watch the grass grow. Maya hasn't been cold, but she hasn't been herself these couple of weeks. It's mostly business between us, which is fine, but damn, it bothers me. I can't help but think I freaked her out. Grossed her out. Something.

Our game tonight is against Chelsea Mountain, a midrange in-conference competitor. I guess I'll see how she reacts to me today. Both sets of parents are going to be in town for the game. With my dad being sick, planning trips like visiting me can be tricky, and I already feel guilty for no reason, other than visiting me is taking them out of their routine. My phone rings, and I dig it from my pocket to answer.

"Hey, Mom."

"Hey, sweetie. How are you?" Her voice is slightly higher than normal. I already know what's coming.

"You guys aren't coming, are you?"

"I'm sorry, Andy. It just didn't work out today. We were about to hit the road and you know…"

"It's all good, Mom. You know I understand."

"The new meds are making him nauseous, and a car ride through the mountains won't help. We'll get up there for another game. I promise."

"Is he okay?"

"He's okay. Just taking a break in his room."

"Okay, good. Listen, I should be getting to the clubhouse. Thanks for the heads-up. I love you."

"I love you, Andrea."

I don't mean to be short, but it's hard not to feel the bite of disappointment. I don't blame them, but that doesn't mean it doesn't suck. Nobody has to be wrong for it to hurt. And man, does it hurt. My dad used to drive me to all my games and tournaments when I was a kid. He was always my number-one fan, and softball was something that bonded us and built a friendship between us. But MS slowly took that from us, and him having to miss this game is just another stolen moment. His MS takes up so much space, sometimes it's hard to believe that I can hold space, too. Now with Maya, I'm also trying to take as little as possible.

But I may overflow.

Maya turns from the locker-room mirror in her all-white Alder uniform. It's our alternate uniform and my personal favorite because if you haven't seen Maya Gonzalez in a skintight, all-white, softball uniform, well, you haven't lived.

"Maya, wow—"

"Hey." She wraps her fingers around my forearm as she guides me to our lockers. She grabs her softball bag and glove. "We should get going, yeah?"

Her energy is soft, languid. I want to say more, but her words contain me. I want to tell her just what that white uniform is doing to me, but she keeps clipping our conversation, pruning it to the necessities. But her eyes, her lingering gaze, are still very much untamed. And that, I will accept.

Walking out to the bullpen is the same for every home game. Emma and Rachel scream my name and wave their silly sign, and the baseball team whistles and hollers if they're there. Jeremy calls for Maya, but instead of running to him, she gives him a short wave. It seems that control is the name of the game for her today.

"Andy!" I hear someone unfamiliar call my name, and I scan the mass of fans along the fence until I find Bailey and Noelle from the Alder Queer Fellowship waving at me.

"Hey, guys. Thanks for coming to support us," I say and give Bailey a high five.

"We're so excited to finally get to see a game," Noelle says.

"I haven't found the space in my schedule to make it to a meeting, yet. But I promise, I'll be there one day."

They exchange a smile. "No worries. We're happy to be here whether you make it to a meeting or not," Bailey says.

I nod toward Maya and say, "I'd better get back, but I hope y'all enjoy the game."

"Good luck," they call in unison.

When we finally make it to the bullpen, Maya tugs me backward by the strap of my bag, and I almost collapse with the shifting of the load. My bag is heavy as hell with all the catching gear in there, but she props me up like it's nothing.

"There they are," she says, still holding on to me.

I squint against the sunshine and the iridescent glow radiating from the damp metal handrails in the stands. My eyes adjust, and I see them, Maya's parents. They stand side by side along the third-base line. Her father wears sunglasses and barks into his phone, though I'm too far to hear what he's saying, and her mother wears a tan leather jacket that looks too hot for this sunny day, skintight black jeans, and heels. Every other parent who attends these games wears an Alder T-shirt and jeans.

"You ready?" Maya asks.

I'm still staring as she pulls me in the direction of Mr. and Mrs. Gonzalez. I ditch my bag before we open the gate and walk out into the crowd. I smooth down my hair and tighten my belt. I'm terrified.

"May, are you sure?"

She stops and turns to me, her eyes focused and determined. She smiles and reaches for my hand, and I let her grab it, knowing we're shielded by the mere fact that women hold hands with their friends sometimes. What a luxury.

"I'm positive. Come on." She tugs me through the mass of Alder fans until we emerge right behind her parents.

"Mom. Dad. Hey."

They turn, and her mother instantly embraces her. I stand as straight as possible and smile. When her mother lets her go, her father lays a single hand on her shoulder and squeezes.

"Maya." Though his entire demeanor screams business, this one word bursts with affection.

"I'm so glad you guys could make it. Oh. This is Andrea Foster, my catcher." She holds out an arm to present me, and I shake her dad's hand.

"It's so great to meet you, Mr. and Mrs. Gonzalez," I say.

"Edgardo and Gloria. We're all adults here. It's a pleasure, Andrea," he says, his voice rich and deep.

Her mom reaches for me and grabs both my cheeks, planting a kiss on my left one. "Oh, Andrea, it's so lovely to finally meet you. Maya has told us so much about you and how great a teammate you are. You must be very special for our Maya to feel that way."

She releases me, and it takes the willpower of a saint to not wipe the wet spot on my face. Maya is all grins and relief.

"Well, she's the best pitcher in the Southeast. Probably the country. I'm just lucky to be along for the ride," I say.

Her mom smiles and reaches for Maya's shirt. "You look sloppy, Maya. Tuck this in nicer."

Maya swats at her mom's hands. "Mom, please. I'm going to go play softball, not host an awards ceremony." I spot Jeremy by the concessions, making his way toward us. Maya clears her throat and tugs on my sleeve.

"We better get going. Gotta warm up," she says.

"Make us proud," her mom says.

"Always," Maya calls back, as we retreat toward the gate.

She releases me when we walk back through the gate, and I grab my bag from the grass and swing it over my shoulder. We let ourselves into the bullpen, finally alone in our sanctuary, and Maya lets out a sigh of relief.

"Holy shit, that was perfect. You were perfect." Before I can process her leaning in, her lips are on my cheek. She presses a soft kiss to me and pulls away as quickly as she came. Unlike when her mom kissed me, my world explodes; it erupts in an exquisite volcano of lust and confusion. I press my fingers to my cheek where the lava scorched me.

"Um, they were really nice. I liked them."

"They loved you." She grabs her glove and walks to the pitching rubber.

"Jeremy was trying to make his way over to say hi. Right before we left." I know she saw him. The timing and urgency of our departure couldn't have been a coincidence. She was avoiding him.

"Was he? Oh well, I'll see him at the party tonight. Ready?"

"*Ugh*, not another baseball party. I think I'm going to skip it."

"What? You have to come. Please, Andy? You can bring Rachel. There are going to be a ton of people there."

I sink into my squat and hold up my mitt. Nothing about this feels right. "Fine. I'll go."

*Thwack.*

"I promise, it will be a blast."

We beat Chelsea Mountain four to one. The game itself was easy, but by the fifth inning, Maya's face had shifted. It was subtle, but the slight arch of her brow and the way she kept shaking out her arm told me she was in pain. And why wouldn't she be? Coach lets her pitch way more than she should. We are having a better-than-expected season, and regionals are finally a possibility for us, so I understand wanting to play Maya as much as possible; it's almost a guaranteed win when she starts. But at what price? What does it matter if we make it to regionals, and Maya can't play because she's injured?

Nothing is worth her pain. The cost is too high.

I finger-comb my hair, toss the towel in the team hamper, put in my hearing aids, and I'm off. My feet carry me past the Lazy, but before I reach Coach Clayton's office, they just stop in their tracks. I look at his office door, then back at my feet. Up to his door. I need to talk to him about this. But when I start to walk, I only manage a stutter step toward his office before I stop again.

I growl at myself.

"What the hell?" I mutter through bared teeth. But I know what the hell. It isn't my place to go behind Maya's back and talk to Coach Clayton. It's her business, and if I have a problem with it, I need to talk to her first.

I wheel around and head back to the locker room, hoping to catch Maya before she leaves. By this time, half the team has left to get ready for the party tonight. I step up to Katie's locker, see her camo coat hanging from the crossbar.

"She's in the training room," she says without looking at me.

"I wasn't…" I shake my head. There's no point in trying. "Are you going to the party tonight?"

"Yeah. Will I see you there?"

"Yeah, yeah. Definitely. I actually have to run," I say, mid-backpedal.

"See ya, weirdo."

I speed walk past the coaches' offices but get caught by Coach Williams. "Andy, one second. I have a favor to ask you."

I take a deep breath and walk into the office. "What's up, Coach?"

She stands and gathers some files into her messenger bag. "I need to run. I'm late for my daughter's basketball game, and Coach Clayton had to leave early to meet with some donors. Can you lock up tonight?"

"Of course. Not a problem."

I follow her out of the office. She pulls a different key from her pocket than the one I have and locks the door. "You're a lifesaver. Call me for anything and don't forget the lights."

"You got it." She rushes to the parking lot, and I continue to the training room. Adrenaline pools into my bloodstream. Finding Maya feels important, pressing.

She sits on one of the padded tables, wrapping ice around her shoulder. She smiles at me as I cross the room to her, take the coiled Ace bandage, and finish wrapping her.

"Where's Eddie?" I ask. He fixes us up and is usually the one to ice Maya after a game. I wrap over her shoulder, under her armpit. Over, under. Her head is at shoulder height as I stand over her, and I can smell the fresh tea tree. A piece of her wet hair lies plastered to her forehead.

"No one else needed anything from him, and I said I didn't need ice. I don't know why. Because I do need ice. He closed up shop and left."

I secure the end of the bandage with the metal butterfly clip and run my fingertips over her forehead, pushing the strand of wet hair behind her ear. With my hands still on her face, she lets her head fall against my stomach. I hold her and stroke her dark hair, watching her head move against me with every breath I take.

"You were already in pain in the fifth inning," I whisper. And stroke.

Maya's ice-free arm wraps around my waist and pulls me between her thighs.

"I can't believe he left you in. You needed to come out. You could tear something. You could get seriously hurt if he overexerts you like that." My hands fall from her face. Anger builds in me, and I want to yell at her. I want to scream at her and Coach Clayton to stop being idiots.

"It's ridiculous, Maya." I step out of her grip and turn to leave. "You're more important to me than any game—"

She snags my hand before I can get away and pulls me around to face her. Her eyes are the deep dark of the Alder wood. The Mariana Trench. I step willingly into her space, and my hands find her face again.

"Andrea…" And goddamn it, I can't take it anymore. I press my forehead against hers. Run a finger from her cheek to her lips. I mean to shush her, but I just drag my fingertip over her softness.

"Shut up. Just shut up, May."

I press my lips to hers, so warm and full. Her fingers dig into the small of my back as I open my mouth to her. Her tongue brushes over mine, and the freezing water from her ice pack drips down my chest, wets my shirt. I shiver against her teeth, and she pulls me closer, kisses my neck. She's fire and ice.

"That's a nice way to shut me up," she whispers against my skin.

I sink against her with the grand plan of murmuring something sexy. "*Argh*." I jump back from her with my hand to my ear.

Maya grins at me while she tugs at her own ear, which is probably ringing like mine from the glass shattering feedback my hearing aid just gave us.

I step toward her, then away in a stupid two-step. "I'm so sorry."

"It's okay. Really. Just get back over here." She holds out her hand. My ringing ear and the cold dampness of my shirt bring me back to reality.

"We can't do this Maya. What even is this?" I hold my arms out in exasperation.

"You know what this is," she says in a slow deliberate cadence.

I nod. "You're right. I do know what this is. But do you? Or better yet, does Jeremy?"

She hops off the training table. "Let me explain."

"You should get going. I have to stay and lock up."

"Andy, can we just talk for a minute?"

I stand by the door, waiting to usher her out. "I'll see you at the party. No hard feelings." *No hard feelings?*

She shakes her head. "Okay. Okay, I'll see you there."

"Are you sure your girlfriend won't get mad that you brought me instead of Rachel?" Emma adjusts the beanie that sits casually on her head in a way that you can tell it's not for warmth. She pulls it off, though.

"She's not my girlfriend, and she said anyone could come."

Corey's house is exactly the same as the last time I was here. Except, since the weather has warmed, there's no chair draped with a pile of coats in the entryway, and people are way drunker and way soberer than the last party. The people who drink during the season are drunker, trying to escape the best they can for the evening. And the people who don't drink during season...well, they aren't drinking.

I spot Kim chatting with some baseball guy I don't recognize. "Come on, let's go say hi." I nod toward the two.

Emma follows on my heels. "Oh. You're, like, cool with everyone now, huh?"

"Yeah. I guess I am." I snag a beer from the inside cooler and crack it for Emma before we hop into conversation.

"Andy!" Kim's smile is wide and squiggly. I guess we're friends now.

"Hey, Kim. You remember my friend Emma?"

Emma raises her beer to greet the tipsy girl across from her.

"Yes. Emma, hi. You're cute." Kim stops and looks down at her beer. "It must be the beer talking, 'cause I'm actually straight. I'm pretty sure."

Emma stifles a chuckle, but I can tell she ate that compliment up. "Well, thank you, Kim. You're quite cute yourself."

Kim looks from me to Emma, and I swear to God, the girl blushes. Full-on red cheeks and all. Emma really could charm anyone into bed. And all of a sudden, this interaction is annoying the hell out of me. I grab Emma's hand and drag her away. "Come on."

"Andy."

I drop Emma's hand and turn, even though I already know that it's Maya calling my name. Even through the obnoxiously loud, obnoxiously bad country music blasting through the house, I know her voice. We lock eyes, and Jeremy waves us over. Of course she's with Jeremy. Fuck that. I pick up Emma's hand and lead her toward the group like she's my trophy wife, and I'm about to show her off. We edge into the circle with Kevin, Jeremy, Corey, and Maya. A lavender floral sundress with a deep V-neck drapes over her body. It's a far cry from the tight little black dress I was expecting, and it takes my breath away. I try not to stare at her. At her body. At her lips.

"Hey, Emma. I didn't know you were coming," Maya says.

Emma loosens her grip on my hand, and I let it fall out of mine, but I lean close to her, hoping her natural flirtatiousness will ooze all over me and paint me as hers. And of course, it does. Emma steps closer and slides her arm around my waist. Maya's gaze follows the movement, right to the point where Emma's thumb strokes the bare skin between my tank top and jeans. Her eyes bore into me.

Making a girl jealous turns out to be quite the delight.

"Rachel bailed to stay with Melissa tonight, so it's just me and Em. All night," I say.

"Right," Maya says.

Jeremy shifts his weight from foot to foot as if he's anticipating something uncomfortable. I focus on Emma's fingers and decide that she can touch me all night long. I'm hers tonight.

"What are we chatting about?" Emma asks, breaking the tension of the circle.

"Kevin here was just being a grade A asshole," Maya says.

"He's kinda right, babe. It just is what it is," Jeremy says as he takes half a step away from her.

"Kev says that softball and baseball are different because girls can't hit off a baseball pitcher. We pitch too fast. So y'all have softball. Slower. Easier," Corey explains.

Maya's body tenses, her hand flexed around her Solo cup. Jeremy takes another step closer to his boys, and Maya is now alone in the circle. I may have an issue with her at the moment...

But fuck these assholes.

I slide out of Emma's grip and stand next to Maya. She arches an eyebrow at me, and I shrug. "I got you," I say, just loud enough for her to hear. Then I turn to the boys. "Are you guys not good at math? Is that what's going on here?" I ask.

"Come on, there's no way you could hit off me," Kevin says.

I want to knock his stupid hat right off his stupid head. "It is quite literally more difficult to hit off a fastpitch pitcher than a baseball pitcher," I say, my heart pounding in my chest.

The boys giggle among themselves, then Corey says, "That is *quite literally* the dumbest shit I've ever heard."

I don't know why I keep coming to these parties. I clear my throat, and when I open my mouth, an avalanche plumes from me. "Like I said before, you guys must not be very good at math, so I'll walk you through it. *Nice and slow.* In baseball, the mound is sixty and a half feet from the plate, and say Kevin happens to pitch at ninety-five miles per hour, which let's be honest, Kev, never happens." I pull out my phone and open the calculator app. "Then the batter has .395 seconds to react to the pitch. Now, in softball, the mound is forty-three feet away, and let's say Maya pitches at seventy miles per hour, which happens for most pitches that aren't a changeup, then"—I tap at the numbers on my phone—"that only leaves .35 seconds to react to the pitch."

"Holy shit," Emma says, her eyes glued to me. All eyes are glued to me.

"You guys think Kevin is such a hotshot, but he barely throws over ninety. Maya throws eighty percent of that speed, and she does it underhanded. Bet she'd whup you if she ever decided to play baseball and pitch overhand. The *easy way*, some would say," I finish.

A small crowd forms around us and fills the room with hoots and hollers. "Go choke on a dick," Corey spits.

Maya steps in front and pushes me behind her. "Aw, so yours is small enough to be a choking hazard? I know Kevin's is." She winks at him.

I didn't know they had a history. This acrid talk and Maya knowing what Kevin's penis looks like and Jeremy standing there just watching everything makes me want to throw up. I have a little bit of word vomit to let out.

I peek over Maya's shoulder. "Penis size has nothing to do with a man's worth or quality of sex. It's okay to be small." The group surrounding us tries to stifle their chuckles as they all stare at Kevin.

Emma busts into uncontrollable laughter, and Maya whirls around to look at me. "Andy, not now," she whispers, eyes wide.

And though I said it sincerely, my words only stoke the flames of Maya's insults.

"Of course, this is coming from the dyke," Kevin says.

"Actually," Emma starts, brushing my shoulder as she also steps in front of me. "Andy's right. Penis size has nothing to do with good sex. In fact, what makes for sex that lasts longer, has significantly more orgasms, and results in significantly fewer STIs is neither partner having a penis. Like, say, *lesbian sex*. So you're probably better off just having a vagina, Kev."

The group of onlookers erupts into laughter and clapping as if having a vagina is the most insulting thing one could suggest to a cis man. I stare at Emma in awe. I shouldn't be surprised that she knows these facts, but damn, that was…sexy.

Corey puts a hand on Kevin's shoulder and says, "I think it's time for y'all to get the fuck out of my house."

"Sounds pretty good to me. What do you say, Andy? Should we leave the men to it and go have some fun?" Emma asks.

Maya rakes me with her gaze, and Kevin's lip curls into a snarl.

I take Emma's hand. "Someone once told me that girls do it better."

As we turn to leave, Maya catches Jeremy's hand.

"J, can we go upstairs for a minute?" He grins and pulls her away from us.

That's all I need to see.

"Take me home, Em."

❖

I toss my wallet and phone on my desk. A different night, I wouldn't be able to resist the unread text from Maya, but tonight, after that party, I'm done caring. I shake my hair out of its French braid and close my hearing aids in their case.

"Well, maybe I'll see you tomorrow?" Emma stands by the door as if not sure if she should step into my intense energy or leave me alone to stew.

I don't want to be alone. Because these days, I'm never alone. Maya is always there. I turn to Emma and make sure to hold her gaze as I pull my tank top over my head and drop it at my feet. "Or you could stay. You were basically my hero tonight with those lesbian sex facts. You've done some research, huh?" She doesn't shy away from watching me. I knew she wouldn't. I unbutton my jeans so there's a sliver of my matching pink underwear showing.

Her eyes flit down my body as she takes a small step toward me. "When you go through life with boys incessantly asking you how two girls can possibly have sex or which one of you wears the strap-on—as if girls *must* have some form of a penis involved—you get tired of it and memorize some facts to throw at them. I bet most lesbians have looked it up."

"Hmm. I've never looked it up. I'm more of a learn-from-experience kind of girl. Feel like helping me do some research tonight?" I ask, pushing away the shock of my own boldness.

She walks toward me, but I turn away and walk into the bathroom. I shut the door and let out a sigh. Has it always been this simple? All I had to do to get Emma was take my clothes off in front of her? I think about how silly it is while I brush my teeth, toothpaste foaming out of my mouth and down my hand.

"It's all yours. Don't be long," I tell Emma when I'm finished.

"Yes, ma'am."

While she's in the bathroom, I slip out of my bra and underwear and into my soft Alder tee and boxers, climb into bed, and lie on my side, facing the wall. The bathroom door opens, and Emma slides in behind me. She must have ditched her pants because her thighs are warm against the backs of mine.

Her body presses against the length of mine, and her hand finds my waist. Her fingers trace up and down my hip bone in long slow strokes until she dips under my shirt and tracks up and down my stomach, from the base of my breast to just inside my waistband. Every trip up, a little higher. Every trip down, a little lower.

I reach over my shoulder and grip the back of her neck, pull her mouth to mine. Her tongue in my mouth is warm and eager. Our first kiss. Second of those for the night, but this one hits a little differently. When her fingers finally find my breast, I push against her, trying to find purchase for all the heat building in me. I pull my mouth from Emma's, bite my lip when her hand reaches into my boxers. I try to push onto her fingers, but she's more patient than I am.

She nibbles my earlobe and dips into me slowly. A groan slides from my lips just as easily as she does.

"I've dreamt about this since high school," she whispers as her fingers roll into me like waves.

She sinks her teeth into my flesh where my neck meets shoulder and sucks hard. I know it's going to leave a mark. And I know what she just said is a lie. But the chemicals in my body build into a humming chord.

I think I hear my phone buzz against the wood of my desk. Though it could just be my ears ringing from the adrenaline, it could also be Maya again. She could need me. And all of a sudden, I don't want to do this anymore.

"Stop, Em. Stop."

She immediately pulls out of me. "Are you okay? Did I hurt you?"

"No. You didn't hurt me. I'm sorry, I just...I don't want to do this."

She leans away and places her hand on my thigh so I can feel my own wetness on her. "Are you sure? Because I don't mean to be an asshole, but it kinda seems like you do want this."

I sit up and pull my shirt back down over my breasts. "I'm sure. I can't do this."

She wipes her hand in her shirt. "Why not?"

I shake my head, a little in disbelief. I think about why I stopped with Maya in the hotel room. Why I stopped with Maya tonight in the training room. Why I stopped just now with Emma. It's all for the same reason.

"Because I think I'm in love with Maya."

Emma lets out a deep breath. "Wow."

"I'm sorry, Em."

"You just needed me to fuck you for you to figure it out?"

I honestly didn't think it was possible to hurt Emma, but the downward pull on her features tells me I have. Of course I have.

"It's not like that." I put my hand on her knee.

She shakes her head. "What's it like, then?"

"You know as well as I do that you could've had this a long, long time ago. And you didn't want it. You don't want me, Emma. We both know this."

"You aren't who you used to be. Don't get me wrong, I've always been attracted to you, but you're different now. Like *activated* or something. More alive."

"Look, this would've been just a fun night—was a fun night—but that's it. I know you love me as a friend, but I had to let go of my hope that you'd see me as more. So I let you go, and Maya...she just came out of nowhere. I may not know where we stand right now, or if she's even available, but I want *her*. You and I are just friends."

She looks at me now. Really looks at me. "I didn't know it was like that with you and her."

"It is...I think. I'm pretty sure. We kissed tonight, and it felt like warm pie, you know? Like running through a sprinkler on a hot day. Like—"

She holds up a hand. "Jesus. Enough. I get it." She chuckles and knocks into me with her shoulder. "I'm sorry I never gave us a shot. I'd be lying if I said I don't regret it."

"You don't need to be sorry. Sometimes, a friend is just a friend, and I really like being your friend."

"I really like being your friend, too. And for what it's worth, I really, really liked having sex with you."

I shove her a little too hard. "Emma!"

She erupts into self-satisfied laughter. "I know you can't say it because you just confessed your great love for Maya or whatever, but I know you liked it, too."

I can't do anything but blush. There's really no denying that.

She gets out of bed and points to my neck. "Good luck explaining that hickey if you get the chance."

I rub at the swollen bruise on my neck. "Of course Emma Wilson marks her lovers like cattle."

She shimmies on her pants and tucks her phone in her back pocket. "How else am I supposed to keep track of all of them?"

"*Ugh*, get out."

"See ya later, lover."

My doors falls shut behind her, and I'm left alone in my bed, extremely unsatisfied. I grab my phone to make sure everything is okay. Two texts from Maya.

Maya: *I'm so sorry about earlier. Guys are assholes.*

And then one from five minutes ago.

Maya: *We need to talk about tonight. Can we hang out after study hall on Monday?*

Me: *Sure.*

One word is all I'm willing to give her right now because even though I've had my love epiphany or whatever, it doesn't mean I'm not still upset with her. I throw my phone across the room onto Rachel's bed. I'm done with that for the night.

I close my eyes and reach into my boxers. I think of Maya's lips and her ice melting on my breast. And that sundress.

## CHAPTER FOURTEEN

After our game and the party, we have a rare day off on Sunday. Our only obligation to see each other is at Mass, and I'm not even sure it's so much a requirement as it is team code. We opt for the service at eleven in the morning, late enough to get a good sleep-in and enjoy the morning but early enough that it still leaves all day.

I pick at my favorite dress and discreetly switch my hearing aids to theater mode with my phone. Though I'd be lying if I said I was paying much attention to Father Kyle's homily.

When I arrived at the chapel, I dillydallied around the stations of the cross, around the different holy water bowls, until I saw Maya slide into our usual pew. She looked around and found me skulking in the back of the church, no doubt with my intentions written all over my face. She nodded at me, then turned to the altar and kneeled in that tight maroon dress like only a Catholic woman knows how. And I watched her until the pew filled up with a barrier of teammates. Then I sat at the opposite end of it between Katie and Kim because I'm avoidant like that. Petty like that? Hiding from the girl I may be falling for?

I just don't like interactions in the nebula. We haven't talked yet, so anything said between us now is just dark matter. Mush. Because neither of us knows what the hell is going on.

"Some of us have this construct of 'hell' in our minds." Father Kyle's voice yanks me from my spiral. "Lake of fire, etcetera,

etcetera. But I challenge you to reframe that idea of hell. Maybe as a place devoid of love."

Mass goes on being Mass for the next half hour. While Father Kyle gives the closing announcements, my fingers twitch with the anticipation of getting out of my dress and enjoying this perfect spring day. The sunshine evaporates the stained glass into a Jolly Rancher haze, beckoning me to go play in it. My knee bounces. Foot jiggles.

Finally, he makes his way down the center aisle, altar boys in tow.

I crane my neck and peer down our pew. "Catch y'all tomorrow." I throw a peace sign for no good reason and slide into the aisle. Their jumbled good-byes send me on my way into the great sunshine—

"Andy. One second."

I take my hand from the chapel door, feeling like I'll never escape this cavern. Maya stands by the small tables of pamphlets and sign-up sheets. A small wave of parishioners starts to fill the little foyer as I sigh and cut through the people toward her.

She smooths her hair. Her breath is quick.

"Did you run?" I look down. "In those shoes? To catch me before I left?"

Her lips quirk into a grin. "What? Run in a church? In these heels? Just to catch up to a girl so I can tell her how beautiful she looks in her green dress with her hair all wavy and free?" She tugs at the end of one of my locks. "Doesn't sound like something I would do."

Her words make me buzz. My body sways toward her like she's my magnetic north, and I can smell her perfume just underneath the dankness of the old chapel. Like a fresh bloom of flowers cutting through the decay of a forest floor. She smiles as if there's nothing wrong. And maybe that's true. But it's only true if she doesn't have a boyfriend. Reckon I should find out.

"Tell me you're single, May."

Her eyes peek over my shoulder at the mass of people flooding past us. Sure, it's crowded, but there's privacy in that. Then she looks only at me and takes my hand.

"I was really hoping we could talk about this alone." Her avoidance tells me she hasn't dumped him yet.

"So you're not?"

"That's not what I said."

I shake my head and pull my hand from hers.

"Andy, you're not listening to—" She dips her head and stares at something that's caught her attention. Her fingers brush my hair over my shoulder and expose my neck. I try to stand straight as I watch her eyes darken and her jaw tighten. She rubs a thumb over the bruised flesh, Emma's stupid trophy.

I will not feel ashamed.

"Last night? After we kissed?" She drops her hand and grits her teeth. "Fucking Emma Wilson." Then her features slacken as if she's tired. She looks around, now seemingly agitated at every single person who crowds the small entryway. She grabs my hand and pulls us to the closest private place, the women's restroom.

The two stall doors hang open, water covers the entire countertop of the sink, and paper towels crawl from the mouth of the trashcan. It smells strongly of old-woman perfume and mildly of shit. Not as sexy as I thought Maya pulling me into a bathroom would be, but nothing about this conversation is sexy.

This is why I avoid the nebula. It's quite a simple rule, really.

The heavy door slams shut behind us and startles us both.

"Last night with Emma—"

"I don't want to hear about it." She waves in surrender. "Not right now, at least. God, it smells horrible in here. Listen, I know this week has been confusing for you, but I just wanted you to know that it hasn't been for me. I wore that sundress last night for you. And I've handled things the best way I could for everyone involved."

"Meaning?"

"Meaning a lot of things, but yes, I broke up with Jeremy. Last night at the party."

"Oh." And it hits me that I massively misread that situation. That she was asking him upstairs to break up with him, not hook up with him. "I thought—"

"Yeah, I know what you thought." Her eyes cut to my neck, and I touch the spot self-consciously.

"Maya—"

"I just wanted to tell you how beautiful you look. I don't want to get into it here." We both look around at the unholy bathroom. "Come over later? Or we can go on a walk. Whatever you want, but I don't want to wait until after study hall to talk. Okay?"

"Okay."

❖

I wait as long as I can.

I want her. And I want her to explain everything to me in the most flattering, perfect way possible, so there is no hesitation scratching at the back of my eyeballs when I climb into her lap and beg her to be mine. I want to tell her Emma meant nothing to me in the most flattering, perfect way possible, so there is no hesitation gnawing at the back of her brain when my weight settles on her thighs, and she tells me she always was.

I linger in my room as long as I can stand. Strip my dress. Choose shorts and a tank top; watch me lean in to warm weather season *hard*. I'm so close to being free, just grabbing my phone from my desk when Rachel busts through our door like a bull out of its pen. *Oh... "bullpen."*

There's a brief stare down. A silence.

Then she hits play.

"You and Emma? Holy shit, Andy." She isn't mad, just shocked. Which kind of offends me, if I'm honest. It's not that hard to bed Emma Wilson. I'm more than capable, clearly.

"What? She told you? It was nothing. It just happened, and now it's done," I explain as I take a step toward the door.

She flops on her bed and rubs her forehead like she's dealing with a misbehaving child. "My head is exploding is all."

"Why? You know I liked her."

"Yeah, but not anymore. It's obvious that you're head over heels for Maya."

"Well, that's who I'm going to talk to right now. Because, yeah, I am. And I need to go explain what happened last night, and she needs to tell me why she hung on to Jeremy for so long so that we can see if maybe we could be anything." I take another small step. "Can we talk about this later?"

She seems to get the point and sighs. "All right. Go get her. But you're not off the hook. I need details, woman."

And now I'm here, outside Maya's door, harvesting the confidence to knock on it. I'll get there, eventually. It's the hope of getting to kiss her again. In her dorm room. On her bed…

*Knock knock knock.*

"Come in," she calls from inside. I open her door in a *whoosh* and am flooded with the scent of her. She changed into an old high school T-shirt and boxers with crew socks. Her messy bun tops off her adorable outfit. Everything about her looks soft and warm, except for how she lounges on her bed. Like a languid tiger.

"Hey, come here," she says.

I sit next to her. "Why is your roommate never here?"

"She's on the swim team."

"Oh."

"Yeah. So—"

"Can I go first?"

She nods and tucks a foot under her thigh, turning her whole body and attention to me.

"You…" I start, but how can I tell her? How are words enough? My shaky fingers find her ankle, and the small connection with her draws a deep, settling breath from me. Her hand covers mine.

"Before you continue," she says, "I want you to know that I'm not angry with you or anything, and this isn't a fight. I hope you feel the same way."

I nod. Her calm welcomes my words. "You know how much I care about you. Getting to be your partner this year was such a sweet, sweet gift. And somewhere along the way, near the beginning, if I'm honest, my feelings for you grew. When I look at you, my heart stutters. Like, literal palpitations when you touch me. I should actually tell my doctor about that." She chuckles, a smooth honey laugh. "I want you so badly. The need is like the dull, constant pain of a toothache. And I can't stand it anymore." My eyes prickle with tears. "I've been so used to shrinking. Making things as easy as possible for my family. Never needing. Never bursting. But you. You make me feel vast. You make me want to flood."

I close my eyes for a moment. Breathe.

She rubs her thumb over my hand. When I open my eyes, she smiles at me. "My turn?"

I nod.

"I'm falling in love with you. I have been since last year."

I burst into laughter. Burst into flames. "Wow. That was succinct."

"I really liked how you said it. What was it? I'm like a toothache?" Her shoulders rumble in a low chuckle.

I laugh. "Shut up. Wait. Last year? As in before January, or when we were freshmen?"

She bites her lip as she considers my question. I think back to our freshman year. Things started well between us. Like Maya said in the hotel, when we were playing ultimate frisbee for our team activity, I felt something between us. I was guarding her and tried to intercept a pass. I stumbled into her, and she fell on top of me. There was a second when her eyes locked on mine, a second of Maya lying on top of me when she should have been trying to get up.

When she realized I had rolled my ankle, she offered to walk me home. She walked me all the way across campus with her arm wrapped tightly around my waist. When I hugged her on the front steps, heat rushed into my cheeks, and butterflies swarmed my stomach. I had a crush on her. But I ruined everything by talking shit about her to Katie.

"I think," Maya starts, snagging my attention. "When we were freshmen. I have always been attracted to you. And when I fell on you in ultimate, it shook something loose inside me. I remember exactly how it felt to have your body underneath me. I remember getting stuck in your eyes. Until you groaned in pain." She laughs. "Then I walked you home and fought the very strong urge to kiss you on your dorm steps."

"Then I ruined it all."

She nods. "Then *we* ruined it all. When I heard you call me crazy, it stung. Because I thought you were on my team. I thought we had this unspoken connection."

"It was one day of getting along, May."

"Come on. You felt it, too."

I look into my lap. "I did. I guess I didn't believe that it was reciprocated. And from the way things were after you overheard me, I just assumed you hated me."

"I did. I hated you so much for not seeing me. And this year, I hated you for being captain. And I hated you for judging me. And for not liking me."

I shake my head. "I've always liked you."

"No, you haven't, Andy. Sure, that day last year was nice, and you liked me then. But you just labeled me and put me away on a shelf after that. The night we had that fight outside of the locker room, and you asked me why I didn't like you...that was my answer. I didn't like you because I felt rejected by you. Even just for friendship, I felt rejected by you. Everything else was just insult to injury."

"And instead of talking to me about it..."

"And instead of talking to you about it, I acted like an asshole." I nod. "What changed for you?"

"You taking the time to tutor me in chemistry. I know it was your job as captain to try to salvage us. I'm not stupid. But I felt like you cared about what happened to me. You didn't have to take your entire day to help, but you did. It was the first time I'd felt connected to you since ultimate frisbee. It was the beginning of our partnership. Not that it's been smooth sailing since then." She chuckles. "What changed for you?"

"I felt the same way you did. I didn't know why things turned cold so quickly between us last year, and I blamed you. I thought you just didn't like me, which was hard to stomach. But the moment you showed the smallest bit of vulnerability, like letting me help you study, things felt like they shifted. I mean, I had hope for a good working relationship." I drop my gaze to her lips. "And for the other side of things…I can't keep my eyes off you. I've wanted you since I met you, but I've kept it buried deep. You had a boyfriend, you're my teammate, I assumed you were straight."

"That's a silly thing to assume. I'm pan, or bi, or whatever." She shrugs. "I'm attracted to all gender identities."

I smile. I'm not just some one-off attraction to her. I have just as much right to be hers as Jeremy did.

"What happened with Jeremy? Why didn't you break up with him sooner?"

"I wanted to, Andy. I'd been feeling distant from him most of this year, and after the hotel, I knew it was done. Well, if I was being honest with myself, I would have realized a lot earlier than that, but Jeremy was comfortable for me. He was easy and safe." She glances at the family photo on her desk. "Honestly, he was like one of my brothers, you know? I liked talking to him about sports, and he didn't require too much from me." Her gaze lands on me, and the variegated sunlight from the window pulls out flecks of brilliant copper from her brown eyes. "I didn't realize what was missing until my feelings for you grew, and it hit me that I need someone to want more from me.

"I texted him that night in the hotel, right when I got into bed, to tell him that we needed to talk, but they had an away series coming up, and I didn't want to do it over the phone. That's why I was trying to keep a little distance from you the last two weeks. I hadn't had the chance to end things, and I didn't want to feel like I was being unfaithful. Jeremy at least deserves that. Anyway, the baseball party was the moment I was looking for to talk to him."

"Oh." My body eases, and my shoulder sinks against hers. This makes sense. I swallow. "Would you have stopped us in the hotel if I hadn't?"

Her hand moves from mine to my thigh, sending tingles through my body. "I don't know. I don't think I could have." She grins and sucks in her lips. Is she seeing me on top of her, grinding into her and losing control? "It was wrong of me to want that to happen because of J, but couldn't you tell I did? The first time you reached for your phone and all of your warmth and weight and beauty rocked against me…I *needed* more of you."

As she tells me how I made her lose control, I feel mine slipping into a warm want. "Tell me what you did about it," I demand.

She smiles and sends her fingertips on a slow journey up and down my leg. While she gathers words, I gather the strength to not jump her bones, but I'm completely melting. "I think the feeling shocked us both. But I wasn't sure how you felt about it, so I held out your phone and told you to try harder to get it. And damn. You did. Then I found desire in your eyes, in the heat of your skin, in the curve of your hips. I put my hands there, on your hips, and it only took the tiniest effort to set you in motion." She shakes her head. "It was incredible. Feeling you against me, watching you lose control on top of me…the answer is no, I wouldn't have been able to stop if you hadn't."

I can't sit here and stare at her lips while she speaks anymore. She's finally mine, and all I want to do is kiss her again. I lean in and press my lips to hers. They're soft and warm and everything I remember but even sweeter. Kissing Maya Gonzalez is like sinking into a hot bath. Her kiss submerges every inch of my body as she sighs into my mouth. I need more. I swing a leg over hers and sink into her lap. Her arms wrap around my waist and pull me against her, stealing my breath.

She pulls away, a little breathless herself, and touches the traitor hickey on my neck. "I hate this. I hate that Emma's mouth was on your skin." She prods at the bruise as if the purple blood of it is Emma's unwelcome presence in her room. Her eyes darken, and she drags her nails over the sensitive skin of my hickey. The rise of her temper and the score on my neck makes my hips grind into her.

"Take it back, then."

Her eyes meet mine, one brow arched in question.

I dig my fingers into her back, matching her pressure at my neck. "I said, make it yours." Her chest rises at my challenge, dragging in a deep breath. She just needs one more little push. I lean in against her ear.

"You've got such pretty teeth. Use them," I whisper.

She growls at my command and sinks her teeth into me. I rock against her as my body shivers from the pressure building in me. She sucks my flesh into her mouth and holds me there, taking what's hers. When she releases, the angry bruise on my neck pulses in rhythm with the rest of me. Her hand slips into the loose leg of my shorts, and she fingers the seam of my underwear. It's a question; she's asking for consent.

She strokes along my seam, and my heart explodes for this woman. It explodes for her strength and her passion, her relentless pursuit of her dreams, and the ferocity of her loyalty. I belong with her. I stare into her eyes as all these words race through my brain. This is not Emma Wilson. This is Maya. My warrior.

"Tell me you're mine," I say.

She kisses me and presses her response into my mouth. "Andrea, I'm yours. If you want me."

I reach into my shorts and pull my underwear to one side. "I'm yours."

She tugs me against her as she traces her fingers through me. I ache for her. I'm swollen for her. I can't get enough of her.

I tighten around her, and as the edges of my body begin to reverberate, I push Maya down onto her bed and pull up her shirt. The sight of her—hot-cheeked, no bra, shirt up to her neck, hand disappearing between my thighs—pushes me over the edge and into oblivion. She steadies me until I come down, then she slips her fingers from me, and I crumble into her.

For all of my confidence in touching her body, and in her touching mine, I'm all of a sudden nervous to overstay my welcome in her room. Maybe it's drilled into my head from every movie and TV show ever, but things are supposed to be awkward now, right? Like, how long should I stay? I wish we were in my room so she was the one who has to stay or leave. We hold each other as the chemicals in my blood dissipate into a steady buzz.

I trust her to tell me what she needs. "Should I go?" I ask as I stroke her stomach.

In a second, Maya is on top of me, stroking my hair and staring into my eyes. The quickness of it and the tenderness of it takes my breath away. "I have wanted you since you gave me that goofy smile when we got assigned lockers next to each other. I wanted you when we played ultimate frisbee, and I learned what it felt like to have your body under mine. I wanted you when you hurt me. I wanted you when you tried to calm me and when you showed concern for me. I wanted you every time you put on that damned uniform. You made me crazy. Every argument we had, I wanted to throw you against a wall and kiss you and touch you and make you *get it*." She presses a tender kiss to my lips. "I just got you. Please don't go."

## CHAPTER FIFTEEN

If focusing on class was hard before I knew what Maya's breasts look like, now it's nearly impossible. I never thought something could shake up my life so violently, especially a girl, but here I sit in my Physiological Psychology class, leg bouncing, eyes darting from the clock on the wall, to my phone, to the door, as if somebody dropped a Mentos in my Coke. I'm not stupid. I know there are literal chemicals being released by my brain, tricking me into thinking that I don't care about school anymore and that the only thing I care about is the fact that I get to see Maya in—my eyes dart to the plastic clock *again*—twenty-seven minutes. Give or take a couple minutes, depending on how quickly I can buy a banana on my way to practice.

An unread text from her has tormented me all class. As my body betrays me for love, I struggle to control even the smallest things, like leaving my phone in my pocket during class so I can concentrate and learn about behavioral neuroscience. Because I *want* to learn. I love my classes and my professors; they are important to me. But I may as well have been texting Maya the entire time because even though I resisted the urge to pull out my phone, my mind has been with her for the last hour and not with Dr. Phillips.

The clock hits 1:15, and Dr. Phillips dismisses us. I shove my notebook and textbook into my bag, barely caring that I bend the pages in my notebook. I fish my phone out of my pocket as I glide through the corridors of Brown Hall. Two texts.

Maya: *Are you feeling as tortured as I am?*
*I need you.*

My eyes are glued to my phone as I turn the corner and run into—

"*Oof.* Careful there, lady. You must be looking at something you like on that thing." She steadies me with a hand on my hip and taps the face of my phone with the other.

"Maya, what are you—"

"Dr. G let us out a little early, so I thought I'd come scoop you up," she says.

My grin stretches to the limits of my lips, and I pull her in for a quick hug. "Yes. I am feeling as tortured as you. I was responding to your text when I ran into this gorgeous girl in the hallway. You might have some competition."

She kisses my cheek and pulls away, her hand finding mine. Her eyes darken. "I can't go through all of practice without touching you. Where can we go? Our dorms are out of the way, and we only have a half hour until we need to be at the club."

I tug her down the hallway. "Come on." We climb two flights of stairs and speed walk to the end of a deserted hallway full of storage closets and auxiliary rooms that remain unused, as the professors' offices and class auditoriums are on the first and second floors. I scan the doors until I find the women's restroom—*the single occupancy* women's restroom. As desperate as I am for Maya, I would never risk fooling around in a storage closet or any public place that doesn't have a lock on the door.

"Here." I pull her into the bathroom and lock the door behind us. The sunlight pouring through the window is hazed with dust, and there are no puddles of water on the floor or on the sink. The trash is empty, and the end of the toilet paper is folded into a neat triangle. It doesn't seem like this bathroom has been used in a long time.

"The stall seems redundant," Maya says.

"Oh my God. It's that short kind you can see over. The kind that's only in nightmares," I say. I peel my eyes from the squat, banana-colored stall and look at Maya. "Isn't it crazy how our brains weave obstacles into our dreams to keep our bodies from doing something in real life?" I point to the stall. "I only come across these monsters in my dreams when I really need to pee, and my brain is like 'No. We can't wet the bed.' So it only gives me the most uncomfortable places to go. Like these mini stalls. Oh, and like, when I'm thirsty—"

"Hey." Maya's warm hand on my cheek steals the rest of my rambles. She looks almost heavenly in the midst of all the golden dust floating around us. "Do I make you nervous?" Her thighs nudge me backward against the sink.

"'Nervous' is the wrong word." I grip the edge of the countertop as she tugs the collar of my shirt and brushes her lips over the spot where she burned Emma's flag and raised her own. I'm basically a battlefield of love. No big deal. My body tenses when her warm breath bathes my neck.

"What's the right word?" She seals her question with small kisses and nips down into my shirt.

"Mm. A couple pop into mind. 'Anxious' for your touch, 'hungry' for your taste." I brush my lips against her ear, and she shivers against me.

My words are like the gunshot to start a race; Maya groans and presses her lips against mine, but my eyes catch the clock in the corner of the old bathroom, and I pull away. "Shoot, May. We're going to be late for practice."

Her fingers work on unbuttoning my jeans. "So we're ten minutes late…I don't care." She dips her hand into my underwear, and I instinctively spread my legs for her. I don't like to be contained anymore; I like to flood. All over her.

Her fingers slide into me, and I hear myself emanate a long, low moan. "Do you care, Andy?" Her words dance on the crests of her breaths, matching each of her thrusts. I don't care. I'm doing me right now.

And so is Maya Gonzalez.

But my phone alarm blares at us from my pocket, and Maya sighs. "No, come on," she whines. She steps back to let me turn off the annoying alarm, the alarm that goes off at the same time every day, telling me it's time to leave the dining hall for practice, and as it turns out, I do care. I'm the *captain*. I can't be late because I'm hooking up with a teammate in an abandoned bathroom.

"We gotta go, May. We're already late, and I'm the captain. And what will they think if we show up late *together*?" I gather my bag and try to splash the red out of my cheeks with cold water as Maya washes her hands. "I am so red."

"I am so grumpy."

"I know, but I'll make it up to you later, come on."

As the weeks pass, it becomes more evident that our dreams of making it to regionals and beyond is actually in the realm of possibility. The way we have been playing has caught the attention of the softball world, and the murmurings we hear from other coaches, the media, and other players tells us that we may even be a shoo-in for the selection show. If we keep it up, that is.

The tournament starts with sixty-four teams. Thirty-two teams are automatically qualified—the Oklahomas, the Alabamas, and the Florida States of the world—while the remaining thirty-two teams are selected by the Division I Softball Committee, which is where teams like Alder come into the mix. I understand it's not comparable to judge us solely on our record when we don't play a major conference schedule, but I hope we get the chance to prove how good of a team we are.

Ashlyn and Katie have both been on home-run streaks, while defensively, we haven't had an error in five games. My arm has been deadly for base runners who have the gall to attempt stealing second, and Maya has been on fire.

"Don't cross the bats." Maya straightens all of the bats that have fallen over each other along the wall of the dugout; superstition is strong in this sport. These moments are rare for her at this point, with most of her passion being channeled in more productive ways, but this is our last regular-season game, our last chance to show the committee what we're worth. Not to mention, finals are coming up. Stress is high.

I walk into the dugout behind her and lay my hand on her lower back. Having learned my way around her in these moments, I don't sleeve tug or berate her or try to douse her passion. I encourage her fire. But instead of throwing crap in her flames and allowing her to smoke everyone out, I feed her dry oak. "Your arm looked great when we were warming up. We're going to crush this game, and you're going to lead us to regionals."

She turns and wraps me in a quick hug. "I'm freaking out," she whispers into my ear.

I smile at her. Her brows are drawn tight with concern. "We're all freaking out. Everything we want is right in front of us. We just need to reach out and grab it, and it's scary because we may miss. But let's just get out there and play. You and me. Together. Let's—"

"Swerve."

"Exactly." I break into a grin. The last month with Maya has been pure bliss. We don't have a ton of spare time right now, but when we do, we're together. Maybe not alone. Ever since our first time in Maya's room, it's been impossible to escape our roommates, but even just studying next to her brings me joy. I never thought Rachel's presence would annoy me, but I'm getting to the point where the only reason I want to go to regionals is to share a hotel room with Maya again. We need privacy soon, or our teammates are going to catch on to our thirstiness.

She pulls her facemask from her cubby, and I clip my chest protector, ready to take the field. She tugs me backward before my cleats hit the dirt. "Hey. Will you go on a date with me?" she whispers. I'm confused because I don't know what a date would look like for us. There's one fancy restaurant in town, and neither of us has the time to leave campus. Not to mention finals are next week, and we're behind in studying because of softball. There's no time, and there's no space for us.

I turn around and cock my head at her. "Um. Sure?"

"Your lack of enthusiasm cuts deep."

"May, of course I want to go on a date with you," I whisper. "But how are we going to do that?"

She looks behind her and over my shoulder to make sure the coast is clear. "Don't worry. Just leave it to me." She squeezes my forearm, her gaze caught on something over my shoulder. "Andy…"

"What?"

"Alex Squared is here," she says.

"What?" I spin around so fast that I almost trip over my cleats. My mom and dad stand posted along the third-base fence with Emma and Rachel. My dad has on all of his Lion gear and waves a homemade sign that reads *That's my kid!* A scruffy-looking lion's mane encircles my mom's head. *A lion's mane.* But I don't even cringe. "Come on, May." I clunk over to them in all of my gear with Maya in tow.

"Wow, Mom. You've really outdone yourself." I unlock the gate and throw myself into her arms. Life is so busy and exciting that I forgot I miss my parents. I miss them a lot.

"Andy Pandy," they both yell. I catch Maya's eyes going wide, and a grin spreads over her lips.

"Why didn't y'all tell me you were coming? We could've done something earlier." I look to the sky and ponder if that's actually true. We've been preparing for this game all day. "Actually, we couldn't have. But what about after?"

"I wanted to surprise you. Felt so bad about canceling the last trip, and I was feeling great today. Nothing was going to stop me from seeing you play your last regular-season game," my dad says.

"Of course, sweetie. Let's all go out to dinner after," my mom says.

"You're not inviting these losers, are you?" I tilt my head to Emma and Rachel, who begin a barrage of objection, and Emma even sneaks in a middle finger when my folks aren't looking.

My mom wraps her arms around Emma's neck and pushes a big kiss to her cheek while her other arm pulls Rachel into a hug. "Of course my girls are coming." Rule number fifty-seven of college is to never reject an invitation to go out to dinner with someone's parents. We're all broke and hungry.

I tug Maya into our weird circle, and she shoots me a nervous look before she straightens her shoulders. "Guys, this is my…Maya Gonzalez, our pitcher." I shake my head at my failure to speak as

I present her to Alex Squared. I'm guessing Maya is someone who excels at interacting with parents.

She shakes their hands and smiles wide. "It's so nice to finally meet you, Mr. and Mrs. Foster."

"Wow," my dad says. "*The* Maya Gonzalez." Her cheeks shade to that pretty rosewood color. "You are making quite the splash in the softball world. Hell, in the sports world at large. I've seen your name on ESPN nonstop. You are quite the athlete, dear."

"Thank you, Mr. Foster. I'm just lucky to be a part of such a talented team this year. And to have such a talented catcher has made all the difference." Her hand finds the small of my back under the cross of my gear straps. "Andy has been an amazing leader. We're here because of her."

My mom lights up like a kid on Christmas. "Maya, you are lovely. Thank you for your kind words. You know, if I had a dollar for every time Andy has said your name—"

"Mom. Please."

Emma shifts her weight from foot to foot, and Rachel grins like she's watching a sitcom. Maya's hand remains on my back, and I can feel the vibration of her chuckles.

"Oh relax, honey. It doesn't seem like I'm telling her anything she doesn't already know." My mom looks pointedly at the two of us, at Maya's arm disappearing behind my back. And if I didn't love her before, I am mad for her, now. She doesn't drop her hand at my mom's insinuation. She looks into my eyes and smiles at me with all the warmth of the Georgia coast in August.

"I'm sure my mom would say the same exact thing about me," she says, eyes still on me. "In fact, I think she actually did."

I ache for the sweetness of this moment, but I break our gaze. "Maya is going to join us for dinner after the game." I turn to her. "That is, of course, if you want to. You might have plans or—"

"Oh my gosh, I would love to join. If that's okay with you, Mr. and Mrs. Foster."

My mom claps and pulls Maya in for a hug. "Of course, sweetie." She releases her and turns to my dad. "You get to have dinner with your favorite athlete."

He looks at Maya and grins. "It must be my lucky day."

I scoff at both of them. "I'm offended that your own daughter isn't your favorite athlete."

"You shouldn't have introduced us to *your* Maya if you felt that way," my dad says. And he winks at us.

"Okay…on that note, we have to get back on the field. Like, now. Love you guys. I'll text you when we're ready." I look at Emma and Rachel. "I hate you both. See y'all after the game."

I pull Maya through the gate back to safety. The grin hasn't left her face.

"Holy shit, Andy. That was—"

"Maya, Andy, let's go!" Coach Clay yells for us to line up for the Anthem. And just like that, we're swept away into the game, and I'm left wondering what Maya was going to say to me.

It was a quick and painless game. We carried on our momentum and will, I hope, go to regionals on a hot streak. Our team dances and sings, and the locker room morphs into a mosh pit. Maya and I celebrate and jump around, too, but we also have a dinner date to attend, so we're the first to shower. I pull on my sweatshirt as Maya approaches her locker, wet from her shower, towel around her body. The music and laughter are loud around us, and no one is paying attention when Maya bends into her locker and lets her towel fall open for the most minuscule of seconds. But it's all I need to snap a picture of her hot, damp body.

"Careful, or we won't make it to dinner," I say.

"You'd better stop staring unless you're ready to spill the beans about us."

I clear my throat and turn away from her. She's right. I'm being reckless.

When we're both dressed and feel that we have spent enough time in celebration with our teammates, we say good-bye to the coaches and walk to my dorm, hand in hand. It may be risky, but I'm finding it hard to care. Even though regionals are around the corner, and I have no idea how our team would react to us being together. We pass the science buildings, then the chapel. The glow from the lamps lining the paths through the quad light up the stone of the campus and set it aglow in the night. It's a beautiful place to be.

"What were you going to say before Coach cut you off? After Alex Squared, you said 'that was'..."

"That was *everything*. That was perfect. Did you tell your parents that we're together? Or did they just sense it?"

I stop and pull her around to face me. "Are we?"

"Are we what?"

"Together. Like, exclusively?" I feel blush bloom on my cheeks.

"I guess we never talked about it, huh?"

I try to read her face, but she's had some form of the same grin since she met my parents. I can't tell if it's just residual happiness or if she's laughing at me inside or if she thinks I'm silly. "No. We haven't."

"That's my bad. I assumed that you must feel about it the same way I feel about it."

I shake my head, trying to stop my mind from going crazy guessing how she feels about it. "How do you feel about it?"

She lets out a long breath, and I steady myself. "If you wanted to see other people, touch other people, be touched by other people"— she shakes her head and swallows—"that would break my heart. I'm in love with you, Andrea. For me, there is no room for other people. I only want you, and I wanted your parents to know that. I want everyone to know that. So what do you say? Will you be my girlfriend?" She tugs my hand, and I trip over my feet into her. "Please."

I drag my finger over her collar and up under her chin. I kiss her and pull away. Tug her down the sidewalk. "Come on. I gotta make sure you fit in with my family before I commit to that."

We continue through the quad toward Wilder Hall. "So what you're saying is, I should be on my best behavior and *not* stab Emma Wilson in her shooting hand with a butterknife?"

"Something like that, yeah."

"Well, if I fail, which I may very well fail, it was nice being yours while it lasted."

I plant one more kiss on her before we walk inside and open my door to find Emma, Rachel, and Alex Squared laughing at something on my mom's phone. *Here we go.*

## CHAPTER SIXTEEN

The library pulses with anxiety, as if its pumping heart is powered by Alder students' blood, sweat, and tears. I kind of love it. Ask me again when I'm a senior, but as of now, I've never had to worry about my grades or how I'll do on my finals. I put in the hours, I'm passionate about the material, and I'm a skilled test-taker. I'm going to kill my finals. But that doesn't mean that I don't take them seriously or that I do anything other than study as much as possible within the limitations of being a student athlete.

I have a sweet little spot in a vacant corner on the fourth floor—the quiet floor—where I can see other people frantically outlining chapters and shuffling through notecards, but nobody notices me. I may have learned how to walk in the spotlight this year, but lurking in a corner, behind the scenes, is still my preferred habitat. I sip my hot coffee and let the steam tickle my nose as I try to refocus on my ethics notes. But I'm struggling to be present in the moment because last night, I had dinner with Maya and my parents. And Rachel and Emma, but they're irrelevant.

My parents drooled over Maya all night. I caught some annoyed looks from Emma every once in a while, but generally, everyone was well behaved. When Emma made a questionable joke at Maya's expense, Maya laughed with all the grace of a patient mother. It made me so proud to call her mine. We gorged ourselves on fresh pasta and roasted veggies, not leaving any room for dessert. My parents dropped everyone off at Wilder, and I walked Maya back across the quad to her dorm.

"Yes," I whispered into her mouth between some of the sweetest kisses I've ever experienced. The glow of the porchlight on the front steps of her dorm dramatized the smile she gave me in response. She didn't have to ask what I was talking about. She knew. She wrapped her arms around my waist and pulled my body into hers, kissing me until my toes curled against the tips of my flats. She asked if she could take me out on our date tonight, and I said, "Fuck yes," which earned me another huge kiss. She loves when I curse.

I open my planner. My heart skips a beat every time I see the Regionals Selection Show on my calendar. Right after finals. In one week. Coaches will order us pizza and set up a projector, and we'll lay out blankets in the outfield to watch the committee announce the teams that are advancing to regionals. I have no doubt in my mind that we will be celebrating that night.

My phones buzzes against the hard surface of my table, and I mouth an apology to the one person in earshot. My stomach does a gymnastics floor routine expecting to see her name.

Maya: *About that date…When can I pick you up?*

Me: *I'm still studying. I have my ethics final in the morning, so I can't be up too late, okay? I can only hang out for two hours.*

Maya: *Hmm. I can't guarantee that.*

Me: *Maya…*

Maya: *Okay, I know I know. How about I scoop you up from the library in an hour?*

Me: *Perfect.*

My focus is completely down the drain. Instead of wasting precious time staring at my notes and not absorbing anything, I pack slowly and head to the most deserted bathroom of the library to make sure I look okay. Maya arrives early, wearing last year's softball sweatshirt and Nike shorts. Her black socks hit just under her calf, and her two-tone Asics pop to life whenever a streetlamp tags them, and a backpack hangs from her shoulders. It's a classic athletic look, but damn. That smile, that messy bun, those legs. When I'm staring at the perfect shelf of muscles above her knees, she snaps me back into focus. Well, redirects my focus.

"I've come to save you from your studies," she says

I lope down the giant steps to meet her on the sidewalk. The night is breezy, the occasional shiver kind of chilly, but for early May, it's mild. The sky shows off its assortment of stars while whisps of clouds gather about the mostly full moon.

"Hey." I pull her into a hug and push my face into her warm neck. I've found many benefits to this. It's warm, she smells amazing, and my hearing aids never give feedback at that angle. She grabs my hand and gives me a quick peck, tugging me away from the library. I pull out my phone as we walk and open the timer app.

Maya side eyes my phone. "For real?"

I set the timer for two hours, a more than generous amount of time, given the fact that I have a final in the morning. "I told you, I have an eight-a.m. final. I really need to get a solid night of sleep."

"All right. Fair enough."

"You can't be surprised."

"I mean, I knew you'd be checking the time every ten minutes, but I have to admit, the timer took me a little off guard." She squeezes my hand. "But if a timer is what makes it possible to take the hottest girl at Alder on a date, then so be it."

The slight goose bumps I had before disappear as if her words are a blowtorch, melting the ice in me. I think I'm a fine-looking girl. Some days, I'd even say I'm damn close to beautiful, but "hottest girl at Alder" is just a little too much of an exaggeration. I love it, but I won't let her get away with it.

"You know, things mean more when said simply. Hyperbole robs meaning." We turn into the arboretum, a place I love, but a place I'm surprised to be led to by Maya. "It's impossible that I'm the most beautiful girl at Alder. I mean, think of our class size alone, and what about—"

She stops walking and whirls me around to face her. "Do you think anyone in this place is more beautiful than I am?" My mind filters through all the familiar faces of this college, but nothing pops into my head except for Maya. I stare at her, half-lit by one of the old, pale streetlamps. A few strands of hair brush over her forehead, and her eyes are almost black in the night.

"No."

She shrugs. "Well, now you can see I'm not being hyperbolic." She runs her fingertips across my forehead, brushing a bit of hair off my face. "Your hair is like sunshine and sand and rust and honey. And your eyes are blue like the sky in April." Her thumb brushes over my bottom lip. "And your lips don't taste sweet but earthy and cool, like fresh moss."

She leans in and kisses me. I slip my arm around her waist and move with her mouth. The feeling of her lips pushing into mine, then pulling away, then brushing over mine, and her warm breath makes me want to tear my clothes off and let her show me how those kisses would feel all over my body. But she breaks away and shakes her head, grabbing my hand again.

"You distracted me. Come on. We're on a schedule here." She tugs me through to the end of the arboretum.

"Are we just on a walk? Where are we going?" I thought we might sit on a bench and chat. Or do *something* in the arboretum before we left.

Maya stops walking about twenty yards from the exit. "Ready?" Before I can respond, she hops the fence out of the arboretum and into the woods. She laces her fingers through the chain link and grins. "Come on, Andy. Time's a tickin'." She taps her wrist where a watch would be.

"What are these woods? Why are they fenced off?"

"They're part of the forestry department. They aren't all the way fenced off, just where the trees butt up to campus. I think it's so they don't get littered with beer cans and cigarette butts. You coming?"

I have not jumped a fence in years, but as it turns out, it's baked into my muscle memory. I grip the metal and dig the tip of my shoe into a gap, then launch myself up and over, landing right next to Maya. She smiles and kisses me.

"That was very attractive."

I tap my imaginary watch, too.

"Right," she says. I follow her into the woods for a good five minutes until we come upon a small clearing about ten feet in diameter. The ground is flat and matted with decayed winter leaves, lending some softness to its surface. The trees stir in the breeze around us, and the moon peeks into our little alcove, bathing us in the perfect amount of light. Maya turns off the flashlight on her phone and opens her bag. She lays down a small wool blanket and hands me a warm thermos.

"Come sit."

"This is the most perfect date I could have ever thought of. How did you know about this place?"

She half grins and looks away. "Jeremy showed me this spot last year. We used to sneak away to this place whenever we couldn't get privacy in the dorms."

My stomach sinks. I know that she doesn't want to be with him anymore, and I *know* that she wants to be with me, but all I can think about is Maya and Jeremy boning in the woods. And if she liked it. And if she liked it more than having sex with me.

She touches my shoulder. "I didn't say that for any other reason than to be honest. I like to keep it one-hundred. Especially with you."

I nod and attempt a smile. "If I'm keeping it one-hundred, too… all I can think about is you and Jeremy having sex here. Maybe we can go somewhere—"

Her lips are on mine, hot and hard. She grips my face and pulls me deeper into her. I open my mouth, desperate to feel her tongue against mine. It's hard to get all keyed up making out with Maya and still think about her with someone else.

"Better?" she asks between kisses.

I nod against her lips.

She pulls away from me to whisper in my ear. "No one has ever come close to you. Ever. If it makes you angry that someone else had me here, right here on this ground, then why don't you do something about it?" A breath puffs out of my open mouth, and my body charges into an intense state of need. I grip the blanket with one hand and dig the other into her lower back. "That's right. Make it yours. Make it so when I think of this spot, I only think of you." She finishes with a nibble of my earlobe, and I flash back to my hickey and the rage it instilled in Maya. And what she did about it…

My turn.

I push her down, and when her back hits the blanket, a small gasp jumps from her lips. I straddle her hips and grip her wrists over her head. Her sweatshirt rides up, exposing bare midriff, telling me that she isn't wearing anything underneath. With my tongue in her mouth and her desperate moans, I lift my weight just long enough to push my hand down the front of her shorts and drag my fingers through her.

I pull her sweatshirt off, balling it up and tucking it under her neck, and she throws her head back, a low moan coasting from her as I lower my mouth to her breast. A shudder runs through me as her sweet and earthy flavor plays on my tastebuds. She tries to fish a hand into my shorts, but I grab it and pin it against the ground. As desperate as I am, I want to be in control.

When she can't take it anymore, she pushes against my shoulders, putting a small gap of space between us. We fill it with heavy breaths as she tucks her thumbs into her waistband and pushes her running shorts down her thighs and over her knees. I take it from there and slide them over her shoes. Maya completely naked except for black crew socks and her purple and black Asics is hands down the sexiest thing I've ever seen.

I lower myself between her thighs and feel the heat against my lips before I even touch her. I gently brush over her slick folds like I'm barely there, and she shivers as I stroke up and down through her, then fill her with my fingers. She grinds into my mouth, into my hand, with every thrust until her breath comes faster and faster. She buries a hand in my hair as her body goes rigid, Asics pointed to the moon. And she melts.

One last small sigh leaves her lips when I slip my fingers out of her and crawl up to meet her. I lie over her body and bury my face in her warm neck, now a little damp, as she drags long strokes down my back and holds me against her.

"I hope you don't think I dragged you to the woods just to have sex with you," she says. Her voice is gentle against the sounds of the night.

"Didn't you?"

"I at least thought we would drink the hot chocolate and have a conversation before."

I slide on top of her again and kiss her breast. "Sometimes, it's fun to order dessert first."

"No truer words."

My phone alarm barrels through the moment like the goddamn Kool-Aid man.

"Shit." Maya grins at my profanity. "Oh, shut up," I say and crawl to my bag to silence the alarm. It's nine thirty. I wouldn't care if it was eleven.

"Time's up, huh?"

I hand Maya her clothes. "No."

"No?" She tugs her sweatshirt over her head and pulls her shorts up.

I pour us a cup of cocoa. "Look, normally, I'd be really strict about this," I say. She chuckles into the thermos cup. "But I only have one final, and it's ethics. I could get zero sleep tonight and still make a hundred on it. My bigger concern is what finals you have tomorrow."

She stays silent, blowing over the top of her hot chocolate.

"Right." I grab my phone and set an alarm for ten thirty. That will get her in bed by eleven for a good night's rest.

"Come on. We don't need to set an alarm," she says.

I sip the cocoa and stare at her. I could rip off her clothes and spend endless hours here with her, competing brands of sneakers knocking through the night. "I don't want to leave, but we have to go soon."

"*Ugh*, okay."

The hot cocoa is warm and has a bit of spice to it. I take another sip and try to hang a memory of this night on the taste of the chocolate, cinnamon, and clove. One day, in the distant future, I'll be minding my own business, drinking hot cocoa and grinning like a fool. *Cinnamon and her.* She sips and gazes at the stars. I hope she only thinks of us now when she thinks of this spot, and when she tastes cinnamon, I hope she thinks of my hands on her body.

"Why were things with Jeremy so easy to end?" I didn't know I was going to ask this question, but being in this place with her makes me curious about what kind of relationship they had. I don't think I'm jealous—anymore—I just want to know more about her.

"I never said it was *easy*." She runs her fingers over the blanket and picks a few pine needles from the wool. Her eyes meet mine. "Do you really want to talk about it? I mean, I'll tell you anything, but none of it matters because it's you. It's you, Andy. Not him, and not anyone else."

"It was a big part of your life. I'd like to know, yeah."

A long breath pours from her mouth. "It wasn't easy to break up with Jeremy. The decision was easy, don't get me wrong, but pulling the trigger was hard. He's a well-intentioned guy who fit into my life nicely. He was never needy and always satisfied what I wanted from our relationship."

"What did you want from your relationship with him?"

"Easy company, someone to stand next to me at parties, good sex, a friend, and he looked good posing in photos with me."

A ribbon of jealousy coils around my gut. Though the things she wanted out of her relationship with Jeremy are simple to achieve in most relationships, I really wish she hadn't said "good sex."

"And what do you want out of our relationship?"

She takes a moment, then grabs my hand and angles her body to me. "J is a friend. I valued his friendship and the ease of our relationship. I only say it was hard to end because I don't want to cheapen what we had, and I don't want to lie to you. But the decision was easy, and I made it quickly, because when you ask me what I want from my relationship with you, my answer is a lot different than what I wanted with him."

"Tell me."

"I want everything from you, Andrea. I want an unwavering partner who is unmatched in her loyalty and dedication to me and everyone else she cares about. I want a woman who is so beautiful, she keeps me up into the morning fantasizing about touching her. I want you to hold me to the highest standards and help me to be the best version of myself I can possibly be. And I want you to love me with no end."

"May—"

"That's just the beginning. I have a tall order for you."

My grin squeezes my eyes almost shut as I let her words find a home in me. "I'm not going to let you down," I say.

She pulls me most of the way into her lap and wraps her arms around my waist, pressing her body against my back. I lean into the warmth of her as her lips brush over my neck.

"Please don't, baby." Her words are whisper soft against my skin, and my toes curl in response. I kiss her. It's as soft as our words at first but quickly ratchets up. And up. Until she accidentally knocks her teeth against mine.

We chuckle at our eagerness, and she presses her fingers to my lips. "Sorry. Got a little overexcited there."

"I think I'm a little overexcited everywhere."

"Oh yeah?"

Her lips find my neck again, and her hands slide down my body. I fight against the hot and cold of my desire. Against the shiver in my spine and the pool of warmth between my legs. Because she has *real* finals tomorrow, and there's not enough time for a round two. I grab her wrist before her hand slips down the front of my shorts.

"We can't. The timer is going to go off soon, and we need to get you to bed."

She groans, and the vibrations of it tickles my neck. "I'll be quick. I promise."

"I want to so badly, but it's not worth messing up your grades over." I crane my head and kiss her on the cheek. "You just said you want me to hold you to the highest standards."

"Can I just feel you?"

I swallow excitement. I don't want to let her win, but deep down, I hope she does. I'm so ready for her. I clear my throat. "Feel me?"

She fingers my waistband. "Feel you."

The ache between my thighs hits me hard, and I uncross my legs. "Okay. But that's it."

She kisses me as her hand pushes into my shorts. I'm completely wasted when her tongue brushes over mine at the same time as her fingers slide into me. And over me. Then into me again. I break away from her kiss to try to catch my breath as I involuntarily rock into her fingers. I can't stop. She knows I can't stop. I reach over my head for her and find a grip on the back of her neck as she keeps her rhythm in my shorts. Her lips are hot against my ear.

"I can stop," she whispers as her fingers go still inside me. I feel my pulse against them.

"I can't." As if to prove my point, I dig my fingers into the back of her neck as my core tightens around her. I need her. I need her fingers to keep moving in me and over me. When I'm about to throw a fit, she slides out of me and rubs against me in small circles. My head falls against her shoulder as the chorus of my body climbs note by note.

"I love you," she says, and her words send me into an earth-combusting orgasm. I press my face into her neck to muffle my cry.

My waistband snaps against my stomach, and I watch as her lips close around her fingers. She wipes her hand on the blanket then pulls me tighter into her. We're quiet as we both come down from the excitement again. The crickets sing with bravado, and the breeze picks up around us.

"I'm serious. I love you, Andrea. I want to be with you."

I stroke her arm and try to dissect the tiny bit of anxiety in her voice. "I love you, too. And you *are* with me. You're my girlfriend. What are you stressing?"

"We're only sophomores," she says.

"Yeah, and that's great. We have so much more time here together."

She sighs. "I know, but maybe we should have met as seniors or after graduation. College relationships rarely last. And I'm your first. First relationships *never* last and I—"

"Hey, it's okay." I squeeze her hand. "You're starting to sound like me over there." She chuckles. "Look, I can't see the future, but I've got a pretty good idea of what the rest of the week looks like. And guess what? We'll still be together. We have everything going for us. We're going to lead our team to the World Series, we're young and in love, and we have two more years together at Alder. When I said I was feeling nostalgic for softball, you told me, 'Don't miss it because you already miss it.' Don't miss us," I say.

She sighs. "You're right. I just feel like I've found a lost treasure, and now that I have it, it's hard to not be afraid of losing it. I just got you."

"I'm not going anywhere." I lean in and kiss her softly, trying my best to comfort her. Her anxiety about losing me breaks my heart in the sweetest way. I'm a shattered mess of rock candy. I feel a tear on my cheek, but my eyes are dry.

She pulls away and wipes her cheek. "We could room together next year. I'm tired of sneaking around trying to find privacy. And I want to tell Coach Clayton and the team."

I think I may have Maya Gonzalez wrapped around my finger. I press a quick kiss to her lips. "Let's see how the summer goes, okay? I'm in it for the long haul with you, but I'm not sure rooming together would be the best thing to get us there. As fun as it would be." I wink.

"You're probably right."

"But when we're not here, we'll both be in Atlanta, and I don't know about your parents, but mine are super chill. You can come over all the time, and we can go upstairs and lock ourselves in my room."

That earns me a smile.

My phone alarm goes off and steals its second moment of the evening. We actually manage to wrap up our date this time and walk back to the dorms together.

I catch my reflection in the vending machine by the bathrooms of Wilder as I walk back to my room. My cheeks are still flushed from Maya and the crisp night, and my limbs are still shaky like Jell-O. I didn't even realize I'd been grinning, which is impressive, given it takes no less than ten muscles in my face to make it happen, as opposed to frowning, which only takes six. Everyone gets those numbers backward.

I float to my dorm room, ready to crumble into bed and relive the best day of my life before passing out hard.

"Hey, girl. We need to talk to you," Rachel says the second I set foot in our room. Emma and Rachel are both on *my* bed, eating greasy pizza, which better not be dripping on my clean sheets.

"Hello to both of you, too. Also, it's way too late for whatever this is. We all have finals tomorrow," I say.

"About your girlfriend. We need to talk to you about your girlfriend. She's playing you, Andy," Emma clarifies.

"Excuse me?" I drop my backpack and stare.

"What's your plan when it comes to Maya?" she asks.

And all of a sudden, the presence of my two friends annoys the shit out of me. Emma can sleep with half the university, and no one cares. Rachel can drag things out in the most hurtful way possible with her ex, and Emma and I are here to support her *gently*. But I finally find my person—I finally *fall in love* for Christ's sake—and these assholes are being…assholes.

I tap my lips. Cock my head. Make it look like I'm thinking hard on this very important question. "Hmm. I think my plan is to have sex with my girlfriend as many times as I possibly can before summer. And during summer. And fall. And—"

"Come on, Andy," Emma interrupts.

I cross my arms. "What's wrong with you guys? Why can't you be supportive? I am literally always here for both of you. And now I'm dating the most beautiful and amazing person at Alder, and y'all can't be happy for me? What the hell?"

"I can't believe you trust that girl. She's the most selfish person I've ever met," Emma says.

I take a step toward her, my anger winning out over every stupid little tool in my stupid little anxiety toolbox. Emma fucking Wilson does not get to call Maya selfish. "That is the most hypocritical thing to have ever been spoken."

She rolls her eyes.

"I have had intense feelings for you for *six years*. Six years, Emma. Which you are very aware of, no doubt, and you used me for whatever you needed." I count on my fingers. "An ego boost, the feel of my bare thigh under your hand, the ever-present fact that a woman wants you." I stare into her eyes. "All you do is take what you want and hope that whatever morsels you leave behind is enough to sustain a friendship. Let me ask you, Emma. Now that I don't want you, now that you can't have me, is there much else left between us? If I told you that when I look at you, I feel *nothing*, would you even care to hang out with me anymore?"

She stares, her mouth crescent-moon open.

"You should think about your answer," I say as I make a scene of looking over her body. "Because I feel *nothing* for you, except the deep desire to not have to look at you anymore. Please get out of my room."

She slides off my bed and grabs her phone from my desk. As she brushes by me, she mumbles, "You've changed."

I watch her walk away, and as the door closes behind her, I yell, "You're damn right. Thanks for noticing."

My doors *clunks* into its frame, and our room is quiet. I turn back to Rachel. I'm not mad at her the way I'm mad at Emma—Rachel has never wronged me—but I am still annoyed at her reaction to me and Maya. I feel one-hundred-percent secure in my relationship, but my friends being so worried makes my stomach ache. Like I'm missing something. Like it's too good to be true. I worry my lip as I watch her, my emotions now caught in an awkward depressurization. I may have the bends. Rachel pats the mattress next to her, and I oblige.

After a few awkward moments, Rachel sighs. "She deserved that," she says.

"I know."

"But she didn't call Maya selfish out of nowhere."

I look at her, scared to ask for details. My brain jumps to the least upsetting explanation. "Em is just jealous that all my attention is on someone else. She can't handle it."

Rachel nods slowly. I appreciate her attempt at being gentle. "You may be right. In fact, don't tell her, but I'm sure you're right."

*Phew.* "Thank you."

"She's in the portal, Andy."

"Emma's transferring? Where?" I shake my head, confused. "Why didn't she tell me? And what does this have to do with Maya?"

Rachel winces. Full-on winces. She slaps her hands together and rubs them in her lap, seemingly preparing to deliver a blow. "Emma isn't in the transfer portal. Maya is."

"What? That…that can't be right." *Can it?* My throat tightens, and my eyes prickle with tears. I am completely blindsided, embarrassed to be the last to know, and straight-up angry. This whole school year, Maya and I have been building a program of excellence. We've been building a partnership. Our team is most likely going to regionals, and our personal relationship is just taking off. How is this even possible after our conversation tonight? She was talking about being together next year at Alder. But she wants to leave? Now? Did she know this whole year that she was going to transfer?

Sure. I could jump to a conclusion and assume the worst about the situation, and given how gutted and vulnerable I feel, I want to prepare myself for the worst, and that means assuming the worst. But I can't do that. Being in a relationship means trusting your partner. I need to talk to her. There must be a reason why she hasn't told me about it.

*But she's in the transfer portal.*

What other reason is there?

I'm spiraling.

I guess I was a good tool for her to use on her way out of here. Build up the team together to boost her appeal as a transfer. Katie's words flash through me like a grease fire: *all she cares about is winning and Instagram followers. If she's being nice to you, it's because she's found you useful for one of those things.*

I close my eyes and breathe.

Rachel lays a hand on my wrist. "Andy."

"I just need twenty seconds. Please."

She waits five, then asks, "You okay?"

I look at her. Speechless. I am a tornado. How could I possibly reach in and pull out words to give her?

"I'm sorry, Andy."

I can't stand to see the organ-grinding pity in Rachel's eyes, and I can't make sense of this tonight. I need to sleep on it. Need space. From everyone.

"I'm just going to go to bed. I'm tired. And finals or whatever," I say.

"Of course. Yeah. I'll see you in the morning."

I lie awake for hours, imagining every possible reason why Maya would be transferring and if it's even a possibility that she isn't. I torture myself until I finally fall asleep at quarter to four.

## CHAPTER SEVENTEEN

We have minimal responsibilities after finals. Just a couple of check-ins here and there. I haven't spoken to Maya about the transfer yet. A couple of short texts have been our only interaction. I'm not technically avoiding her. I just haven't gone out of my way to see her this week. And though I haven't *wanted* to see her—because I'm scared to know the truth—we also haven't been forced to be around each other since our date. But I can't keep the distance for much longer. She knows something is off.

*God, that date.* Every time I think about that night, my body wants to implode from all of the opposing signals and chemicals it receives. Dopamine first, then cortisol. Ten face muscles, then six. My heart swells, then breaks. All of the neurons in my brain fire Roman candles at each other instead of neurotransmitters.

It sucks. I can barely sleep more than four hours.

But tomorrow is the selection show for regionals, so regardless, if it's a smile or a frown, dopamine or cortisol, my body will have a solid response because tomorrow, I'll see Maya. And tomorrow, I'll find out what the hell is going on.

The next morning, I wake up to what is now a familiar ache of dread. My temple pulses in beat with my headache, and my eyelids are heavy, my lack of sleep catching up with me. I try my absolute best to reset my attitude. We have all day off until the selection show party on the field tonight, so I take a long shower and treat myself to a decadent breakfast in the dining hall. Part of trying to force myself into a positive mindset means extending that positive energy to Maya.

Me: *Hey. I know I've been MIA this week, but I am really excited to see you tonight. Maybe after the selection show we can take a walk and catch up. I want hear all about how the rest of your finals went.*

I may have typed that text through gritted teeth, but I'm trying to manifest here.

Maya: *Finally. Yes, of course. I miss you so much. Just come to my dorm after. It's a little more intimate than a walk.*

The winky face at the end of her text annoys the shit out of me. She is perfectly happy and clueless while I've had to shoulder all the worry and doubt and exhaustion.

Stop. Just stop.

I know nothing. Everything is going to be okay.

❖

Right center field has morphed into a small movie theater with a projector casting ESPN onto the outfield fence. More pizzas than our team could possibly eat are scattered around the grass like mines, and there are blankets and lawn chairs for lounging. An excited energy buzzes among our team and coaches as we wait for the show to begin. Girls are doing cartwheels and filming TikToks, and I'm just sitting on my blanket trying to act natural.

Maya finishes a silly dance with Kim and Ashlyn, then crouches next to me.

"Hey, there was something in the clubhouse I wanted to show you. Come with me real quick," she says.

I point to the ESPN hosts. "It's about to start. After?"

She grabs my hand and pulls me off the blanket. "It will be quick. I promise, we won't miss it."

We walk in silence through the home dugout, and she turns right when we should turn left to go to the clubhouse. I follow without complaint because I trust her. *I trust her.* I shouldn't have to keep reminding myself of that. We only walk a second longer before we cross behind the concession booth, out of view, and she whips around and pins me against the wood paneling.

"I couldn't wait until tonight," she says. She kisses me like I've just come home from war, and I kiss her like I may never get the chance to kiss Maya Gonzalez ever again. I let my worry go and try to memorize every sensation. Her mouth tastes like pizza, and her body melts into mine. The cheap paneling behind me claws and tugs at my hair.

My favorite part is her hand, firm around the back of my neck, her fingers dragging through my baby hairs, then squeezing me tight. I can't get a word in, which is probably best. She breaks away and pulls me along behind her. "Stop trying to make out with me all night, Foster. We have a selection show to watch." Maya acts completely normal. As if nothing is off. As if she's *not* planning to cut and run on me and the rest of our team at the end of the season. I drop my shoulders when I feel them inching toward my ears and force myself to let go of the worry until we talk later tonight.

We return to our teammates and sit next to each other for the show. The ESPN hosts reveal the thirty-two teams that have automatically made it to regionals and their rankings. Oklahoma is number one—no surprise there—and Alabama is number two. After they announce the host schools for the tournament, they begin to announce the Division I Softball Committee's selections for the remaining thirty-two slots. Paula Wise, one of the hosts and softball *legend*, begins to list the four teams in the Tallahassee regional.

"And as the number three seed for the Tallahassee regional, pitted against the fierce Florida State, we have the Alder University Lions." Our whole team gasps, then jumps around in a mosh pit of hugging and cheering. "Alder U has come up slowly and could be the dark horse of this tournament, Frances." Paula's words fill our hearts, and I grab Maya's hand as a highlight reel of her pitching glows in front of us.

"Absolutely, Paula. And how about that Maya Gonzalez? Those Florida State hitters better say a prayer or two before they meet her in Tallahassee."

"You know, Frances, there have been few pitchers who have caught my eye the way Gonzalez has. Not only does she bring the heat, but her ball movement and placement are impeccable. I can't wait to see what she and the Lions can make happen in this regional."

Everything fades, and the only thing that matters in this moment is her. I pull Maya down and plant a kiss on her cheek. Our outfield is in chaos; no one can see. "I could not be prouder of you, Maya. You deserve it all. Everything Paula Wise just said. Congratulations," I say into her ear.

She pulls back and looks into my eyes. Her face is the most radiant shade of jubilant that I have ever seen. And though celebration erupts around us like a volcano of joy, before she lets the lava take her, she dips her mouth to my ear and says, "This is *our* moment, not mine." She lets me go and zigzags through our team, high-fiving everyone. A whiplash of emotions paralyzes me as I watch her. I can't fully let go of the dread and potential hurt, but I miss her so much. It's only been a week, but I miss feeling one-hundred-percent about us.

When the show wraps up, I stand in front of my teammates and coaches. "Congratulations," I yell. And everyone cheers. "We've worked so hard to get here, but we won't stop at regionals, and we won't stop at super regionals. We won't stop until we're playing the final game of the World Series." I wait for the hollering to die down to continue. "I think I speak for the whole team when I say, thank you, Coach Williams, Coach Clayton, and the rest of the coaching staff. Thank you for believing in us and helping us to reach this point." Coach Clay points at me and winks. I find Maya on the edge of the team next to Katie. "And one more thing, Maya. Thank you for pushing us as a team and for being the fierce spirit that we need. Let's kick some butt!"

After the show, we all pitch in to clean up. The coaches bail early on us, and Maya has to go meet someone, so Katie volunteers to stay late and lock up the clubhouse with me. I relish every moment of the being in the clubhouse after hours, the peacefulness of it. I slide the leftover pizzas into the fridge.

"Want to have one more slice with me?" I ask Katie before I close the door.

She rips two paper towels from the roll and sits at one of the round tables. "Hell, yeah. I miss you, bud."

A little pang of guilt hits me in the belly. When my phone rings loudly in my pocket, the pang doubles to the point of me being relieved that my appendix is on the other side of my body.

"Who's calling?"

"It's just my mom calling to congratulate us for regionals. I've been bad at keeping in touch with them lately. It's been a whirlwind. You know, finals…"

Katie wipes at a spot of pizza sauce on her mouth. "Mm-hmm. And Maya."

I almost choke on a stringy bit of mozzarella in the back of my throat. Not only do I not want the team to find out until after the postseason, but at this point, I have no idea if there will be a relationship to tell them about. Or if she'll be gone. At UGA, I assume.

I clear my throat. "What about Maya?"

"Relax, Andy. I know you guys are together, and I really don't care. Y'all keep it tight and super professional around the team, and that's all that matters. And your happiness, obviously."

"Oh. Okay. Um, how did you know?" Her response is pretty ideal. If that's how everyone will feel about two teammates getting together, then there'll be nothing to worry about.

"Well, you guys have been inseparable, and not in the *forced together* kind of way like last semester. Also, I heard Kim gossiping with Taylor about how she thinks Maya and Jeremy broke up."

"What made her think that?" I ask.

"Because he's transferring."

I put down my slice of pizza, wipe my hands, and take a giant gulp of air that surprises me. "He's transferring, huh? That's a big move. Do you know where?"

"Yeah. UGA. He'll probably ride the bench, but I guess it's more important to him to say that he plays in the SEC than to actually play. Our baseball team is pretty good this year. I mean, not as good as we are, but good enough to contend. Weird decision, in my opinion." She shrugs.

The pizza in my stomach sours, and my vision narrows on a grease spot soaked through my paper towel. *They're transferring to UGA together.* Maya and Jeremy had this planned all along. I was just a means to an end and a fun romp in the woods. An athlete doesn't just casually enter the transfer portal. It's a decision that holds weighty consequences. Once they put their name in the portal, they have to be prepared to surrender their scholarship at the end of the semester and lose their spot on the team, their coaches being absolved of their commitment to the athlete.

"You okay? It's a good thing, right?" she asks.

I nod.

"Her ex will be out of the picture. What am I missing? Why do you look like I just told you Santa isn't real?"

A battle rattles through my brain. Do I lie to Katie again? I really don't want to break Maya's trust or jeopardize the harmony that our team has finally achieved. If word gets out that Maya is bailing on us next year for Georgia, then the postseason will be a mess. But I also feel like I'm going to explode. I need a friend to talk to, and Rachel and Emma aren't an option right now. Katie looks at me with genuine concern. It's decided.

"Because you just told me Santa isn't real."

Her head falls back, and she lets out a yelp of laughter. "Shoot, Andy. I knew you weren't the most 'experienced' of the bunch, but there comes a time in everyone's life when they must let go of the man in red. You know, the tooth fairy isn't real either."

I laugh and shake my head. "Oh, shut up."

"And the Easter bunny…"

"Okay, I get it. I get it." I look at my plate.

"What's really going on?" she asks.

"Katie, you have to swear not to tell anyone. I really don't want to mess with the team's groove. Especially right before regionals."

She pushes her pizza aside and gives me her full attention. No more jokes. "Of course. I'll always put the team first."

I blow out a breath and spill. "Maya is in the transfer portal."

Katie's brows shoot for the sky, and she slaps the table. "What. The. Fuck. What the actual fucking fuck?"

"I'm really trying not to jump to conclusions before I talk to her, but now that I know Jeremy is transferring to UGA, it's really hard not to assume that they're going together. Especially since Georgia is the one that got away for Maya." What other school would she risk everything for? It's the only place she wanted to go.

"Wow."

"That's all you have for me? Wow?"

She rubs her hands together. "I'm digesting the information. Patience please."

My leg bounces under the table as I wait to hear an outsider's prospective of what the hell is going on here. Her opinion means a lot to me, and I don't think Katie is one for exaggeration. Her take will be a solid one.

"Did she tell you that she is in the portal, or did you find out somehow?"

"Rachel and Emma told me. They overheard their coaches chatting about it."

"And have y'all talked about next year at all?"

I sigh in exasperation. "All the time. And every time we talk about it, it involves me and her together *at Alder*. The girl even wanted to room together."

"So you were weirded out to hear that she's in the portal, and when I told you about Jeremy, your first thought was that they have a plan to leave for UGA together. Do I have that right?"

"I mean, yeah." The thought sounds absurd when I hear it aloud. "But I'm trying not to rush to any conclusions. I'm going to go talk to her after this."

Getting clarity in this situation scares the hell out of me. Sure, at the end of the day, I want to know the truth, but right now, Maya is still mine. Once I walk into her dorm room and we talk things over, I don't know what will happen. Heads or tails...

"Look, I'm not going to sugarcoat it. It's pretty shady that they're both in the portal. Especially since she seemingly dated him right up until—maybe even a little during—getting with you." She points her pizza crust at me, then drops it again. "But it also doesn't really add up. If it was their plan all along to run away together, why would she even get with you? No offense, but that just seems weird. If she was happy with J, why break up with him?"

I shake my head. "I don't know. Maybe she really likes us both, and it's just which school she'd rather go to that's the determining factor."

She shrugs. "Maybe. Reckon you'd better go find out."

"Yeah. Thanks for the help."

We throw away our trash, lock up the clubhouse, and walk to the athletic dorms. Katie drops me off at Maya's dorm and wishes me luck.

A girl I recognize from the track-and-field team lets me into Carter Hall, and I walk to Maya's room. As I approach her door, I see that it's open, the dead bolt blocking the door from shutting in its frame. Normal enough; everyone does that when they're feeling social. It's code for *pop in and say hi.*

I knock once as I push open the door. I freeze, taking a snapshot of what I just walked in on.

Maya and Jeremy stand in the middle of her room. His hands are on her hips. Her fingers stroke behind his neck, and I want to fucking die. They stare into each other's eyes...until they whip their heads around to me, the intruder. She drops her hand and turns ketchup red.

"Andy..."

She steps out of his arms, and he throws his head back, letting out a baleful laugh. A laugh that makes me take a small step backward. "Of course it's fucking Andy. For Christ's sake, can you please do everyone a favor and just disappear?"

Maya looks at me, eyes wide, shoulders tight like a loaded spring. "Don't go. Andy, I can explain." She turns back to Jeremy. "You need to leave right now."

They argue with each other in a slurry of profanities as I fade in and out of the moment, trying desperately to grab on to something.

But all I come up with is the snapshot of them holding each other. Just now. Right in front of me. And it all hits me.

*She chooses him.*

My phone blares in my pocket, drawing everyone's attention, and I snatch it up like it's a lifeline.

"Andrea," Maya says again.

I'm not sure why she keeps saying my name. What does she want from me? *Mom* lights up on my home screen, and I lift it to show Maya, as if I'm bound by the universe to answer this call. As if there is no other thing in the world more important than listening to my mom tell me how proud she is of us. *Regionals!*

I swipe up on my screen and press the phone to my ear.

"Andrea. Honey." Her tone is dark and clipped. My world snaps back into sharp focus. Something is seriously wrong. I turn away from the stupid implosion happening in front of me and yank out my opposite hearing aid so I can zone in on my call.

"Mom, what's wrong?"

"Your dad—"

"What happened?"

"Everything is okay, but he's in the hospital. He's not able to hold down any food right now, and he's been running a high fever for four days."

"Is it the new medicine? Why is this happening now?"

"They're trying to figure that out. Listen, Dr. Anderson is walking into the room. I'll call you back as soon as we learn more, okay? I love you."

"I love you."

With all the adrenaline in my blood, it's easier and more satisfying to rip my other hearing aid out to make it even. But I'm so scattered in the moment that I reach for my ear and suck in a sharp breath at the feedback I just gave myself. "Shit." I shove them in opposite pockets, not bothering to turn them off.

Maya's hand falls on my shoulder, and I swear to God, I think I hear her say my name again. I shirk out from under her. Then, all of the chemicals in my body just stop…and I'm suddenly exhausted.

"I can't," I say.

"You can't what? Is everything okay? What's happening with your mom?"

"I can't handle whatever this is. Not tonight."

"Andrea."

One more flash of anger hits me. "Stop. Stop saying my name like that. I have to go."

Does she think I'm just going to fall into her arms and tell her everything my mom just said? Fat chance. I can't deal with Maya *and* my dad. And after witnessing that sickening show, I choose to focus on my dad. I turn on a heel and bail.

## CHAPTER EIGHTEEN

I don't sleep.

The only positive thing I've found in this terrible pit of worry and insomnia the last two days is that, oddly enough, I'm not suffering from any panic attacks. Maybe because I've already fallen into the depths, and anxiety attacks hit when I'm merely peeking over the ledge. It's more like a steady depression.

Maybe I'm not panicky because I know my dad is going to die. And I've always known this. Only back then, I didn't have a timeline. It was a distant threat that felt more like a fable, like how one day the sun will explode, or all the animals on Earth will gradually suffocate with the changing of our atmosphere. So far away that it almost feels fake. But it's not fake; it's fate. One day, some sorry sons-of-bitches are going to get exploded by the sun or suffocate slowly.

And my dad will die before I turn twenty-one.

I know this because I researched it. I'm not a child, yet my mom still struggles to give it to me straight. "There's no telling how long. He could make it another ten years. We just don't know, honey." It's bullshit. There *is* telling how long. My father just turned sixty, and he's in the hospital recovering from pneumonia that he got from aspirating his food. He aspirated his food because he has developed dysphagia, which causes difficulties swallowing. It can be a side effect of MS. They inserted a feeding tube through his abdomen, so he no longer has to chew and swallow.

But the thing about the feeding tube is that for older patients with MS, once they're on one, they most likely die within two years. The possibility of my dad making it to ten…well, sorry, Mom, but it's around five percent.

I ignore everyone in my life except for my parents. People die all the time, and maybe I'm being a little dramatic, but I'm really fucking sad. He's not even dead, and I'm already mourning him. Mourning the fact that he probably won't see me graduate, will never see me play another softball game, or be at my wedding. The fact that this man has suffered for so long just to die young. I'm processing these things. And I need space to do it.

I called Coach Clayton this morning and told him I couldn't make it to practice today. It's just too much, the stuff with my dad, and I can't face Maya right now. He gave me some old-guy bullshit about pushing through even if you're sick until I told him that I'm not sick. In fact, it's a mental-health day. I could literally feel his gears grinding through the phone. After what I assume was an intense internal debate, he wished me well and told me he'd see me tomorrow for our solo meetings. Coaches want to meet with each of us individually before the tournament starts in five days.

Rachel is home for two weeks until their basketball camp starts, but Emma is still on campus for a few more days. I've considered texting her. Even though we didn't leave things in a great place, I'm craving the comfort of someone who knows my family—knows my dad—beyond a couple of random meetups. But I don't want to have to deal with the argument we had in order to receive the comfort I want. Katie has texted to check on me but respected my request for space when I asked for it. Maya has texted consistently since I walked in on her and Jeremy. She's blowing me up.

My phone vibrates. It's her: *I know you don't want to see me right now or talk to me. I just wanted to let you know I can't stop thinking about you. I hope you're okay. Can I please come see you today?*

Me: *I just don't have the space for us right now.*

Maya: *Nothing happened with him. We were just talking. He needed closure.*

I don't respond. Instead, I force myself to get dressed and try to eat some food in the dining hall. Just like everything else in my life, I mentally set a time limit for my wallowing: the rest of the day, that's all I'll allow myself. Tomorrow, I will wake up and resume being a human in this world.

❖

The next morning, I try to fulfill my promise to myself. I text Coach that all is well, and I will be at my meeting this afternoon. Campus is quiet now that most of the students have gone home for summer vacation, and I take a walk through the old buildings, harvesting peace from my adoration of them. My dad is sick, and I can't control that. Obsessing over the statistics of his mortal timeline will not do me or my family any favors. As of this moment, he is alive. That is our current reality, and instead of mourning him, I need to take advantage of whatever time is left with him.

"Hey, Dad. How are you doing today?"

"Andy"—he takes a long, dry swallow—"Pandy. My girl." His words wobble, but he begins speech therapy today. "I'm okay. Don't be worrying about me."

"Hah. Easier said than done. I'll try to pick something else to worry about."

"Regionals. That's very exciting. We're so proud of you." He pivots the conversation to greener pastures.

"Yeah, it's great..." The melancholy slips into my words. I can't help it. I want him to hear it and ask me what's wrong because even in his fragile state, I want to unload everything on him. I want to burden him with my worries and make him take care of me. Funny how after all these years of trying so hard to be the easiest child possible, when my father is at his most vulnerable, all I want to do is talk about myself. All I want to do is tell him about the girl who is currently breaking my heart.

"Well, I can't wait to watch my favorite team. I'm going to pass you to your mom, now. Love you."

My mom and I catch up briefly before we're interrupted by a nurse coming to take my dad's blood, and I'm left hollowed out. I stop walking and look around. The quiet of campus feels eerie now instead of peaceful, and I walk back to Wilder feeling oppressively alone.

I have never felt so lonely.

❖

"What are—"

Emma wraps her arms around me and pulls me into her the instant I walk into my room.

"Emma, I'm fine." But I'm not fine, and the sharp crack in my voice punctuates that very obvious fact. Her shoulder is wet from my tears before I realize I'm crying. I grab her sweatshirt for dear life and sob. She holds me tight as I drench her clean clothes with my uncontrollable mucus and tears.

"I got you," she says against my hair.

I pull away from her and rub my swollen face into my shirt. "How did you know I needed you?" I ask through hiccupping gasps of air.

"I'd been wanting to come talk to you after our fight, then your mom called and updated me on what's been going on with your dad. I'm so sorry, Andy." I nod and sniffle. "I'm not sure where you're at with the Maya situation, but I thought you could use a friend. You might have refused to see me if I asked to come over, so I just showed up. And you never lock your door..." She shrugs. "Here I am."

I burry my face in her shoulder again. Sometimes, words aren't necessary. And though I feel like this could be one of those moments, I want to apologize.

"I'm sorry." My words muffle against the damp cotton of her sweatshirt.

"Me, too. I honestly wanted it all to explode in your face but not like this."

I step away from her. "What?"

"I'm trying to be as honest as possible here. It's ugly, but it's the truth. I was so jealous, I couldn't stand to even be in the same room as you two. And when I had to be, like at dinner with Alex Squared, I could barely look at you."

"But you don't want me..."

She shakes her head. "Seeing you with someone else is driving me crazy. You gave me a lot, and I was totally happy being single and settling for hookups because I had you. I didn't want to be tied down, and I didn't want to risk our friendship by trying to pursue you. I guess that amounted to using your love without giving much back." She shudders as if she's just now realizing how shitty she was to me. "I didn't understand that I was using you until I lost you to Maya." She swallows hard.

I drum my fingers on my thigh and digest her words. "I don't understand. Are you saying you have feelings for me?"

She sighs and drops onto my bed. "Of course I have feelings for you, Andy. All you seem to focus on from our past is that we never actually got together. But don't you remember me always begging to hang out with you? Don't you remember talking for hours at that little park by the Chattahoochee while we ate Sour Patch Kids until our mouths turned raw? It felt like a gray area of flirting and touching between us, but we always landed safely back in the friend zone." She studies me. "You never made a move."

I hold up my arms. "Emma. You knew."

"You're trying to tell me that you didn't?"

I open my mouth to speak, but I'm stumped. Am I as culpable as Emma for our missed romance?

"Look, all I'm saying is that it's painful to lose the possibility of you. I don't know if it would be a giant disaster if we tried a relationship for real, but I hate losing the chance. She sighs. "I kind of always thought it would be us in the end."

I cross my arms and sit next to her. This is all I've ever wanted to hear her say. That she hasn't just been leading me on all these years but is stuck in the same hesitation as me. Scared to ruin a friendship. It's hard not to wonder about what would have happened for me and Emma if we hadn't missed our opportunity to be together. But it doesn't matter anymore because I'm with Maya. *I think.*

"Where does this leave us now? I value our friendship, and I want it back. Even if it looks a little bit different than it used to," I say.

I see pain etched in her face as she chews her lip. It looks as if she's trying to clear a mental hurdle. I hope she can move past it because I miss her, but I can't be involved with a friend who pines for me. That's not fair to Emma, and it's not fair to Maya. She looks at me and smiles. "I think it leaves us with a brand-new friendship. A healthier one. If you'll still have me, that is."

I pull her in for a quick hug, and when I release her, I see a grimace hidden under her grin. I choose to trust her words instead of her body language. "I could use a friend like that."

As I fill Emma in on everything that has been going on with my dad, I can feel my body begin to loosen and let go of some of the stress I've been clenching lately. Now I have someone to put it on. Emma sits quietly, nodding along as she listens to the words gushing from my mouth.

"And what about you and Maya? Have you cleared things up?" she asks when we finish talking about my dad.

I fall back on my mattress in a huff. "That's the other thing that's been going on. I found out Jeremy is also in the transfer portal. He's going to UGA."

Emma's back hits my mattress next to me. "Oh."

"Yeah."

"That's where she wanted to go originally, right?"

"Exactly. I went to Carter to talk to her about it. Her door was cracked, and when I opened it all the way, Jeremy and her were holding each other." I drop my hand over my eyes.

"Like a hug?"

"Yeah, but there was like disgusting gazing into each other's eyes, and his hands were on her hips, and her hand was gripping the back of his neck. It felt really inappropriate."

Emma groans. "Ew. What happened? What'd you say?"

"Maya snapped out of it and told him to leave. He freaked out, and then my mom called to tell me my dad is in the hospital. I answered my phone in front of them. Then I told Maya I couldn't deal with this right now and left. That's the last time I've seen her, but we have individual meetings with the coaching staff tonight, so I'll most likely see her."

"It's probably not how it looked. I know what I said, but honestly, it was mostly out of jealousy. I can't deny the chemistry between you guys. You should give her the benefit of doubt."

"I know. I'm trying. I just can't believe she's in the portal. That's a decision only *she* could make and a decision that had to have been made in the last couple months."

"Benefit of doubt."

I groan. "Fine."

After Emma leaves, I text Maya: *When is your meeting tonight?*

Maya: *Hey! I'm so happy to hear from you. It's at six thirty. When's yours?*

Me: *Seven. Maybe we can chat between our meetings.*

Maya: *Of course, but it's not much time. We could grab dinner together when you finish yours.*

Me: *Maybe. Let's just see how it goes, okay?*

Maya: *Yeah. Okay.*

I already feel way too vulnerable just from texting her. I take a deep breath, trying to calm the anxiety bubbling up my esophagus. Knowing I have to talk to Maya tonight floods my system with cortisol and pushes me into fight-or-flight mode, but there's no running from this. I have to face her.

## CHAPTER NINETEEN

My phone reads six forty-five. I tug my backpack straps until I feel like someone is holding me as I pace outside the clubhouse waiting for Maya to come out of her meeting.

"Andy." Maya walks out of the clubhouse and wraps me in a tight hug. I drop my arms to my sides and stiffen in her embrace.

"Hey," I say.

Her eyebrows scrunch in concern, and she grabs my hand. "Come on. Let's go talk."

She leads me around the back of the clubhouse to the bench where we had our big fight last semester. We both sit and take a moment to gather our thoughts.

She turns her face to the sun, and it bathes her skin in a golden bath. Then she turns to me. "That night—"

"His hands were on your hips." I look at her in disbelief. No matter what excuse she was about to throw at me, the way they were touching was *unacceptable*. She doesn't respond. "Do you know how that felt for me to walk in on? And you completely reciprocated the intimacy. You were stroking his damn neck, Maya."

She lays her hand on my knee and ducks her head to see past the wall of hair that has fallen in front of my eyes. "How you feel is completely valid."

I swing my knee away from her touch. "Don't give me that appeasing therapist bullshit." My anger catches me off guard, but I double down. "Can you imagine opening my door to find me and Emma holding each other like that?"

"I mean, I kind of have."

"That is completely different, and you know it. We weren't in a relationship at that point. But you were..."

She takes a deep breath. "He asked if we could talk after the selection show. When I broke up with him at Corey's party, it was too fast. I messed it up. I was just desperate to do the right thing, especially after we kissed, that I didn't give Jeremy what he deserved from me in that moment. Which was the time to have a real conversation and give him closure."

"I know he's transferring to UGA, Maya."

She looks at me, confused. "Well, yeah. He's been planning on that all year. That embrace you walked in on was a good-bye. We talked, and I told him the truth about everything. That's why he got so angry to see you. He blames losing me on you." She takes another deep breath. "And since the boys didn't make regionals this year, he was going home to Birmingham the next day. We were saying good-bye forever."

I squint against the falling sun, trying to stare into her eyes. "Forever, huh?"

She tilts her head to one side. "Yes."

"I know you're in the transfer portal. You're going with him to Georgia, aren't you? Why are you lying to me right now?" My voice rises with the exasperation building in my chest.

She runs a hand through her hair. "How did you find out about that?"

I laugh into my hands and rub my face. "So it is true. Wow. I never thought you would hurt me this way."

"What? I'm not transferring, Andy."

I check my phone and stand. "Then why are you in the portal, May? And why is your boyfriend going to your dream school next year?" I shake my head. "You probably entered it when we were just getting together."

"My boyfriend, huh? Nice, Foster." I can practically see the armor covering her like a Power Ranger.

"I have to go to my meeting."

I turn away from her silence and walk to the front of the clubhouse. Coach Williams and Coach Clayton welcome me into the office. I sit in the chair opposite them and begin to fidget. Every part of my life is beginning to unravel around me, and I'm starting to feel like this meeting might go the same way.

"Andy, thanks for joining us," Coach Williams says.

"Yeah. Of course."

"We were sorry to hear about the developments with your father," Coach Clay says.

I stare at him. I never told him what was going on with my dad. He must sense my confusion. "I asked Katie if you were okay yesterday, and she gave us the highlights," he says.

I nod. I did tell Katie what was going on when she texted to check in.

He clears his throat. "Anyway, let's talk softball. Coach Williams and I are extremely happy with your performance on and off the field this semester. You've worked hard to develop your arm, and the results were clear in your throw-outs." He looks at the statistics printout on his clipboard. "And you raised your batting average to .365. Very impressive."

"Thank you."

Coach Williams leans on the desk. "We wanted to touch base before we head into the postseason and see where everyone is at. How do you feel like our team did this year? And do you have any concerns that you want to address before we head to Tallahassee?"

I look at Coach Williams and realize that I am wildly unprepared for this meeting. I don't even know what I'm going to say when I open my mouth to speak. "Um, I think we've grown a lot this year and are in a strong position heading into regionals." They nod along. "I guess my only concern is my father's health. He's stable right now and could remain stable for a long time. But things could also turn for the worse pretty quickly. I just want to be clear that he will be my priority if things go badly."

"We completely understand, and if the day comes when you need to go handle your family business, we'll be here, ready to work through that with you. Whether that's in the middle of the World Series or next year during the off-season," Coach Williams says.

I sigh in relief.

"Let's just keep our communication open. We not only have high hopes for you in this postseason but also for next year," Coach Clay says.

"Thanks, Coach. For everything. I'm really excited to see where this program can go."

Coach Clay shoots a nervous glance to Coach Williams. *What is happening?* "Yes. It's very exciting times for Alder softball," she says. She swallows before she continues. "Speaking of next year, Andy, there is one other thing we wanted to talk about."

I scratch at the scar tissue—gained from more wipeouts than I can count—on my knee. "Okay," I say. This must be where they break it to me that I'm losing my star pitcher, and my girlfriend, to the Bulldogs and Jeremy.

"It has come to our attention that you and Maya are involved in a relationship that extends past teammates or friendship," she says.

My whole body caves in on itself and combusts into flames of terror. I can't help but feel like I'm in deep shit. Not only that, but I probably don't even have a relationship to talk about at this point. I'm pretty sure I ruined everything. I stay silent, not sure in which direction I should take the conversation. Surely the red in my face speaks for itself. My fingers are trembling, for Christ's sake.

"It's okay, Andy. We just want to address it and make sure everyone is on the same page about it. In our minds, as long as you two keep it professional, nothing has to change next year," Coach Clayton says.

I go to speak, then shake my head. "Next year?"

They look at each other in confusion. "Well, yeah. Unless you two break up before then," Coach Clay says, his hands up in question. Coach Williams cringes. Everyone is uncomfortable.

"Um. It's just that...isn't Maya in the transfer portal?" This is information the coaches have access to. It should come as no surprise to them.

"Well, yes—"

"So won't she be at UGA next year?"

"No," Coach Williams says. "I'll let her explain the details, but she declined their offer. Scholarship and all."

My mouth cracks open, but I don't speak. Coach Clayton jumps in. "She didn't want to enter the portal, but she'd had the goal of transferring to UGA since we signed her, so we told her she needed to. Just to keep her options open. We thought maybe she was making a brash decision to stay at Alder because of alternate reasons." He looks pointedly at me. "Not to say we aren't ecstatic to keep her. We just wanted to protect her interests."

"She made us promise to save her spot on the team and her scholarship if she entered the portal," Coach Williams adds.

"I don't understand. She never wanted to transfer?" I ask.

"She came to us in December and told us her goals had changed. And that's when we started to notice her relationship with you change. It's our job to pay attention," Coach Clay says.

I've made a giant fucking mistake.

"We don't know exactly why she doesn't want to go to UGA. We'll leave that for you to discuss with her."

"So you guys were trying to do everything you could to get our best player to transfer?" I ask. It sounds like a challenge, but I'm just trying to catch up. "And you enlisted me to help?"

"First of all, Maya settling down and developing her skills was a benefit to our team no matter what she decided to do about the transfer portal. And, yes, we believed you could help her achieve her full potential, which you did. Second of all, I don't care how competitive the world of sports is, our primary responsibility is to honor our student athletes. That means helping them get to wherever they want to go, even if Alder is just a stepping-stone," he says.

"Are you okay, Andy?" Coach Williams asks.

I nod. "Yeah. I'm sorry. I just assumed she was leaving when I heard she was in the portal. But I was wrong. Clearly."

"How did you hear about that anyway?" Coach Clay asks.

"My friends on the basketball team overheard their coaches talking about it."

He bites his lip and shakes his head. "We have got to stop inviting Carson to get drinks with us. That guy can't keep his mouth shut about anything."

"Um. Is there anything else you guys wanted to talk about? It's time for your next meeting." I nod to the clock on the wall.

"That's it, kid. Keep doing what you're doing," he says.

"And maybe go talk to Maya," Coach Williams adds with a wink.

I stand and shoulder my backpack. "Thank you both." I clear my throat. "For uh...for everything."

"Of course. Send Ashlyn in if you see her on your way out."

"Sure thing."

There's no sign of Ashlyn as I leave the clubhouse. I quicken my pace to a speed walk as I pass the batting cages, hoping Maya hasn't left yet. The possibility that she's still sitting on that bench after how I treated her is low but not zero. I hit the door with such momentum that my body slams into it a second before my hands find the crash bar to open it. My body bounces off the door in a loud *thwack*, and I'm momentarily stunned at my failure to operate my being.

I hear a quiet knock on the other side of the door, which is technically an emergency exit and locked to the outside.

"Everything okay in there?" I hear Maya's muffled question.

I crack it open slowly so it doesn't hit my girlfriend in the face. When I see that she's clear of its radius, I swing it wide. One of Maya's brows stands slightly taller than the other, as if she's not sure if I'm going to yell at her or kiss her. I launch myself into her arms, and she stumbles backward, receiving me with a thud. Her hands immediately put me at ease, one wrapped tightly around my waist and the other stroking my hair.

"I'm so sorry, Maya. I didn't trust you, and I am so sorry." My nose instantly clogs with mucus, and tears begin to gather. I've cried more in this past week than I have in my entire life.

"I know. I know. It's okay," she whispers, trying to soothe me.

"I assumed the worst about you, and...and my dad is dying." As the mucus and tear-coated words leave my mouth, the truth of the statement hits me in a new way, a harder way. As if I was waiting to discover the exact shape and depth of this pain until I was in a safe space. Until I was in Maya's arms. My chest tightens between painful heaves, and she absorbs it all.

"Let's get you home. Can I walk you?"

I nod against her chest before stepping out of her warmth and wiping my swollen face with my shirt. She leans in and kisses my gross cheek at the same time that Ashlyn walks through the emergency exit with a vape in her hand. Maya slowly pulls away from me.

Ashlyn takes a hit and shrugs, the vapor twisting from her nose and mouth like she's a dragon. "All right. I guess I could see this working out." She waves a finger at us, seemingly not noticing that I've been crying.

"Um. Thanks, girl," Maya says. "We're going to get out of here. See you tomorrow."

"See y'all."

We walk wordlessly across the quad to Wilder Hall. The sun falls behind the mountains, and the summer air is silky and fresh against my raw face. Maya holds my hand, her grip firm and unwavering. Unlike me. I wavered *hard*. I try to tame the wild shame that curls around my throat.

Maya squeezes my hand and drops it when we arrive at my dorm.

"Why don't you go take a moment for yourself. Have dinner, chill, and I'll come by around nine. We can talk then," she says.

My stomach drops as I trade the shame for worry. I know she loves me, but will she be able to forgive me? "Okay. Yeah, let's do that."

She raises an eyebrow at my expression. "You and I"—she pops another small kiss to my cheek—"we're still us. I don't want you to be worrying about that. Okay?"

I nod and wipe at my bleary eyes. "Okay."

## CHAPTER TWENTY

D o you have your key?" Maya asks.
I shake the dead bolt hanging from the fence. "No. I didn't think we'd end up at the field."

"Well, I guess fence jumping is just a thing we do on our dates now." She squeezes my hand. "I promise to take you on a real date one day. If you can hang with me through the breaking and entering, there are fancy dinners in our future."

This is the second time she has mentioned our future together on this walk from my dorm to our softball field. The part of my brain that thought I jeopardized our relationship by making the wrong assumptions about her relaxes a little each time. I've wiped my tears, showered, and fed myself since Maya dropped me off at my dorm earlier, and I feel a thousand times better. I drop her hand and curl my fingers around the chain link. "I don't need a fancy restaurant." I catapult over the top of the fence, and for the split second that I'm flying, I feel completely invincible. I land in a squat and straighten up to look at Maya. "Just need some grass stains and you."

She smiles underneath the faded glow of the remote streetlamps and jumps over to join me on the field. Her hand finds mine again, and we stroll toward the outfield, the crisp green grass of it softly glowing under the moonlight. "Our field looks good like this," I say.

She spins to soak in the place at night but ends up just looking at me. The trees rustle in the summer breeze as she wraps her arms around me and pulls me into her. I tilt my head up to look into her eyes, and she kisses me. Her lips are gentle on mine, but when I peek at her face, her eyes are squeezed shut with such force that crow's feet ripple from their corners.

I pull back. "What's wrong?"

She tugs me down to sit next to her in the soft grass of center field. "Nothing is wrong."

"I peeked at you when we were kissing. You looked pained."

She picks at the grass, her stare focused on home plate in the distance. "I'm just so relieved I didn't lose you." She looks at me, her eyes still reflecting some of that pain. "I know what you saw between Jeremy and I was completely inappropriate, and on top of that, you were dealing with the news of your dad. But just so you know, I was a fucking mess after you left my room that night." She shakes her head. "Not only did I possibly ruin our relationship, but I couldn't be there for the person I care about most in this world, and that fact rotted me hollow." She strokes my cheek with a tenderness that makes my teeth ache. "So to be here with you means *everything* to me. When I kissed you, I guess I needed a place to put all my emotion, so I squeezed my eyes shut to save your lips from getting crushed."

She grins and drops her hand to my thigh.

"I'm not so passionless, you know," I say.

She tilts her head. "What do you mean?"

"I understand we're human, and that things are rarely so cut and dry. When you broke up with Jeremy, sure, you drew a line between the two of you, but that doesn't mean that the love you shared and the respect you have for one another just vanishes. Things don't always stay where they're supposed to. Things bleed." I take a moment to gather the rest of this thought before I lose the thread completely. "And I think it's normal that all the love you guys shared bled through while you were saying good-bye."

She nods along with my thoughts. "That's generous of you."

"The reason I so quickly jumped to the worst possible scenario— even though I was trying desperately not to—was because Emma and Rachel overheard their coaches talking about how you were in the transfer portal."

She drops her head back and groans at the stars.

"Then, Katie casually tells me that Jeremy is transferring to UGA," I add.

"Oh no." Her head falls to her chest.

"Yeah. I was operating under a lot of misinformation when I walked in on you guys hugging. Then my mom called, and I think I used my dad as an excuse to avoid you."

"That must have been so confusing for you." She pulls my hand into her lap and strokes my palm. "They made me enter the portal. Coach Clay and Coach Williams. I told them I wasn't interested in transferring anymore, but they wanted me to have the option in case I changed my mind."

I nod. "Yeah. They told me in my meeting. They kind of insinuated that you didn't want to transfer because of me and that they made you enter the portal in case we didn't work out." She chuckles into the sap-soaked air. My blood pressure raises at the thought that I may have held Maya back from something she really wanted. That's the complete opposite of what I want for her. "Did you stay because of me? Because I want you to have everything you want from this life, Maya. If that's transferring to UGA, you need to go. Please."

She takes a deep breath. "That was always my goal, yeah. But things were different then. I'm not going to sit here and say that falling in love with you had nothing to do with my decision to stay at Alder. Because it did. How could it not?"

"I don't—"

She holds up a hand to quiet me. "Things bleed, Andy. But besides our relationship, we built something special here together, and it's this team. If I had to bet on who will go further in the postseason between UGA and Alder, I'd bet on us. Hands down. Every time. My goal is to win the World Series one day, and I believe I have a better shot at that being a Lion than being a Bulldog. So let's see…" She scrunches her face and pretends to count on her fingers. "That adds up to absolutely zero reasons to transfer."

I spring from my spot and push her back into the cool grass. I duck my head like I'm going to kiss her and pull up. She groans in protest, but I just stare at her.

"I hope we make it. It just feels too good to be true, you know? It almost feels impossible that we could last forever."

She sits up and reaches behind her neck to unclasp her gold chain. I hold my breath as she reaches behind me, knuckles skimming my neck, and fastens it around my neck. The St. Rita medallion feels warm against my chest, as if all of Maya's power and strength and passion are being transferred into my heart. She considers her chain on my neck and smiles.

"Maya, I can't accept this. It's yours. Didn't your parents give it to you or something?"

She shakes her head. "I bought it for myself."

"Of course you did." I grin.

"The thing about *forever* is that it's a choice we make. We have the power to decide we'll be together forever. And for the things that are out of our control, it will take a little luck, a little faith." She fingers the warm medallion on my chest. "A little bit of the impossible."

I press my lips to hers. "You know, I looked up St. Rita," I say, medallion in hand.

"Oh yeah?"

"Yeah. You didn't mention that she's also the patron saint of baseball."

She shrugs. "That's only because of a movie. Besides, I prefer softball."

"Bet you can't hit off me," I say in my best impersonation of Kevin.

She giggles in confusion. "What?"

I stand and pull her up. "I'm an All-American. And a boy. No way you can hit off me." I tug her along to the infield.

"Andy, what are you—"

I stand on the pitching mound and direct her to the batter's box. I toss an imaginary ball in the air then focus as if I'm receiving my pitch call from the catcher.

Maya breaks into a huge grin and points to the outfield. "I'm taking it to left center for a double," she calls.

"Calling your shot, huh? Okay, okay. We'll see about that."

I make a slow, exaggerated pitching motion, and Maya swings away.

"*Pop*," she yells, and I track the imaginary ball in the sky while she trots to first. When she rounds the base, I call for my ghost centerfielder to throw me the ball. I catch it and jog to pretend tag her out.

"I'm going to get you, Gonzalez." Coaches may kill me for kicking up the dirt of our perfectly raked field, but the sounds of Maya laughing as I chase her to third base make it completely worth it.

"In your dreams, Foster," she calls over her shoulder as she approaches home.

I catch up to her, wrap my arms around her waist, and pull her down to the dirt with me.

"Our clothes are ruined," I say as we roll around in the amber plumes.

She sits up and wipes the loose dirt from her old T-shirt. "Yeah, but you saved an in-the-park home run. Totally worth it. Plus, I've always wanted to make out with a girl on home plate. A hot catcher, maybe." She pushes me back into the dirt and rolls on top of me to show me just what I've been missing out on with this sexy home-plate fantasy.

After my hair is at its dirt-holding capacity, we do our best to shake off the rest of the dust and climb back over the fence. Maya holds my hand as she walks me back to Wilder. She checks her phone a couple of times and replies to some texts.

"Ashlyn was so funny earlier," she says.

I stutter step to avoid a cockroach crossing the stone path. "Yeah. I guess us being together isn't that big of a deal to people. Coaches didn't seem to be concerned."

"Maybe we should just tell everyone. Now that Ashlyn knows, it feels weird to keep it from the rest of the team." She taps another quick message on her phone.

I think about how desperately I wanted to save breaking it to the team until the off-season, but now, I have the utmost faith that they'll understand.

"I agree. Katie guessed it, so other girls probably have, too."

"Cool. Done deal." She squeezes my hand. "Andy?"

"Yeah?"

"We haven't really talked about your dad. I'm so sorry things turned bad so quickly."

"It's okay. When you think about it, it wasn't quick at all. He's been headed to this place for a long time, now. Not much we can do about it at this point." I shrug. I fill her in on the feeding tube and his probability of passing away before I graduate. On the fact he'll need constant medical support at this point, and our home life will never be the same.

She pulls me around to face her. "I'll be right here with you. Every step of the way, okay?"

Her eyes are bright and intense. "Okay."

"We'll take it day by day."

"Yeah." I let out a heavy breath. "I'm going to miss him so much."

She wraps me into her, and her body heat envelops me like a heated blanket. I sink into her. It will be a hard, scary couple of years for me and my family, but now, I have someone to help me carry it.

We stop at the front door of Wilder, and she checks her phone *again*.

I nod to her phone. "Everything all right on there?" I ask.

She smiles and tucks it in her pocket. "This is going to sound weird, but you trust me, right?"

I nod. "Of course, but you're kind of freaking me out."

"Go put on a bathing suit."

Twigs snap and nip at my ankles as Maya and I walk through the dark Alder woods down a path I've never been on before. For as many times as I've gone exploring in this place, I continue to be surprised by all the hidden gems I've yet to discover. Maya reaches behind for my hand, and I grab hers, ducking under a low-hanging oak limb and trying to keep pace with her. A flutter reverberates in my belly at the thought of taking a night swim with Maya. She seems a little nervous, too, which is completely out of character for her and leaves me a on guard.

When the path takes a ninety-degree turn right, she drops my hand and continues straight into the brush ahead, parting it as best she can for me. She grins as I walk past her onto a new trail, smaller and more faded than the one we were on before.

"Where are you taking me?" I ask.

"I told you, just a nice little swimming hole. It's just around that bend up there." She tilts her head down the wooded path. "Can you hear that?" she asks.

I shake my head. "I didn't wear my hearing aids because we're swimming."

"Gotcha." She plants a kiss on my cheek and extends a hand. "After you."

I give her a skeptical look as I pass, then keep my eyes peeled for roots that could trip me on the dark path. As I near the bend up ahead, the rustling of the breeze through the trees tickles my ears. I pause. *Is that laughter?* I turn back to Maya, arching my eyebrow in confusion.

"Go on," she says.

I follow the sound of shouts and laughter around the bend until I stumble upon one of the most beautiful places I've ever seen. The moonlight ignites the small stream that bubbles silver water into a swimming hole bordered by smooth, expansive rocks. And on those rocks, my teammates lounge and play fight one another, giggling into the night and passing around Bud Light from a Styrofoam cooler. Kim and Daniella float on a cheap-looking raft that they must have gotten from Walmart when they were buying the beer.

"Andy," Kim shouts as all the girls turn to greet Maya and I.

"What—"

"I thought you could use a fun distraction. After your meeting, I texted Katie and asked her to rally the troops for a night swim. Finals are over, and we have a lot to celebrate. Think of this as my team activity for the week," Maya says.

I can't help but smile. This is *perfect.*

"Come on guys, grab a beer. The water is warmer than you'd think." Ashlyn says.

Maya snags a cold can for herself and holds one out for me. "No pressure," she says.

I grab it and crack it open. "I'm not feeling any pressure. Not tonight." I take a small sip and groan. "How can it taste watery and bitter at the same time?"

Ashlyn laughs and slaps me on the back. "You'll get used to it."

"Can we please invite the baseball team now?" Kim whines from her raft.

"No, come on. Boys ruin everything," Maya says as she pulls off her clothes and eases into the water. "Come on, Andy."

I hesitate for a second before I join Maya in the dark, cool water. We wade around Daniella and Kim.

"No, boys make everything more fun," Kim says.

Maya slips under the water as Kim continues to complain to Daniella about how much she wishes the baseball team could be here. I see Maya's small air bubbles pop on the surface of the water, popping closer and closer to the girls' raft.

"Hey, Kim," I say. She turns to me, waiting for me to continue. "Plug your nose."

She tilts her head. "What are you—" She doesn't get the chance to finish her sentence because Maya flips their raft from underneath them, sending Kim and Daniella flying into the water. The whole team erupts in laughter, and the energy ratchets up to party mode as the beer flows, and all the girls join us for a swim. It's a war of splashing water, chicken, and shotgunning beers. The moonlight illuminates our summertime smiles and fans the flame of excitement that burns through each of us. Excitement for regionals.

I wipe water from my eyes and let gratitude wash over me like this stream.

Kim's gaze falls on me…on my chest, actually. Am I that attractive all of a sudden?

"Why are you wearing Maya's chain?" she asks, and all eyes fall on me. On my chest. The moonlight catches St. Rita, pulling everyone's gaze to her brilliant glow. I grasp it, speechless. *Shit.*

"Because I gave it to her," Maya says from behind Katie.

I let go of the medallion, allowing it to shine bright again.

"Yeah. Because, um, we're together," I add.

The girls look around at one another, and Kim chokes on her beer. I hold my breath as she tries to cough the Bud Light out of her lungs. Ashlyn and Katie sport amused grins while they watch everyone digest the news.

Kim clears her throat one more time, hand over chest. "Oh," she says. "Well, that would make sense."

"I knew it," Daniella shouts.

"Well, that's that. Congrats, guys," Katie says. "Now who wants to play sharks and minnows?" Everyone's attention is sucked back into the water wars. Everyone's attention except for mine and Maya's. I catch her gaze across the water and squeeze my St. Rita medallion. She smiles and wades over to me.

"Are you having fun?" she whispers.

"Yes. This was exactly what I needed." I grab her hand under the night-soaked water and watch Katie try to drown Kim. The pieces of my world are beginning to put themselves back together.

I am not wearing jeans. Today, I match my teammates in our Adidas navy and maroon team swag. We match down to the shoes. We match in our team gear because we're basically professional athletes. No big deal. I'm also pretty sure it's so the coaches can keep track of us through the airport, our form of the backpack leash. As we move through Hartsfield-Jackson, pride swells in my chest. I know most people haven't heard of Alder University, and most people would have no idea that we are headed to regionals, but I can't help but love the lingering eyes on us. This is our moment.

Our team lounges around on the dirty airport carpet for some reason instead of sitting in the mildly cleaner chairs. They laugh over *Cosmo* articles and TikTok videos and procure last-minute snacks from newsstands. Maya and I sit together next to the gate and watch our silly teammates run around, unable to contain their excitement.

She knocks my knee. "If I told you in August that we'd be sitting in the Atlanta airport as a couple waiting to board a plane to the Tallahassee regionals, would you have believed me?" she asks.

I lean closer to her. "I would have said it's impossible."

# EPILOGUE

I ndomitable."

"Indomitable?" Maya chuckles over her cup of coffee, the steam curling around and framing her face. The sun warms my back as I watch the most beautiful girl ruminate over my words. "That's the one word you would pick to describe me? Do I even want to know what it means?"

I laugh and squeeze her thigh under the table. "I can keep you in the dark if you want. But I like you, so I wouldn't pick a negative word to describe you," I say.

"Indomitable sounds like you're describing that deranged snowman thing." She cringes.

"That's 'abominable,' and I would never use that to describe you." I look up to the bright blue summer sky and arch my brow. "Almost never." I wink.

Maya gives my shoulder a shove. "Tell me what it means."

"It means, to be repulsive."

"*Ugh*." She grabs two fistfuls of my T-shirt in feigned desperation. "Not that one. Tell me what 'indomitable' means."

The corners of my mouth tug up when the definition pops into my head because this word encapsulates Maya Gonzalez so wholly, so perfectly, it's basically her aura, the reason I would follow her anywhere, into anything. I lean in and steal a coffee kiss. I can't help but linger in her space. "Unconquerable," I whisper into her ear, as if the definition is a secret only she gets to know.

She kisses me, and I so badly want to sink into her, but the hustle and bustle of students brings me back to the very public space that we're in. "I don't know. I'm feeling pretty conquered by a certain girl," she says.

I wave her off. "We're on the same side. If I tried to conquer you, you'd have to sentence me to death for treason."

Her brows reach for her hairline. "That took a fast turn into grim."

I suck in the corner of my lip and sigh. "Yeah. Sorry. Tell me mine, now."

"One word to describe Andrea Foster." She taps her teeth. "Hmm. This is hard."

"Oh, come on. My word for you popped in my head in seconds. You must not think very highly of me..." I knock her knee under the table.

"I just have so many words and feel so many things. How can I possibly pick just one to describe you?"

I arch an eyebrow. "I did. Fair is fair."

She huffs and picks at the cardboard sleeve of her coffee cup. "Okay. Just give me a minute." She catches me staring. "And don't look at me. I have to concentrate."

"Okay, okay. I'll just be over here anguishing over which word my girlfriend is going to choose. It's a big moment. A defining moment. Lots of pressure to pick the perfect one. My entire identity hangs in this moment. What if—"

"Magnanimous."

My cheeks warm at her description of me. *Magnanimous.* My new favorite word. My mouth hangs open, but now I can't find words to say.

"It means—"

"I know what it means, May." I press my lips to hers, and she deepens the kiss. In the back of my mind, I know we're being disgusting. Making out in public is not a thing I do. *Usually.* When Maya's hand slides up my thigh, and I begin to feel the heat of laser eyes boring into us, I pluck her hand and pull her up. "Come on. Meeting time."

❖

A hum of excited chatter bounces around the Lazy as our team files in and waits for Coach Clay to begin the meeting.

Katie falls into the open chair next to Maya. "Hey, y'all."

"Katie, what's up, girl?" Maya asks.

"Hey, Katie," I say.

She takes a big swig from her water bottle and wipes the dribble from her chin with the back of her hand. "I'm ready for this meeting." She turns in her seat and combs the rest of the Lazy with her eyes. "But I thought we'd get some treats, ya know." She sighs. "Man, I'd kill for a bagel."

Maya pats her on the back. "I heard only teams who *win* the World Series get to have bagels at their pre-season meetings."

Coach Clayton walks to the front of the Lazy, and the three of us muffle the rest of our chuckles, ready to listen. He adjusts his Alder Softball cap and grabs the blue Expo marker. Even when he's not writing anything on the whiteboard, he likes to have it in his hand when he's addressing the team. I think it's his emotional support animal or something.

"All right, ladies. Settle in, settle in." He waits for the rustling in the back to stop before he continues. Just when there's silence in the Lazy, he throws a bomb of disruption in the room by hollering, "What a season we had!" Our team erupts with cheers and chants and excitement.

"And we'll do it again," Ashlyn yells from the back.

"Hell, yeah," Katie adds.

A giant grin breaks across Coach Clay's face as he watches us completely unravel with celebration *again*. My throat is still recovering from how much I screamed when we beat UW in the Super Regionals to advance to the World Series. Sure, we lost in the first round, but we lost in the first round to the *championship team*. And we eked out a win on them in our first game of the series. So really, we've *beaten* the championship team.

As it happens, UGA did not make it past Super Regionals.

"Okay, ladies, listen up." He holds up his hands to get our attention back. "This year is going to look a lot like last year in terms of the lineup. We were lucky to only have to say good-bye to a few seniors. I'm going to go ahead and list the starters for the season." As coach writes the names of all the starters on the board, I think back to this moment last year. I think about being terrified when I heard my name called. Now, I would be completely shocked if I *didn't* hear my name called. The thought makes me sit up straighter, proud of how far I've come.

"And Andy will be our starting catcher. Congratulations, everyone. We have a very exciting season coming up," he says. Maya shoots me a quick grin. The only real wild card this year is who will be named captain, but no matter which name comes out of his mouth, I know Maya and I will lead our team together. Just like we did last season.

Coach clears his gunky throat. "One more thing, ladies. Quiet, please." He waits a moment for the chatter to die. "I am beyond pleased to announce that Andrea Foster"—Maya squeezes my hand under the table in congratulations—"*and* Maya Gonzalez will be our captains this year."

"Nice," I hear Kim say under her breath. Congratulations pours from our teammates, and I can't help but nod and think...*Maya and I are the best damn captains a team could ask for.*

"All right, y'all. That's it. Get out of here and enjoy the sunshine," Coach says.

I check my watch and lay a hand on Maya's shoulder. "Let's roll. The meeting starts in a half hour, and I want to be there early," I say.

❖

Maya and I walk into Dr. Martin's classroom in Brown Hall, where most of my psychology classes are located. We're fifteen minutes early, but the room is already mostly full, with members milling about and greeting one another. I spot Bailey and Noelle at the front of the room talking to a boy with pink hair, two blond girls, and a man I assume to be Dr. Martin.

"Wow. This club gets quite the turnout. I didn't know that Alder had such a big queer community," Maya says as she looks around the room.

I grab her hand and pull her toward the front. "Doesn't everywhere?"

"I guess so," she says.

Bailey squeezes one of the blond girl's shoulders as Noelle laughs at whatever the pink-haired boy just said. I take one more step toward their group, trying to ignore my nerves. Why am I even nervous? Maya pulls me out of my anxiety with a squeeze of my hand. She smiles and nods at me. "Go on," she mouths.

I nod and turn back to the group. "Bailey, hey," I say.

She and Noelle snap their attention to us. "Andy," they holler in unison. Noelle slings her arms around me and pulls me into one of the warmest hugs I've ever received.

"You came," she says. She pulls away and wraps Maya in a similar hug. I grin as she stiffens in the stranger's arms. "I'm Noelle," she says after she releases Maya.

"Maya Gonzalez." She smooths down her shirt.

"It's so great to have you both. I'm Bailey." Bailey shakes Maya's hand and squeezes my shoulder. "Well, I'd like to officially welcome you to the Alder Queer Fellowship. This is the man, the myth, the legend, Dr. Steve Martin." Maya and I exchange a grin. "No jokes about his name, please. He's very sensitive."

Dr. Martin musses up Bailey's hair. "You are such a pain in my ass. 'Steve' is fine. Welcome to AQF. And congratulations are in order. These two took the softball team to the World Series for the first time in school history," he says over his shoulder to the rest of the group.

After a round of congratulations, the boy with pink hair introduces himself as Robert.

"I'm Ashley. Welcome to AQF. It's pretty all right here, I guess." She shrugs. "Just kidding. You're going to love it."

"Thanks. Nice to meet you, Ashley."

The other blond girl fills in behind her. "And I'm Cassie. I run the religious outreach part of AQF and am the last of the board members. We're so glad you're both here, and congratulations again on your season." Her smile is warm and genuine.

"Thank you," Maya says for both of us.

Bailey finishes talking to another member and joins me and Maya again with two papers in hand. "Just a quick form for new members to fill out. Your preferred form of communication, what you hope to gain from AQF, etcetera." She hands us each a paper and checks her phone. "Go ahead and sit wherever you want. We'll get rolling here shortly."

We tuck ourselves near the back of the room and fill out the papers. Maya taps her eraser against her teeth as she considers what she wants out of her AQF membership, and I watch her.

Last year was a complete whirlwind full of so many ups and downs, but here I sit next to Maya, watching her do that sexy thing with her pencil as I burst with gratitude. We made it to the World Series. And when we were both back in Atlanta for the short summer break that we had left, Maya was with me every step of the way as my mom and I got my dad situated back in our house. It wasn't an easy transition for him, but we all took it day by day, and now he's settled and comfortable.

She never dropped my hand or faltered through any of it.

"Maya…"

"I don't know what the hell I want out of this club." She taps the eraser harder against her teeth. "I just want to be where you are, and you're here." She shrugs. "Can I write that?"

I grab her hand and hold it in my lap. "Maya."

She looks at me with those deep brown eyes, and I want to crawl into her lap and stay in her arms forever. "What's up?" she asks.

"I think I'm *catching feelings*," I say, biting back a smile.

She quirks an eyebrow, then shakes her head. "Andy, no. Stop." Her lips tug into a smile.

I elbow her in the ribs. "Get it? Because I'm the *catcher*." I chuckle.

She buries her face in her hands and groans. "That was the worst pun ever. I cannot believe I am dating such a nerd."

I smack a kiss on her cheek. "You'd better believe it. Someone once told me that anything is possible."

Bailey announces something to the room, but I miss it. All of my focus is on Maya Gonzalez and the intensity in her gaze as she stares into me. Her eyes are narrowed, and that perfectly sharp canine pinches over the top of her bottom lip. My neck tingles from knowing exactly how it feels to have her teeth rake over the thin skin of my throat. I shift in my seat as she leans in, heat pooling low in my belly from her proximity and the promise of something sweet coming from her lips.

"You know why I love you so much, Andrea Foster?" she whispers.

I shake my head gently, not wanting to disrupt this moment anymore than is necessary.

"Because you're such a *screwball*."

"Maya!" I whisper-yell at her and shove her in the side. Her shoulders shake with silent laughter. "An, here I was, bracing myself for a sweet declaration of love."

"I've got one more." She clears her throat. "A softball diamond is my second favorite…" she says and looks at me, nodding as if waiting for me to guess the punchline.

I quirk my brow. "*Ugh*. Don't tell me a baseball diamond is your first favorite."

She rolls her lips under her teeth and shakes her head. "The diamond I'm going to slip on your finger one day. That's my favorite diamond."

I stare at her, failing to push any words out of my open mouth as my entire body hums at the idea of Maya proposing. *Play it cool.* I don't want her to know that a dumb softball pun has me white knuckling the edge of my seat, trying not to fall over in excitement. I shake my head. "That was bad joke, May."

She pulls my hand into her lap and fingers the bare skin where a ring would be. "It's not a joke," she says.

"What? I don't—"

"I want to marry you, Andrea. Not a doubt in my mind. After we graduate. We can live in Atlanta and open a sports psychology practice together. You'll handle the sessions, and I'll handle the business side of everything. We'll buy a house with a huge yard where we'll play with our kids and raise them to be athletes. If they want, of course." She rubs my finger and watches me. "What do you think?"

I grin. "I think you missed a step. I need to get my PhD before we start a practice."

She groans and leans back in her chair. "You're killing me, Foster. Of all the things to—"

"Yes, Maya." She straightens and locks eyes with me, her breathing slow and deliberate as if she's trying to rein in her own overflowing reaction to my words. "I don't need a ring. I'd say yes to you tomorrow. Would've said yes to you yesterday." I throw my hands up in exasperation. "Hell, I probably would've hobbled down the aisle on my ankle you sprained freshman year."

She leans in and pushes a sweet kiss to the corner of my mouth. "This is valuable information."

Bailey's voice returns, pulling us out of our moment. As Maya turns to face the front of the classroom, I drop my gaze to my lap. To my bare ring finger.

If forever is a choice, I choose Maya Gonzalez.

# About the Author

Ana is an author of lesbian romance. She has been named a finalist for the Foreword Indies Book of the Year Award, the Next Generation Indie Book Awards, and the Golden Crown Literary Awards. She worked in the Pacific Northwest wine industry for seven years and now lives in her hometown of Atlanta, Georgia, with her wife, their fluffy German shepherd, and mildly evil cat. She loves all things fermented, walking the local trails, and eating pastries. So many pastries. She is currently writing her next book and working at a local distillery.

# Books Available from Bold Strokes Books

**A Good Chance** by Ali Vali. Harry, Desi, and Desi's sister Rachel are so close to getting everything they've ever wanted, but Desi's ex-husband is coming back to get his revenge and rip apart their chance at happiness. (978-1-63679-023-7)

**A Perfect Fifth** by Jaycie Morrison. Streetwise pianist Zara Keller and Lady Jillian Stansfield couldn't be more different; yet their connection brings a new awareness of who they are and what they truly want in their lives—including each other. (978-1-63679-132-6)

**Catching Feelings** by Ana Hartnett Reichardt. Andrea Foster expected to catch a lot of pitches from the Alder Lion's star pitcher, Maya, but she didn't expect to catch feelings. (978-1-63679-227-9)

**Defiant Hearts** by Lee Lynch. In these stories, you'll find your lovers, friends, and lesbians you wish you knew—maybe even yourself. (978-1-63679-237-8)

**Love and Duty** by Catherine Young. All Princess Roseli wants is to marry her three lovers, but with war looming, she must instead marry Princess Lucia to establish a military alliance between their planets. (978-1-63679-256-9)

**Murder at Union Station** by David S. Pederson. Private Detective Mason Adler struggles to determine who killed a woman found in a trunk without getting himself killed in the process. (978-1-63679-269-9)

**Serendipity** by Kris Bryant. Serendipity brings jingle writer Annie Foster and celebrity pop star Bristol Baines together, and their undeniable attraction keeps them close, but will their different paths drive them apart? (978-1-63679-224-8)

**The Haunted Heart** by Jane Kolven. A ghost, a ring, and a quest to find a missing psychic—it's a spell for love. (978-1-63679-245-3)

**The Rules of Forever** by Nan Campbell. After reconnecting at their high school reunion, Cara and Lauren agree to embark on a textbook definition friends-with-benefits relationship, but trying to keep it uncomplicated is harder than it seems. (978-1-63679-248-4)

**Vision of Virtue** by Brey Willows. When virtue and desire come together, be prepared for sparks in this next installment of the Memory's Muses series. (978-1-63679-118-0)

**Cherry on Top** by Georgia Beers. A chance meeting leaves Cherry and Ellis longing for a different life, but when Ellis's search for truth crashes into Cherry's insta-filter world, do they have any hope at all of a happily ever after? (978-1-63679-158-6)

**Love and Other Rare Birds** by Angie Williams. Ornithologist Dr. Jamie Martin and park ranger Rowan Fleming are searching the Alaskan wilderness for a bird thought to be extinct and they're about to discover opposites really do attract. (978-1-63679-108-1)

**Parallel Paradise** by Mayapee Chowdhury. When their love affair is put to the test by the homophobia of their family, community, and culture, Bindi and Rimli will need to fight for a chance at love. (978-1-63679-204-0)

**Perfectly Matched** by Toni Logan. A beautiful Cupid named Hannah, a runaway arrow, and just seventy-two hours to fix a mishap that could be the best mistake she has ever made. (978-1-63679-120-3)

**Royal Exposé** by Jenny Frame. When they're grouped together for a class assignment, Poppy's enthusiasm for life and love may just save Casey's soul, but will she ever forgive Casey for using her to expose royal secrets? (978-1-63679-165-4)

**Slow Burn** by Missouri Vaun. A wounded wildland firefighter from California and a struggling artist find solace and love in a small southern town. (978-1-63679-098-5)

**The Artist** by Sheri Lewis Wohl. Detective Casey Wilson and reclusive artist Tula Crane are drawn together in a web of passion, intrigue, and art that might just hold the key to stopping a killer. (978-1-63679-150-0)

**The Inconvenient Heiress** by Jane Walsh. An unlikely heiress and a spinster evade the Marriage Mart only to discover true love together. (978-1-63679-173-9)

**A Champion for Tinker Creek** by D.C. Robeline. Lyle James has rescued his dad's auto repair business, but when city hall condemns his neighborhood, Lyle learns only trusting will save his life and help him find love. (978-1-63679-213-2)

**Closed-Door Policy** by Erin Zak. Going back to college is never easy, but Caroline Stevens is prepared to work hard and change her life for the better. What she's not prepared for is Dr. Atlanta Morris, her gorgeous new professor. (978-1-63679-181-4)

**Homeworld** by Gun Brooke. Headed by Captain Holly Crowe, the spaceship Velocity's crew journeys toward their alien ancestors' homeworld, and what they find is completely unexpected—and they're not safe. (978-1-63679-177-7)

**Outland** by Kristin Keppler & Allisa Bahney. Danielle Clark and Katelyn Turner can't seem to stay away from one another even as the war for the wastelands tests their loyalty to each other and to their people. (978-1-63679-154-8)

**Secret Sanctuary** by Nance Sparks. US Deputy Marshal Alex Trenton specializes in protecting those awaiting trial, but when danger threatens the woman she's falling for, Alex is in for the fight of her life. (978-1-63679-148-7)

**Stranded Hearts** by Kris Bryant, Amanda Radley, Emily Smith. In these novellas from award winning authors, fate intervenes on behalf of love when characters are unexpectedly stuck together. With too much time and an irresistible attraction, anything could happen. (978-1-63679-182-1)

**The Last Lavender Sister** by Melissa Brayden. Aster Lavender sells her gourmet doughnuts and keeps a low profile; she never plans on the town's temporary veterinarian swooping in and making her feel like anything but a wallflower. (978-1-63679-130-2)

**The Probability of Love** by Dena Blake. As Blair and Rachel keep ending up in the same place despite the odds, can a one-night stand turn into forever? Or will the bet Blair never intended to make ruin their happily ever after? (978-1-63679-188-3)

**Worth a Fortune** by Sam Ledel. After placing a want ad for a personal secretary, a New York heiress is surprised when the woman who got away is the one interested in the position. (978-1-63679-175-3)

**A Fox in Shadow** by Jane Fletcher. Cassie's mission is to add new territory to the Kavillian empire—murder, betrayal, war, and the clash of cultures ensue. (978-1-63679-142-5)

**Embracing the Moon** by Jeannie Levig. Just as Gwen and Taylor are exploring the new love they've found, the present and past collide, threatening the future they long to share. (978-1-63555-462-5)

**Forever Comes in Threes** by D. Jackson Leigh. Efficiency expert Perry Chandler's ordered life is upended when she inherits three busy terriers, and the woman she's referred to for help turns out to be her bitter podcast rival, the very sexy Dr. Ming Lee. (978-1-63679-169-2)

**Heckin' Lewd: Trans and Nonbinary Erotica** by Mx. Nillin Lore. If you want smutty, fearless, gender diverse erotica written by affirming own-voices folks who get it, then this is the book you've been looking for! (978-1-63679-240-8)

**Missed Conception** by Joy Argento. Maggie Walsh wants a relationship with Cassidy, the daughter she's only just discovered she has due to an in vitro mix-up. Heat kindles between Maggie and Cassidy's mother in a way neither expects. (978-1-63679-146-3)

**Private Equity** by Elle Spencer. Cassidy Bennett spends an unexpected evening at a lesbian nightclub with her notoriously reserved and demanding boss, Julia. After seeing a different side of Julia, Cassidy can't seem to shake her desire to know more. (978-1-63679-180-7)

**Racing the Dawn** by Sandra Barrett. After narrowly escaping a house fire, vampire Jade Murphy is unexpectedly intrigued by gorgeous firefighter Beth Jenssen, and her undead existence might just be perking up a bit. (978-1-63679-271-2)

**Reclaiming Love** by Amanda Radley. Sarah's tiny white lie means somehow convincing Pippa to pretend to be her girlfriend. Only the more time they spend faking it, the more real it feels. (978-1-63679-144-9)

**Sol Cycle** by Kimberly Cooper Griffin. An encounter in a park brings Ang and Krista together, but when Ang's attempts to help Krista go spectacularly wrong, their passion for each other might not be enough. (978-1-63679-137-1)

**Trial and Error** by Carsen Taite. Attorney Franco Rossi and Judge Nina Aguilar's reunion is fraught with courtroom conflict, undeniable chemistry, and danger. (978-1-63555-863-0)

**A Long Way to Fall** by Elle Spencer. A ski lodge, two strong-willed women, and a family feud that brings them together, but will it also tear them apart? (978-1-63679-005-3)

**Barnabas Bopwright Saves the City** by J. Marshall Freeman. When he uncovers a terror plot to destroy the city he loves, 15-year-old Barnabas Bopwright realizes it's up to him to save his home and bring deadly secrets into the light before it's too late. (978-1-63679-152-4)

**Forever** by Kris Bryant. When Savannah Edwards is invited to be the next bachelorette on the dating show When Sparks Fly, she'll show the world that finding true love on television can happen. (978-1-63679-029-9)

**Ice on Wheels** by Aurora Rey. All's fair in love and roller derby. That's Riley Fauchet's motto, until a new job lands her at the same company—and on the same team—as her rival Brooke Landry, the frosty jammer for the Big Easy Bruisers. (978-1-63679-179-1)

**Inherit the Lightning** by Bud Gundy. Darcy O'Brien and his sisters learn they are about to inherit an immense fortune, but a family mystery about to unravel after seventy years threatens to destroy everything. (978-1-63679-199-9)

**Perfect Rivalry** by Radclyffe. Two women set out to win the same career-making goal, but it's love that may turn out to be the final prize. (978-1-63679-216-3)

**Something to Talk About** by Ronica Black. Can quiet ranch owner Corey Durand give up her peaceful life and allow her feisty new neighbor into her heart? Or will past loss, present suitors, and town gossip ruin a long-awaited chance at love? (978-1-63679-114-2)

**With a Minor in Murder** by Karis Walsh. In the world of academia, police officer Clare Sawyer and professor Libby Hart team up to solve a murder. (978-1-63679-186-9)

**Writer's Block** by Ali Vali. Wyatt and Hayley might be made for each other if only they can get through nosy neighbors, the historic society, at-odds future plans, and all the secrets hidden in Wyatt's walls. (978-1-63679-021-3)